CONTENTS

INTRODUCTION

MOST PEOPLE who don't know anything about either science or science fiction think that we have "conquered space" with the Russian Sputniks and our own space vehicles. Not a few of them have personally sympathized with me, as an editor of science fiction anthologies, because—as they put it—"science has caught up with science fiction," so why bother reading science fiction anyhow?

Nothing could be wronger than that idea! I do not have to go deep into the science or technology of astronautics (cosmonautics, as the Russians more sensibly call it) to show you that we have some distance to go, yet, before we even know if it is feasible to send living beings safely through the possibly lethal Van Allen Radiation Belts, which englobe the earth in a layer ranging between 5,000 and 15,000 miles high. That's a long way up!—compared to our achievements in manned space travel as of the beginning of 1963. The maximum height of an orbiting *manned* satellite has been under 200 miles. Probably the highest at the time this book appears will still be the first manned one of all, the Soviet *Vostok I,* which reached a height of 187.66 miles in its single orbit around the earth with Yuri Gagarin aboard, April 12, 1961.

According to theoretical interpretations of data returned by our *unmanned* satellites in the DISCOVERER series and other types of information, the Van Allen Belt radiation hazards can be conquered. That is, the radiations (probably) can be shielded from human beings in a space ship at our present level of radiation protection technology—except when one of those almost unpredictable, monstrous, incomprehensibly powerful nuclear explosions known as *solar flares* occurs. The experts say they do not believe we can, as of now, protect a moon-going space ship from such a violent radiation attack. Undoubtedly, that particular hazard will be conquered eventually—but we really cannot say so for sure, yet. Meanwhile, science fiction explores not only the moon and our solar planets, but also other star systems. It finds not only new planets around those stars, but also new forms of life on those planets. In general, it runs fancy free and wonderfully wild in the unknowns of outer space.

In all likelihood, even the Solar System will remain science-fictional for some time after this book appears. As for the stars, they will be unapproachable for a period which I hesitate to estimate. However, it is most unlikely that even the younger readers of this book (not to mention myself, an old hand, born less than a year after the airplane was first shown to be practical when the Wright Brothers flew 852 feet in 59 seconds on December 17, 1903), will live to witness even the basic scientific discoveries which must be made before we can travel to the nearest star, 26 TRILLION (26,-000,000,000,000) miles, or four and a third lightyears, away from us. That the human race will eventually make that trip, I am convinced. That it will be soon, I am very, very doubtful indeed.

In the meantime, we can all explore the wonders of our galaxy through the disciplined imaginations of our scientifically-oriented science fiction writers, some of the best of whom you will find in the pages that follow. When I say "scientifically oriented," though, I do not want you to assume that all of the "science" in these stories is real. If it were, they would not be science fiction. What I can say is that for the most part (with one or two exceptions) nothing in them is inherently impossible.

As a matter of fact, the "realm of the possible" in

science fiction is expanding at an almost frightening rate. New discoveries, and amplifications of old discoveries, are coming up almost every other day: and they make it the utmost in foolishness for anyone to say that something that does not flatly violate proven facts of Nature and of Science is impossible. (And even some of those violations may turn out to be possible, in time, for some "facts" of Nature and of Science are changeable, too—as witness what happened to Newton's laws after Einstein got hold of them!)

But the realm of the possible does have certain strict limitations. There are many people who believe in ghosts, I am told, and go along with superstitions about witches, werewolves, and other such creatures. These are the sort of primitive monsters that haunt some people's dreams, but never bother scientists—when they are awake, at least. Scientists know that these nightmares cannot in any conceivable way be bent so that they will fit into some natural fact.

On the other hand, voyaging to the stars, discovering life forms there which are entirely inconceivable to us oxygen-breathers, and many of the other science-fictional ideas encountered in this book, are thoroughly believable. They are not in violation of any "natural law" (so-called), nor are they impossible from the point of view of science as we know it.

I'll make it even clearer. Space travel, as I have said, violates no known facts of nature or of science. Time travel, either backwards or forwards, does—except for that strange oddity of time which Einstein imagined when he theorized about people traveling near the speed of light: they could "travel in time" to the extent that they would find a marked difference between "subjective" time in their space ship, and the "objective" passage of time back home. (This is too complicated for me either to explain or, as a matter of fact, to understand; we will just take Einstein's word for it!)

But space travel is scientifically, technologically, and psychologically possible. This we know from even the

limited orbital flights which have been made thus far. Therefore we can only believe that before another decade or so Man will have reached the Moon and perhaps Mars and Venus. These goals we have already set ourselves as a nation, as have the Russians. When we achieve them, the stories in Part One of this book will perhaps be proved false. (Perhaps not!)

As for travel to the stars: the stories in Part Two of this collection will remain "possible" for many generations to come. They may, indeed, eventually turn out to be real. I hope Arthur C. Clarke does not sue me— he is the famous English expert on space travel and aqualunging (he knows and writes about the former, and practices and writes about the latter), who is also author of one of the best stories in this book—for saying he once felt that travel beyond the speed of light has not yet been proved impossible. With such travel speeds, exploration of some of the stars will become at least feasible—and if it is feasible, some members of the human race unquestionably will try it! How it will be done, no one knows. That it ever will be done is highly uncertain today. That it is impossible, only the unimaginative and the scientifically bigoted will state.

But more than scientific extrapolation is involved in this book: and that is, quite simply, entertainment. Every story, I think you will agree, is fun to read— even when it may turn out to be terrifying or even tragic. Each one is an enlargement of the world we know, performed by adventurous human beings. Each tale expands our horizons, spreads the wings of our imaginations, and gives us a chance to fly high—while sitting in our easy chairs or lying on our beds.

After all, the *first* requirement of any book of fiction, be it novel or collection of short stories, is: It must keep you interested. And *that*, I guarantee, this book will do!

GROFF CONKLIN

LESTER DEL REY

THE WINGS OF NIGHT

This sharply to-the-point story of the discovery of the last surviving member of a strange, non-human, intelligent race on the Moon was published over twenty-one years ago, in March, 1942. It has since become one of the classics of space travel science fiction, and for more than one reason. First, its daring dream of a subterranean moon life form is thrilling—and also still a not impossible concept. Second, the story's strong plea for a hard-boiled idealism (which pays off), an absence of prejudice, racial or human-alien (which also earns its own rewards), and a philosophy of live-and-let-live (which actually saves the lives of the earth protagonists) is particularly apt for our times.

Read this story then, and think—hard!

"Damn all Martians!" Fats Welch's thin mouth bit out the words with all the malice of an offended member of a superior race. "Here we are, loaded down with as sweet a high-rate cargo of iridium as ever came out of the asteroids, just barely over the Moon, and that injector starts mis-metering again. If I ever see that bulbous Marshy—"

"Yeah." Slim Lane groped back with his right hand for the flexible-shaft wrench, found it, and began wriggling and grunting forward into the mess of machinery again. "Yeah. I know. You'll make mince meat out of him. Did you ever figure that maybe you were making your own trouble? That maybe Martians are people after all? Lyro Bmachis told you it would take two days to make the overhaul of the injector control hookup, so you knocked him across the field, called his ancestors dirty dogs, and gave him just eight hours to finish repairs. Now you expect his rush job to be a labor of love for you— Oh, skip it, Fats, and give me the screwdriver."

What was the use? He'd been over it all with Fats a dozen times before, and it never got him anywhere. Fats was a good rocket man, but he couldn't stretch his imagination far enough to forget the hogwash the Reconstruction Empire was dishing out about the Destiny of Man and the Divine Plan whereby humans were created to exploit all other races. Not that it would do Fats much good if he did. Slim knew the value of idealism—none better.

He'd come out of college with a bad dose of it and an inherited fortune big enough for three men, filled with the old crusading spirit. He'd written and published books, made speeches, interviewed administrators, lobbied, joined and organized societies, and been called things that weren't complimentary. Now he was pushing freight from Mars to Earth for a living, quarter owner of a space-worn freighter. And Fats, who'd come up from a tube cleaner without the help of ideals, owned the other three quarters.

Fats watched him climb out of the hold. "Well?"

"Nothing. I can't fix it—don't know enough about electronics. There's something wrong with the relays that control the time interval, but the indicators don't show where, and I'd hate to experiment out here."

"Make it to Earth—maybe?"

Slim shook his head. "I doubt it, Fats. Better set us down on Luna somewhere, if you can handle her that far. Then maybe we can find out what's wrong before we run out of air."

Fats had figured as much and was already braking

the ship down, working against the spasmodic flutter of the blasts, and swearing at the effects of even the Moon's weak gravity. But the screens showed that he was making progress toward the spot he'd chosen—a small flat plain with an area in the center that seemed unusually clear of debris and pockmarks.

"Wish they'd at least put up an emergency station out here," he muttered.

"They had one once," Slim said. "But nobody ever goes to Luna, and there's no reason for passenger ships to land there; takes less fuel for them to coast down on their fins through Earth's atmosphere than to jet down here. Freighters like us don't count, anyway. Funny how regular and flat that place is; we can't be over a mile up, and I don't see even a meteor scar."

"Luck's with us, then. I'd hate to hit a baby crater and rip off a tube or poke a hole in the shell." Fats glanced at the radio altimeter and fall indicator. "We're gonna hit plenty hard. If— Hey, what the deuce?"

Slim's eyes flicked to the screen just in time to see the flat plain split into two halves and slide smoothly out from under them as they seemed about to touch it; then they were dropping slowly into a crater of some sort, seemingly bottomless and widening out rapidly; the roar of the tubes picked up suddenly. Above them, the overscreens showed a pair of translucent slides closing together again. His eyes stared at the height indicator, neither believing nor doubting.

"Hundred and sixty miles down, and trapped in! Tube sounds show air in some amount, at least, even up here. This crazy trap can't be here; there's no reason for it."

"Right now, who cares? We can't go through that slide up there again, so we go down and find out, I guess. Damn, no telling what kind of landing field we'll find when we reach bottom." Fats' lack of excess imagination came in handy in cases like this. He went about the business of jockeying down the enormous crater as if he were docking at York port, too busy with the uncertain blast to worry about what he might find at the bottom. Slim gazed at him in wonder, then fell back to staring at the screens for some indication of the reason behind this obviously artificial trap.

Lhin scratched idly through the pile of dirt and rotten shale, pried out a thin scrap of reddened stone his eyes had missed the first time, and rose slowly to his feet. The Great Ones had been good to him, sending a rockslide just when the old beds were wearing thin and poor from repeated digging. His sensitive nostrils told him there was magnesium, ferrous matter, and sulphur in abundance, all more than welcome. Of course, he'd hoped there might be copper, even as little as the end of his finger, but of that there seemed no sign. And without copper—

He shrugged the thought aside as he had done a thousand times before, and picked up his crude basket, now filled half with broken rock and half with the lichenlike growth that filled this end of the crater. One of his hands ground a bit of rottenstone together with shreds of lichen and he popped the mixture into his mouth. Grace to the Great Ones who had sent the slide; the pleasant flavor of magnesium tickled his tongue, and the lichens were full-flavored from the new richness of the soil around them. Now, with a trace of copper, there would have been nothing left to wish for.

With a rueful twitch of his supple tail, Lhin grunted and turned back toward his cave, casting a cursory glance up at the roof of the cavern. Up there, long miles away, a bright glare lanced down, diffusing out as it pierced through the layers of air, showing that the long lunar day was nearing noon, when the sun would lance down directly through the small guarding gate. It was too high to see, but he knew of the covered opening where the sloping walls of the huge valley ended and the roof began. Through all the millennia of his race's slow defeat, that great roof had stood, unsupported except for the walls that stretched out around in a circle of perhaps fifty miles diameter, strong and more lasting than even the crater itself; the one abiding monument to the greatness that had been his people's.

He knew without having to think of it, that the roof was artificial, built when the last thin air was deserting the Moon, and the race had sought a final refuge here in the deepest crater, where oxygen could be trapped and kept from leaking away. In a vague way, he could sense the ages that had passed since then and wonder at the permanence of the domed roof, proof against all time.

Once, as the whole space about him testified, his had been a mighty race. But time had worked on them, aging the race as it had individuals, removing the vigor of their youth and sending in the slow creepers of hopelessness. What good was existence here, cooped up in one small colony, away from their world? Their numbers had diminished and some of their skill had gone from them. Their machines had crumbled and vanished, unreplaced, and they had fallen back to the primitive, digging out the rocks of the crater walls and the lichens they had cultured to draw energy from the heat and radioactive phosphorescence of the valley instead of sunlight. Fewer young were planted each year, and of the few, a smaller percentage proved fertile, so that their original million fell to thousands, then to hundreds, and finally to a few grubbing individuals.

Only then had they awakened to the danger of extinction, to find it too late. There had been three elders when Lhin was grown, his seed being the only fertile one. Now the elders were gone long years since, and Lhin had the entire length and breadth of the crater to himself. And life was a long series of sleeps and food forages, relieved only by the same thoughts that had been in his mind while his dead world turned to the light and away more than a thousand times. Monotony had slowly killed off his race, but now that its work was nearly done, it had ended. Lhin was content with his type of life; he was habituated, and immune to boredom.

His feet had been moving slowly along with the turning of his thoughts, and he was out of the valley proper, near the door of the shelter carved into the rocky walls which he had chosen from the many as his home. He munched another mouthful of rock and lichen and let the diffused sunlight shine on him for a few minutes more, then turned into the cave. He needed no light, since the rock walls about had all been rendered radioactive in the dim youth of his race, and his eyes were adapted to wide ranges of light conditions. He passed quickly through the outer room, containing his woven lichen bed and few simple furnishings, and back into the combination nursery and workshop, an illogical but ever-present hope drawing him back to the far corner.

But, as always, it was reasonless. The box of rich earth, pulped to a fine loam and watered carefully, was barren of life. There was not even the beginnings of a small red shoot to awaken him to hope for the future. His seed was infertile, and the time when all life would be extinct was growing near. Bitterly he turned his back on the nursery bed.

So little lacking, yet so much! A few hundred molecules of copper salt to eat, and the seeds he grew would be fertile; or those same copper molecules added to the water would render the present seeds capable of growing into vigorous manhood—or womanhood; Lhin's people carried both male and female elements within each member, and could grow the seeds that became their children either alone or with another. So long as one member of the race lived, as many as a hundred young a year could be reared in the carefully tended incubating soil—if the vital hormone containing copper could be made.

But that, it seemed, was not to be. Lhin went over his laboriously constructed apparatus of hand-cut rock bowls and slender rods bound together into tubes, and his hearts were heavy within him. The slow fire of dried lichen and gummy tar burned still, and slow, drop by drop, liquid oozed from the last tube into a bowl. But even in that there was no slightest odor of copper salts. Well, he had tried that and failed. The accumulation of years of refining had gone into the water that kept the nursery soil damp, and in it there had been too little of the needed mineral for life. Almost dispassionately he threw the permanent metal rolls of his race's science back into their cylinders and began disassembling the chemical part of his workshop.

That meant the other solution, harder, and filled with risks, but necessary now. Somewhere up near the roof, the records indicated, there was copper in small amounts, but well past the breathable concentration of air. That meant a helmet and tanks for compressed air, long with hooks and grapples to bridge the eroded sections of the old trail and steps leading up, instruments to detect the copper, and a pump to fill the tanks. Then he must carry many tanks forward, cache them, and go up to make another cache, step by step, until his supply line would reach the top and—perhaps—he could find copper for a new beginning.

He deliberately avoided thinking of the time required and the chances of failure. His foot came down on the little bellows and blue flames licked up from his crude forge as he drew out the hunks of refined metal and began heating them to malleability. Even the shaping of it by hand to the patterns of the ancient records was almost impossible, and yet, somehow, he must accomplish it correctly. His race must not die!

He was still working doggedly hours later when a high-pitched note shot through the cave. A meteor, coming into the fields around the sealing slides of the roof, and a large one! In all Lhin's life there had been none big enough to activate the warning screens, and he had doubted that the mechanism, though meant to be ageless and draw Sun power until the Sun died, was still functioning. As he stood staring at the door sense-lessly, the whistling note came again.

Now, unless he pressed his hand over the inductance grid, the automatic forces would come into play, twist-ing the meteor aside and beyond the roof. But he gave no thought to that as he dashed forward and slapped his fingers against the grilled panel. It was for that he had chosen this rock house, once the quarters of the Watchers who let the few scouting rockets of dim past ages in and out. A small glow from the grid indicated the meteor was through, and he dropped his hand, let-ting the slides close again.

Then he waited impatiently for it to strike, moving out to the entrance. Perhaps the Great Ones were kind and were answering his prayers at last. Since he could find no copper here, they were sending a token from outer space to him, and who knew what fabulous amounts it might contain—perhaps even as much as he could hold in one hand! But why hadn't it struck? He scanned the roof anxiously, numb with a fear that he had been too late and the forces had thrown it aside.

No, there was a flare above—but surely not such as a meteor that size should make as it sliced down through the resisting air! A sharp stinging whine hit his ears finally, flickering off and on; and that was not the sound a meteor would logically make. He stared harder, wondering, and saw that it was settling down-ward slowly, not in a sudden rush, and that the flare struck down instead of fading out behind. That meant —could only mean—intelligent control! A rocket!

Lhin's mind spun under the shock, and crazy ideas of his ancestors' return, of another unknown refuge, of the Great Ones' personal visit slid into his thoughts. Basically, though, he was severely logical, and one by one he rejected them. This machine could not come from the barren moon, and that left only the fabled planet lying under the bottom of his world, or those that wandered around the Sun in other orbits. Intelli-gence there?

His mind slid over the records he had read, made when his ancestors had crossed space to those worlds, long before the refuge was built. They had been unable to colonize, due to the oppressive pull of gravity, but they had observed in detail. On the second planet were only squamous things that slid through the water and curious fronds on the little dry land; on his own primary, gigantic beasts covered the globe, along with growth rooted to the ground. No intelligence on those worlds. The fourth, though, was peopled by more familiar life, and like his own evolutionary forerunners, there was no division into animal and vegetable, but both were present in all. Ball-shaped blobs of life had already formed into packs, guided by instinct, with no means of communication. Yet, of the other worlds known, that seemed the most probable as a source of intelligence. If, by some miracle, they came from the third, he abandoned hope; the blood lust of that world was too plainly written in the records, where living mountainlike beasts tore at others through all the rolls of etched pictures. Half filled with dread, half with anticipation, he heard the ship land somewhere near, and started toward it, his tail curved tightly behind him.

He knew, as he caught sight of the two creatures outside the opened lock of the vessel, that his guess had been wrong. The creatures were bifurcate, like himself, though massive and much larger, and that meant the third world. He hesitated, watching carefully as they stared about, apparently keenly enjoying the air around them. Then one spoke to the other, and his mind shook under a new shock.

The articulation and intonation were intelligent, but the sounds were a meaningless babble. Speech—that! It must be, though the words held no meaning. Wait—in the old records. Slha the Freethinker had touched on some such thought; he had written of remote days when the Lunarites had had no spech and postulated that they had invented the sounds and given them arbitrary meaning, and that only by slow ages of use had they become instinctive in the new-grown infants—had even dared to question that the Great Ones had ordered speech and sound meanings as the inevitable complement of intelligence. And now, it seemed, he was right. Lhin groped up through the fog of his discovery and tightened his thoughts into a beam.

Again, shock struck at him. Their minds were hard to reach, and once he did find the key and grope forward into their thoughts, it was apparent that they could not read his! Yet they were intelligent. But the one on whom his thoughts centered noticed him finally, and grabbed at the other. The words were still harsh and senseless, but the general meaning reached the Moon man. "Fats, what's that?"

The other turned and stared at Lhin's approach. "Dunno. Looks like a scrawny three-foot monkey. Reckon it's harmless?"

"Probably, maybe even intelligent. It's a cinch no band of political refugees built this place—nonhuman construction. Hi there!" The one who thought of himself as Slim—massive though he appeared—turned to the approaching Lunarite. "What and who are you?"

"Lhin," he answered, noting surprised pleasure in Slim's mind. "Lhin—me Lhin."

Fats grunted. "Guess you're right, Slim. Seems to savvy you. Wonder who came here and taught him English."

Lhin fumbled clumsily, trying to pin down the individual sounds to their meanings and remember them. "No sahffy Enlhish. No who came here. You—" He ran out of words and drew nearer, making motions toward Slim's head, then his own. Surprisingly, Slim got it.

"He means he knows what we're thinking, I guess. Telepathy."

"Yeah? Marshies claim they can do it among themselves, but I never saw one read a human mind. They

claim we don't open up right. Maybe this Ream monkey's lying to you."

"I doubt it. Take another look at the radioactivity
meter in the viability tester—men wouldn't come here
and go home without spreading the good word. Anyway, his name isn't Ream—Lean comes closer to the
sound he made, though we'll never get it right." He
half sent a thought to Lhin, who dutifully pronounced
his name again. "See? His liquid isn't . . . it's a glottal
stop. And he makes the final consonant a labial, though
it sounds something like our dental. We can't make
sounds like that. Wonder how intelligent he is."

He turned back into the ship before Lhin could
puzzle out some kind of answer, and was out a moment
later with a small bundle under his arm. "Space English
code book," he explained to Fats. "Same as they used
to teach the Martians English a century ago."

Then to Lhin: "Here are the six hundred most useful
words of our language, organized, so it'll beat waiting
for you to pick them up bit by bit. You look at the
diagramed pictures while I say and think the word.
Now. One—w-uh-nn; two—t-ooo. Getting it?"

Fats watched them for a while, half amused, then
grew tired of it. "O. K., Slim, you molly-coddle the
native awhile and see what you learn. I'm going over to
the walls and investigate that radioactive stuff until
you're ready to start repairs. Wish radios weren't so
darned limited in these freighters and we could get a
call through."

He wandered off, but Lhin and Slim were hardly
aware of it. They were going through the difficult task
of organizing a means of communication, with almost
no common background, which should have been
worse than impossible in terms of hours. Yet, strange
as the word associations and sounds were, and odd as
their organization into meaningful groups, they were
still only speech, after all. And Lhin had grown into
life with a highly complex speech as natural to him as

breathing. He twisted his lips over the sounds and nailed the meanings down in his mind, one by one, indelibly.

Fats finally found them in Lhin's cave, tracing them by the sound of their voices, and sat down to watch, as an adult might watch a child playing with a dog. He bore Lhin no ill will, but neither could he regard the Moon man as anything but some clever animal, like the Martians or the primitives of Venus; if Slim enjoyed treating them as equals, let him have his way for the time.

Lhin was vaguely conscious of those thoughts and others more disturbing, but he was too wrapped up in the new experience of having some living mind to communicate with, after nearly a century of being alone with himself. And there were more important things. He wriggled his tail, spread his arms, and fought over the Earth sounds while Slim followed as best he could.

Finally the Earth man nodded. "I think I get it. All of them have died off except you, and you don't like the idea of coming to a dead end. Um-m-m. I wouldn't either. So now you hope these Great Ones of yours— we call 'em God—have sent us down here to fix things up. How?"

Lhin beamed, his face contorting into a furrowed grimace of pleasure before he realized Slim misinterpreted the gesture. Slim meant well. Once he knew what was needed, perhaps he would even give the copper gladly, since the old records showed that the third world was richest of all in minerals.

"Nra is needed. Life comes from making many simple things one not-simple thing—air, drink stuff, eat stuff, all that I have, so I live. But to begin the new life, Nra is needed. It makes things begin. The seed has no life—with Nra it lives. But I had no word."

He waited impatiently while Slim digested that. "Sort of a vitamin or hormone, something like Vitamin E$_6$, eh? Maybe we could make it, but—"

Lhin nodded. Surely the Great Ones were kind. His

hearts were warm as he thought of the many seeds carefully wrapped and stored that could be made to grow with the needed copper. And now the Earth man was willing to help. A little longer and all would be well.

"No need to make," he piped happily. "Simple stuff. The seed or I can make, in us. But we need Nra to make it. See." He pulled a handful of rock from the basket lying near, chewed it carefully, and indicated that it was being changed inside him.

Fats awoke to greater attention. "Do that again, monkey!" Lhin obliged, curious to note that they apparently ate nothing other life had not prepared for them. "Darn. Rocks—just plain rocks—and he eats them. Has he got a craw like a bird, Slim?"

"He digests them. If you've read of those half-plant, half-animal things the Martians came from, you'll know what his metabolism's like. Look, Lhin, I take it you mean an element. Sodium, calcium, chlorine? No, I guess you have all those. Iodine, maybe? Hm-m-m." He went over a couple of dozen he could imagine having anything to do with life, but copper was not among them, by accident, and a slow fear crept up into the Lunarite's thoughts. This strange barrier to communication—would it ruin all?

He groped for the answer—and relaxed. Of course, though no common word existed, the element itself was common in structure. Hurriedly he flipped the pages of the code book to a blank one and reached for the Earth man's pencil. Then, as Slim and Fats stared curiously, he began sketching in the atomic structure of copper, particle by particle, from the center out, as the master physicists of his race had discovered it to be.

It meant nothing to them! Slim handed the paper back, shaking his head. "Fella, if I'm right in thinking that's a picture of some atom, we've got a lot to learn back on Earth. *Wheoo!*"

Fats twisted his lips. "If that's an atom, I'm a fried

egg. Come on, Slim, it's sleepy time and you've fooled away half a day. Anyhow, I want to talk that radio-active business over with you. It's so strong it'd cook us in half an hour if we weren't wearing these portable nullifiers—yet the monkey seems to thrive on it. I got an idea."

Slim came back from his brown study and stared at his watch. "Darn it! Look, Lhin, don't give up yet; we'll talk all this over tomorrow again. But Fats is right; it's time for us to sleep. So long, fella."

Lhin nodded a temporary farewell in his own tongue and slumped back on his rough bed. Outside, he heard Fats extolling a scheme of some kind for getting out the radioactives with Lhin's help, somehow, and Slim's protesting voice. But he paid no attention. The atomic structure had been right, he knew, but they were only groping toward it in their science, and their minds knew too little of the subject to enable them to grasp his pictures.

Chemical formulas? Reactions that would eliminate others, one by one? If they were chemists, perhaps, but even Slim knew too little for that. Yet, obviously, un-less there was no copper on Earth, there was an answer somewhere. Surely the Great Ones whom they called God would never answer generations of faithful prayer with a mockery! There was an answer, and while they slept, he would find it, though he had to search through every record roll for clues.

Hours later he was trudging across the plain toward the ship, hope again high. The answer, once found, was simple. All elements formed themselves into families and classes. Slim had mentioned sodium, and copper was related in the more primitive tables, such as Earth might use. More important, its atomic number was twenty-nine by theory elementary enough for any race that could build rockets.

The locks were open, and he slipped through both, the wavering half-formed thoughts of the men leading him to them unerringly. Once in their presence, he stopped, wondering about their habits. Already he had learned that what held true for his people was not necessarily the rule with them, and they might not approve of his arousing a sleeper. Finally, torn between politeness and impatience, he squatted on the metal floor, clutching the record roll, his nostrils sampling the metals around him. Copper was not there; but he hadn't expected so rare an element, though there were others here that he failed completely to recognize and guessed were among the heavy ones almost lacking on the Moon.

Fats gurgled and scrimmaged around with his arms, yawned, sat up, still half asleep. His thoughts were full of some Earth person of the female element which Lhin had noted was missing in these two, and what he'd do "when he got rich." Lhin was highly interested in the thought pictures until he realized that it would be best not to intrude on these obviously secret things. He withdrew his mind just as the man noted him.

Fats was never at his best while waking up. He came to his feet with a bellow and grabbed for something. "Why, you sneaking little monkey! Trying to sneak up and cut our—"

Lhin squealed and avoided the blow that would have left him a shapeless blob, uncertain of how he had offended, but warned by caution to leave. Physical fear was impossible to him—too many generations had grown and died with no need of it. But it came as a numbing shock that these beings would actually kill another intelligent person. Was life so cheap on Earth?

"Hey! Hey, Fats, stop it!" Slim had awakened at the sound of the commotion, and a hasty glance showed Lhin that he was holding the other's arms. "Lay off, will you? What's going on?"

But now Fats was fully awake and calming down. He dropped the metal bar and grinned wryly. "I dunno. I guess he meant all right, but he was sitting there with that metal thing in his hands, staring at me, and I figured he meant to cut my throat or something.

I'm all right now. Come on back, monkey; it's all right."

Slim let his partner go and nodded at Lhin. "Sure, come back, fella. Fats has some funny ideas about non-humans, but he's a good-hearted sort, on the whole. Be a good doggie and he won't kick you—he might even scratch your ears."

"Nuts." Fats was grinning, good nature restored. He knew Slim meant it as a crack, but it didn't bother him; what was wrong with treating Marshies and monkeys like what they were? "Whatcha got there, monkey? More pictures that mean nothing?"

Lhin nodded in imitation of their assent gesture and held out the roll to Slim; Fats' attitude was no longer unfriendly, but he was an unknown quantity, and Slim seemed the more interested. "Pictures that mean much, I hope. Here is Nra, twenty-nine, under sodium."

"Periodic table," Slim told Fats. "At least, it looks like one. Get me the handbook, will you? Hm-m-m. Under sodium, No. 29. Sodium, potassium, copper. And it's No. 29, all right. That it, Lhin?"

Lhin's eyes were blazing with triumph. Grace to the Great Ones. "Yes, it is copper. Perhaps you have some? Even a gram, perhaps?"

"A thousand grams, if you like. According to your notions, we're lousy with the stuff. Help yourself."

Fats cut in. "Sure, monkey, we got copper, if that's the stuff you've been yelling about. What'll you pay for it?"

"Pay?"

"Sure, give in return. We help you; you help us. That's fair, isn't it?"

It hadn't occurred to Lhin, but it did seem fair. But what had he to give? And then he realized what was in the man's mind. For the copper, he was to work, digging out and purifying the radioactives that gave warmth and light and life to the crater, so painfully brought into being when the place was first constructed, transmuted to meet the special needs of the people who were to live there. And after him, his sons and their sons, mining and sweating for Earth, and being paid in barely enough copper to keep Earth supplied with laborers. Fats' mind filled again with dreams of the other Earth creature. For that, he would doom a race to life without pride or hope or accomplishments. Lhin found no understanding in it. There were so many of those creatures on Earth—why should his enslavement be necessary?

Nor was enslavement all. Eventually, doom was as certain that way as the other, once Earth was glutted with the radioactives, or when the supply here dropped below the vital point, great as the reserve was. He shuddered under the decision forced upon him.

Slim's hand fell on his shoulder. "Fats has things slightly wrong, Lhin. Haven't you, Fats?"

There was something in Slim's hand, something Lhin knew dimly was a weapon. The other man squirmed, but his grin remained.

"You're touched, Slim, soft. Maybe you believe all this junk about other races' equality, but you won't kill me for it. I'm standing pat—I'm not giving away my copper."

And suddenly Slim was grinning, too, and putting the weapon back. "O. K., don't. Lhin can have my share. There's plenty on the ship in forms we can spare, and don't forget I own a quarter of it."

Fats' thoughts contained no answer to that. He mulled it over slowly, then shrugged. Slim was right enough about it, and could do as he wanted with his share. Anyhow— "O. K. Have it your way. I'll help you pry it off wherever it is, or dig it out. How about that wire down in the engine locker?"

Lhin stood silently watching them as they opened a small locker and rummaged through it, studying the engines and controls with half his mind, the other half quivering with ecstasy at the thought of copper—not just a handful, but all he could carry, in pure form, easily turned into digestible sulphate with acids he had already prepared for his former attempt at collecting it. In a year, the crater would be populated again, teeming with life. Perhaps three or four hundred sons left, and as they multiplied, more and yet more.

A detail of the hookup he was studying brought that part of his mind uppermost, and he tugged at Slim's trouser leg. "That . . . that . . . is not good, is it?"

"Huh? No, it isn't, fella. That's what brought us here. Why?"

"Then, without radioactives, I can pay. I will fix it." A momentary doubt struck him. "That is to pay, is it not?"

Fats heaved a coil of wonderful-smelling wire out of the locker, wiped off sweat, and nodded. "That's to pay, all right, but you let those things alone. They're bad enough, already, and maybe even Slim can't fix it."

"I can fix."

"Yeah. What school did you get your degree in electronics from? Two hundred feet in this coil, makes fifty for him. You gonna give it all to him, Slim?"

"Guess so." Slim was looking at Lhin doubtfully, only half watching as the other measured and cut the wire. "Ever touched anything like that before, Lhin? Controls for the ion feed and injectors are pretty complicated in these ships. What makes you think you can do it—unless your people had things like this and you studied the records."

Lhin fought for words as he tried to explain. His people had had nothing like that—their atomics had worked from a different angle, since uranium was almost nonexistent on the Moon, and they had used a direct application of it. But the principles were plain to him, even from what he could see outside; he could feel the way it worked in his head.

"I feel. When I first grew, I could fix that. It is the way I think, not the way I learn, though I have read all the records. For three hundred million years, my people have learned it—now I feel it."

"Three hundred million years! I knew your race was

old when you told me you were born talking and reading, but—galloping dinosaurs!"

"My people saw those things on your world, yes," Lhin assured him solemnly. "Then I shall fix?"

Slim shook his head in confusion and handed over a tool kit without another word. "Three hundred million years, Fats, and during almost all that time they were farther ahead than we are now. Figure that one out. When we were little crawling things living off dinosaur eggs, they were flitting from planet to planet—only I don't suppose they could stay very long; six times normal gravity for them. And now, just because they had to stay on a light world and their air losses made them gather here where things weren't normal, Lhin's all that's left."

"Yeah, and how does that make him a mechanic?"

"Instinct. In the same amount of time, look at the instincts the animals picked up. He has an instinct for machinery; he doesn't know all about it, probably, but he can instinctively feel how a thing should work. Add to that the collection of science records he was showing me and the amount of reading he's probably done, and there should be almost nothing he couldn't do to a machine."

There wasn't much use in arguing, Fats decided, as he watched what was happening. The monkey either fixed things or they never would leave. Lhin had taken snips and disconnected the control box completely; now he was taking that to pieces, one thing at a time. With a curious deftness, he unhooked wires, lifted out tubes, uncoupled transformers.

It seemed simple enough to him. They had converted energy from the atomic fuel, and they used certain forces to ionize matter, control the rate of ionization, feed the ions to the rocket tubes, and force them outward at high speed through helices. An elementary problem in applied electronics to govern the rate and control the ionization forces.

With small quick hands he bent wires into coils,

placed other coils in relation, and coupled a tube to the combination. Around the whole, other coils and tubes took shape, then a long feeder connected to the pipe that carried the compound to be ionized, and bus bars to the energy intake. The injectors that handled the feeding of ions were needlessly complicated, but he let them alone, since they were workable as they were. It had taken him less than fifteen minutes.

"It will now work. But use care when you first try it. Now it makes all work, not a little as it did before."

Slim inspected it. "That all? What about this pile of stuff you didn't use?"

"There was no need. It was very poor. Now it is good." As best he could, he explained to Slim what happened when it was used now; before, it would have taken a well-trained technician to describe, even with the complicated words at his command. But what was there now was the product of a science that had gone beyond the stumbling complications of first attempts. Something was to be done, and was done, as simply as possible. Slim's only puzzle was that it hadn't been done that way in the first place—a normal reaction, once the final simplification is reached. He nodded.

"Good. Fats, this is the business. You'll get about 99.99% efficiency now, instead of the 20% maximum before. You're all right, Lhin."

Fats knew nothing of electronics, but it had sounded right as Lhin explained, and he made no comment. Instead, he headed for the control room. "O. K., we'll leave here, then. So long, monkey."

Slim gathered up the wire and handed it to Lhin, accompanying him to the air lock. On the ground as the locks closed, the Moon man looked up and managed an Earth smile. "I shall open the doors above for you to go through. And you are paid, and all is fair, not so? Then—so long, Slim. The Great Ones love you, that you have given my people back to me."

" 'Dios," Slim answered, and waved, just before the

doors came shut. "Maybe we'll be back sometime and see how you make out."

Back at the cave, Lhin fondled the copper and waited for the sounds the rockets would make, filled with mixed emotions and uncertainties. The copper was pure ecstasy to him, but there were thoughts in Fats' mind which were not all clear. Well, he had the copper for generations to come; what happened to his people now rested on the laps of the Great Ones.

He stood outside the entrance, watching the now-steady rocket blast upward and away, carrying with it the fate of his race. If they told of the radioactives, slavery and extinction. If they remained silent, perhaps a return to former greatness, and passage might be resumed to other planets, long deserted even at the height of their progress; but now planets bearing life and intelligence instead of mere jungles. Perhaps, in time, and with materials bought from other worlds with ancient knowledge, even a solution that would let them restore their world to its ancient glory, as they had dreamed before hopelessness and the dark wings of a race's night had settled over them.

As he watched, the rocket spiraled directly above him, cutting the light off and on with a shadow like the beat of wings from the mists of antiquity, when winged life had filled the air of the Moon. An omen, perhaps, those sable wings that reached up and passed through the roof as he released the slides, then went skimming out, leaving all clear behind. But whether a good omen or ill, he had not decided.

He carried the copper wire back to the nursery.

And on the ship, Slim watched Fats wiggle and try to think, and there was amusement on his face. "Well, was he good? As good as any human, perhaps?"

"Yeah. All right, better. I'll admit anything you want. He's as good as I am—maybe he's better. That satisfy you?"

"No." Slim was beating the iron while it was hot. "What about those radioactives?"

Fats threw more power into the tubes, and gasped as the new force behind the rockets pushed him back into his seat. He eased up gently, staring straight ahead. Finally he shrugged and turned back to Slim.

"O. K., you win. The monkey keeps his freedom and I keep my lip buttoned. Satisfied?"

"Yeah." Slim was more than satisfied. To him, also, things seemed an omen of the future, and proof that idealism was not altogether folly. Some day the wings of dark prejudice and contempt for others might lift from all Earth's Empire, as they were lifting from Fats' mind. Perhaps not in his time, but eventually; and intelligence, not race, would rule.

"Well satisfied, Fats," he said. "And you don't need to worry about losing too much. We'll make all the money we can ever spend from the new principles of Lhin's hookup; I've thought of a dozen applications already. What do you figure on doing with your share?"

Fats grinned. "Be a damned fool. Help you start your propaganda again and go around kissing Marshies and monkeys. Wonder what our little monkey's thinking."

Lhin wasn't thinking, then; he'd solved the riddle of the factors in Fats' mind, and he knew what the decision would be. Now he was making copper sulphate, and seeing dawn come up where night had been. There's something beautiful about any dawn, and this was very lovely to him.

JEROME BIXBY

THE HOLES
AROUND MARS

*This is not one of those science fictions
which you should automatically assume
may be likely to happen. Of course, nothing of its sort can actually be proved to
be impossible; and the Universe is, indeed,
full of extraordinary things. In view of
the theoretically "real" nature of collapsed matter in certain types of stars
(see any moderately advanced book on
modern astronomy*), I suppose Mr. Bixby's concept has to be filed among those
that "might be." In any event, the author
has written about it in such a convincing
way that it does seem thoroughly real—
and that is what makes it fun to read.*

SPACESHIP CREWS should be selected on the basis of
their non-irritating qualities as individuals. No chronic
complainers, no hypochondriacs, no bugs on cleanliness

* As, for example, Fred Hoyle's superb *Astronomy* (1962),
in which Hoyle estimates that material from the center of the
white dwarf star known as the Pup, companion of Sirius, which
we know as the Dog Star, is so densely packed that "a single
matchboxful would weigh several tons." Another source has
made it more specific by estimating that one-tenth of a cubic
inch would weigh 1,300 pounds at the Earth's surface; and that
a 150-pound Earth man, if he were made of collapsed material
and was on the surface of the Pup, would weigh around 250,000
tons!

—particularly no one-man parties. I speak from bitter experience.

Because on the first expedition to Mars, Hugh Allenby damned near drove us nuts with his puns. We finally got so we just ignored them.

But no one can ignore that classic last one—it's written right into the annals of astronomy, and it's there to stay.

Allenby, in command of the expedition, was first to set foot outside the ship. As he stepped down from the airlock of the *Mars I*, he placed that foot on a convenient rock, caught the toe of his weighted boot in a hole in the rock, wrenched his ankle and smote the ground with his pants.

Sitting there, eyes pained behind the transparent shield of his oxygen-mask, he stared at the rock.

It was about five feet high. Ordinary granite—no special shape—and several inches below its summit, running straight through it in a northeasterly direction, was a neat round four-inch hole.

"I'm *upset* by the *hole* thing," he grunted.

The rest of us scrambled out of the ship and gathered around his plump form. Only one or two of us winced at his miserable double pun.

"Break anything, Hugh?" asked Burton, our pilot, kneeling beside him.

"Get out of my way, Burton," said Allenby. "You're obstructing my view."

Burton blinked. A man constructed of long bones and caution, he angled out of the way, looking around to see what he was obstructing view *of*.

He saw the rock and the round hole through it. He stood very still, staring. So did the rest of us.

"Well, I'll be damned," said Janus, our photographer. "A hole."

"In a rock," added Gonzales, our botanist.

"Round," said Randolph, our biologist.

"An *artifact*," finished Allenby softly.

Burton helped him to his feet. Silently we gathered around the rock.

Janus bent down and put an eye to one end of the hole. I bent down and looked through the other end. We squinted at each other.

As mineralogist, I was expected to opinionate. "Not drilled," I said slowly. "Not chipped. Not melted. Certainly not eroded."

I heard a rasping sound by my ear and straightened. Burton was scratching a thumbnail along the rim of the hole. "Weathered," he said. "Plenty old. But I'll bet it's a perfect circle, if we measure."

Janus was already fiddling with his camera, testing the cooperation of the tiny distant sun with a light-meter.

"Let us see *weather* it is or not," Allenby said.

Burton brought out a steel tape-measure. The hole was four and three-eighths inches across. It was perfectly circular and about sixteen inches long. And four feet above the ground.

"But why?" said Randolph. "Why should anyone bore a four-inch tunnel through a rock way out in the middle of the desert?"

"Religious symbol," said Janus. He looked around, one hand on his gun. "We'd better keep an eye out— maybe we've landed on sacred ground or something."

"A totem *hole*, perhaps," Allenby suggested.

"Oh, I don't know," Randolph said—to Janus, not Allenby. As I've mentioned, we always ignored Allenby's puns. "Note the lack of ornamentation. Not at all typical of religious articles."

"On Earth," Gonzales reminded him. "Besides, it might be utilitarian, not symbolic."

"Utilitarian, how?" asked Janus.

"An altar for snakes," Burton said dryly.

"Well," said Allenby, "you can't deny that it has its *holy* aspects."

"Move your hand, will you, Peters?" asked Janus.

I did. When Janus's camera had clicked, I bent again and peered through the hole. "It sights on that low ridge over there," I said. "Maybe it's some kind of surveying setup. I'm going to take a look."

"Careful," warned Janus. "Remember, it may be sacred."

As I walked away, I heard Allenby say, "Take some scrapings from the inside of the hole, Gonzales. We might be able to determine if anything is kept in it. . ."

One of the stumpy, purplish, barrel-type cacti on the ridge had a long vertical bite out of it . . . as if someone had carefully carved out a narrow U-shaped section from the top down, finishing the bottom of the U in a neat semicircle. It was as flat and cleancut as the inside surface of a horseshoe magnet.

I hollered. The others came running. I pointed.

"Oh, my God!" said Allenby. "Another one."

The pulp of the cactus in and around the U-hole was dried and dead-looking.

Silently Burton used his tape-measure. The hole measured four and three-eighths inches across. It was eleven inches deep. The semicircular bottom was about a foot above the ground.

"This ridge," I said, "is about three feet higher than where we landed the ship. I bet the hole in the rock and the hole in this cactus are on the same level."

Gonzales said slowly, "This was not done all at once. It is a result of periodic attacks. Look here and here. These overlapping depressions along the outer edges of the hole—" he pointed— "on this side of the cactus. They are the signs of repeated impact. And the scallop effect on *this* side, where whatever made the hole emerged. There are juices still oozing—not at the point of impact, where the plant is desiccated, but below, where the shock was transmitted—"

A distant shout turned us around. Burton was at the rock, beside the ship. He was bending down, his eye to the far side of the mysterious hole.

He looked for another second, then straightened.

"They line up," he said when he reached us. "The bottom of the hole in the cactus is right in the middle when you sight through the hole in the rock."

"As if somebody came around and whacked the cactus regularly," Janus said, looking around warily.

"To keep the line of sight through the holes clear?" I wondered. "Why not just remove the cactus?"

"Religious," Janus explained.

The gauntlet he had discarded lay ignored on the ground, in the shadow of the cactus. We went on past the ridge toward an outcropping of rock about a hundred yards farther on. We walked silently, each of us wondering if what we half-expected would really be there.

It was. In one of the tall, weathered spires in the outcropping, some ten feet below its peak and four feet above the ground, was a round four-inch hole.

Allenby sat down on a rock, nursing his ankle, and remarked that anybody who believed this crazy business was really happening must have holes in the rocks in his head.

Burton put his eye to the hole and whistled. "Sixty feet long if it's an inch," he said. "The other end's just a pinpoint. But you can see it. The damn thing's perfectly straight."

I looked back the way we had come. The cactus stood on the ridge, with its U-shaped bite, and beyond was the ship, and beside it the perforated rock.

"If we surveyed," I said, "I bet the holes would all line up right to the last millimeter."

"But," Randolph complained, "why would anybody go out and bore holes in things all along a line through the desert?"

"Religious," Janus muttered. "It doesn't *have* to make sense."

We stood there by the outcropping and looked out along the wide, red desert beyond. It stretched flatly for miles from this point, south toward Mars' equator —dead sandy wastes, crisscrossed by the "canals,"

which we had observed while landing to be great
straggly patches of vegetation, probably strung along
underground waterflows.

BLONG - G - G - G - . . . st - st - st - . . .

We jumped half out of our skins. Ozone bit at our
nostrils. Our hair stirred in the electrical uproar.

"L - look," Janus chattered, lowering his smoking
gun.

About forty feet to our left, a small rabbity creature
poked its head from behind a rock and stared at us in
utter horror.

Janus raised his gun again.

"Don't bother," said Allenby tiredly. "I don't think
it intends to attack."

"But—"

"I'm sure it isn't a Martian with religious convic-
tions."

Janus wet his lips and looked a little shamefaced. "I
guess I'm kind of taut."

"That's what I *taut*," said Allenby.

The creature darted from behind its rock and, looking at us over its shoulder, employed six legs to make
small but very fast tracks.

We turned our attention again to the desert. Far out,
black against Mars' azure horizon, was a line of low
hills.

"Shall we go look?" asked Burton, eyes gleaming at
the mystery.

Janus hefted his gun nervously. It was still crackling
from the discharge. "I say let's get back to the ship!"

Allenby sighed. "My leg hurts." He studied the hills.
"Give me the field-glasses."

Randolph handed them over. Allenby put them to
the shield of his mask, and adjusted them.

After a moment he sighed again. "There's a hole. On
a plane surface that catches the Sun. A lousy damned
round little impossible hole."

"Those hills," Burton observed, "must be thousands
of feet thick."

The argument lasted all the way back to the ship.

Janus, holding out for his belief that the whole thing was of religious origin, kept looking around for Martians as if he expected them to pour screaming from the hills.

Burton came up with the suggestion that perhaps the holes had been made by a disintegrator-ray.

"It's possible," Allenby admitted. "This might have been the scene of some great battle—"

"With only one such weapon?" I objected.

Allenby swore as he stumbled. "What do you mean?"

"I haven't seen any other lines of holes—only the one. In a battle, the whole joint should be cut up."

That was good for a few moments' silent thought. Then Allenby said, "It might have been brought out by one side as a last resort. Sort of an ace in the hole."

I resisted the temptation to mutiny. "But would even one such weapon, in battle, make only *one* line of holes? Wouldn't it be played in an arc against the enemy? You know it would."

"Well—"

"Wouldn't it cut slices out of the landscape, instead of boring holes? And wouldn't it sway or vibrate enough to make the holes miles away from it something less than perfect circles?"

"It could have been very firmly mounted."

"Hugh, does that sound like a practical weapon to you?"

Two seconds of silence. "On the other hand," he said, "instead of a war, the whole thing might have been designed to frighten some primitive race—or even some kind of beast—the *hole* out of here. A demonstration—"

"Religious," Janus grumbled, still looking around.

We walked on, passing the cactus on the low ridge.

"Interesting," said Gonzales. "The evidence that whatever causes the phenomenon has happened again and again. I'm afraid that the war theory—"

"Oh, my God!" gasped Burton.

We stared at him.

"The ship," he whispered. "It's right in line with the holes! If whatever made them is still in operation. . ."

"Run!" yelled Allenby, and we ran like fiends.

We got the ship into the air, out of line with the holes to what we fervently hoped was safety, and then we realized we were admitting our fear that the mysterious hole-maker might still be lurking around.

Well, the evidence was all for it, as Gonzales had reminded us—that cactus had been oozing.

We cruised at twenty thousand feet and thought it over.

Janus, whose only training was in photography, said, "Some kind of omnivorous animal? Or bird? Eats rocks and everything?"

"I will not totally discount the notion of such an animal," Randolph said. "But I will resist to the death the suggestion that it forages with geometric precision."

After a while, Allenby said, "Land, Burton. By that 'canal.' Lots of plant life—fauna, too. We'll do a little collecting."

Burton set us down feather-light at the very edge of the sprawling flat expanse of vegetation, commenting that the scene reminded him of his native Texas pear-flats.

We wandered in the chilly air, each of us except Burton pursuing his specialty. Randolph relentlessly stalked another of the rabbity creatures. Gonzales was carefully digging up plants and stowing them in jars. Janus was busy with his cameras, recording every aspect of Mars transferable to film. Allenby walked around, helping anybody who needed it. An astronomer, he'd done half his work on the way to Mars and would do the other half on the return trip. Burton lounged in the Sun, his back against a ship's fin, and played chess with Allenby, who was calling out his moves in a bull roar. I grubbed for rocks.

My search took me farther and farther away from the others—all I could find around the 'canal' was gravel, and I wanted to chip at some big stuff. I walked toward a long rise a half-mile or so away, beyond which rose an enticing array of house-sized boulders.

As I moved out of earshot, I heard Randolph snarl, "Burton, *will* you stop yelling, 'Kt to B-2 and check?' Every time you open your yap, this critter takes off on me."

Then I saw the groove.

It started right where the ground began to rise—a thin, shallow, curve-bottomed groove in the dirt at my feet, about half an inch across, running off straight toward higher ground.

With my eyes glued to it, I walked. The ground slowly rose. The groove deepened, widened—now it was about three inches across, about one and a half deep.

I walked on, holding my breath. Four inches wide. Two inches deep.

The ground rose some more. Four and three-eighths inches wide. I didn't have to measure it—I *knew.*

Now, as the ground rose, the edges of the groove began to curve inward over the groove. They touched. No more groove.

The ground had risen, the groove had stayed level and gone underground.

Except that now it wasn't a groove. It was a round tunnel.

A hole.

A few paces farther on, I thumped the ground with my heel where the hole ought to be. The dirt crumbled, and there was the little dark tunnel, running straight in both directions.

I walked on, the ground falling away gradually again. The entire process was repeated in reverse. A hairline appeared in the dirt—widened—became lips that drew slowly apart to reveal the neat straight four-

inch groove—which shrank as slowly to a shallow line of the ground—and vanished.

I looked ahead of me. There was one low ridge of ground between me and the enormous boulders. A neat four-inch semicircle was bitten out of the very top of the ridge. In the house-sized boulder directly beyond was a four-inch hole.

Allenby winced and called the others when I came back and reported.

"The mystery *deepens*," he told them. He turned to me. "Lead on, Peters. You're temporary *drill* leader."

Thank God he didn't say *Fall in*.

The holes went straight through the nest of boulders —there'd be a hole in one and, ten or twenty feet farther on in the next boulder, another hole. And then another, and another—right through the nest in a line. About thirty holes in all.

Burton, standing by the boulder I'd first seen, flashed his flashlight into the hole. Randolph, clear on the other side of the jumbled nest, eye to hole, saw it.

Straight as a string!

The ground sloped away on the far side of the nest —no holes were visible in that direction—just miles of desert. So, after we'd stared at the holes for a while and they didn't go away, we headed back for the canal.

"Is there any possibility," asked Janus, as we walked, "that it could be a natural phenomenon?"

"There are no straight lines in nature," Randolph said, a little shortly. "That goes for a bunch of circles in a straight line. And for perfect circles, too."

"A planet is a circle," objected Janus.

"An oblate spheroid," Allenby corrected.

"A planet's orbit—"

"An ellipse."

Janus walked a few steps, frowning. Then he said, "I remember reading that there *is* something darned near a perfect circle in nature." He paused a moment. "Potholes." And he looked at me, as mineralogist, to corroborate.

"What kind of potholes?" I asked cautiously. "Do you mean where part of a limestone deposit has dissol—"

"No. I once read that when a glacier passes over a hard rock that's lying on some softer rock, it grinds the hard rock down into the softer, and both of them sort of wear down to fit together, and it all ends up with a round hole in the soft rock."

"Probably neither stone," I told Janus, "would be homogeneous. The softer parts would abrade faster in the soft stone. The end result wouldn't be a perfect circle."

Janus's face fell.

"Now," I said, "would anyone care to define this term 'perfect circle' we're throwing around so blithely? Because such holes as Janus describes are often pretty damned round."

Randolph said, "Well . . ."

"It is settled, then," Gonzales said, a little sarcastically. "Your discussion, gentlemen, has established that the long, horizontal holes we have found were caused by glacial action."

"Oh, no," Janus argued seriously. "I once read that Mars never had any glaciers."

All of us shuddered.

Half an hour later, we spotted more holes, about a mile down the 'canal,' still on a line, marching along the desert, through cacti, rocks, hills, even through one edge of the low vegetation of the 'canal' for thirty feet or so. It was the damnedest thing to bend down and look straight through all that curling, twisting growth . . . a round tunnel from either end.

We followed the holes for about a mile, to the rim of an enormous saucerlike valley that sank gradually before us until, miles away, it was thousands of feet deep. We stared out across it, wondering about the other side.

Allenby said determinedly, "We'll burrow to the *bottom* of these holes, once and for all. Back to the ship, men!"

We hiked back, climbed in and took off.

At an altitude of fifty feet, Burton lined the nose of the ship on the most recent line of holes and we flew out over the valley.

On the other side was a range of hefty hills. The holes went through them. Straight through. We would approach one hill—Burton would manipulate the front viewscreen until we spotted the hole—we would pass over the hill and spot the other end of the hole in the rear screen.

One hole was two hundred and eighty miles long.

Four hours later, we were halfway around Mars.

Randolph was sitting by a side port, chin on one hand, his eyes unbelieving. "All around the planet," he kept repeating. "All around the planet. . ."

"Halfway at least," Allenby mused. "And we can assume that it continues in a straight line, through anything and everything that gets in its way. . ." He gazed out the front port at the uneven blue-green haze of a 'canal' off to our left. "For the love of Heaven, why?"

Then Allenby fell down. We all did.

Burton had suddenly slapped at the control board, and the ship braked and sank like a plugged duck. At the last second, Burton propped up the nose with a short burst, the ten-foot wheels hit desert sand and in five hundred yards we had jounced to a stop.

Allenby got up from the floor. "Why did you do that?" he asked Burton politely, nursing a bruised elbow.

Burton's nose was almost touching the front port. "Look!" he said, and pointed.

About two miles away, the Martian village looked like a handful of yellow marbles flung on the desert.

We checked our guns. We put on our oxygen-masks. We checked our guns again. We got out of the ship and made damned sure the airlock was locked.

An hour later, we crawled inch by painstaking inch up a high sand dune and poked our heads over the top.

The Martians were runts—the tallest of them less than five feet tall—and skinny as a pencil. Dried-up and brown, they wore loincloths of woven fiber.

They stood among the dusty-looking inverted-bowl buildings of their village, and every one of them was looking straight up at us with unblinking brown eyes.

The six safeties of our six guns clicked off like a rattle of dice. The Martians stood there and gawped.

"Probably a highly developed sense of hearing in this thin atmosphere," Allenby murmured. "Heard us coming."

"They thought that landing of Burton's was an earthquake," Randolph grumbled sourly.

"Marsquake," corrected Janus. One look at the village's scrawny occupants seemed to have convinced him that his life was in no danger.

Holding the Martians covered, we examined the village from atop the thirty-foot dune.

The domelike buildings were constructed of something that looked like adobe. No windows—probably built with sandstorms in mind. The doors were about halfway up the sloping sides, and from each door a stone ramp wound down around the house to the ground—again with sandstorms in mind, no doubt, so drifting dunes wouldn't block the entrances.

The center of the village was a wide street, a long sandy area some thirty feet wide. On either side of it, the houses were scattered at random, as if each Martian had simply hunted for a comfortable place to sit and then built a house around it.

"Look," whispered Randolph.

One Martian had stepped from a group situated on the far side of the street from us. He started to cross the street, his round brown eyes on us, his small bare feet plodding sand, and we saw that in addition to a loincloth he wore jewelry—a hammered metal ring, a bracelet on one skinny ankle. The Sun caught a copperish gleam on his bald narrow head, and we saw a band of metal there, just above where his eyebrows should have been.

"The super-chief," Allenby murmured. "Oh, *shaman* me!"

As the bejeweled Martian approached the center of the street, he glanced briefly at the ground at his feet. Then he raised his head, stepped with dignity across the exact center of the street and came on toward us, passing the dusty-looking buildings of his realm and the dusty-looking groups of his subjects.

He reached the slope of the dune we lay on, paused —and raised small hands over his head, palms toward us.

"I think," Allenby said, "that an anthropologist would give odds on that gesture meaning peace."

He stood up, holstered his gun—without buttoning the flap—and raised his own hands over his head. We all did.

The Martian language consisted of squeaks.

We made friendly noises, the chief squeaked and pretty soon we were the center of a group of wide-eyed Martians, none of whom made a sound. Evidently no one dared peep while the chief spoke—very likely the most articulate Martians simply squeaked themselves into the job. Allenby, of course, said they just *squeaked by*.

He was going through the business of drawing concentric circles in the sand, pointing at the third orbit away from the Sun and thumping his chest. The crowd around us kept growing as more Martians emerged from the dome buildings to see what was going on. Down the winding ramps of the buildings on our side of the street, plodding through the sand, blinking brown eyes at us, not making a sound.

Allenby pointed at the third orbit and thumped his chest. The chief squeaked and thumped his own chest and pointed at the copperish band around his head. Then he pointed at Allenby.

"I seem to have conveyed to him," Allenby said dryly, "the fact that I'm chief of our party. Well, let's try again."

He started over on the orbits. He didn't seem to be getting anyplace, so the rest of us watched the Martians instead. A last handful was straggling across the wide street.

"Curious," said Gonzales. "Note what happens when they reach the center of the street."

Each Martian, upon reaching the center of the street, glanced at his feet—just for a moment—without even breaking stride. And then came on.

"What can they be looking at?" Gonzales wondered.

"The chief did it too," Burton mused. "Remember when he first came toward us?"

We all stared intently at the middle of the street. We saw absolutely nothing but sand.

The Martians milled around us and watched Allenby and his orbits. A Martian child appeared from between two buildings across the street. On six-inch legs, it started across, got halfway, glanced downward—and came on.

"I don't get it," Burton said. "What in hell are they *looking* at?"

The child reached the crowd and squeaked a thin, high note.

A number of things happened at once.

Several members of the group around us glanced down, and along the edge of the crowd nearest the center of the street there was a mild stir as individuals drifted off to either side. Quite casually—nothing at all urgent about it. They just moved concertedly to get farther away from the center of the street, not taking their interested gaze off us for one second in the process.

Even the chief glanced up from Allenby's concentric circles at the child's squeak. And Randolph, who had been fidgeting uncomfortably and paying very little attention to our conversation, decided that he must answer Nature's call. He moved off into the dunes surrounding the village. Or rather, he started to move.

The moment he set off across the wide street, the little Martian chief was in front of him, brown eyes wide, hands out before him as if to thrust Randolph back.

Again six safeties clicked. The Martians didn't even blink at the sudden appearance of our guns. Probably the only weapon they recognized was a club, or maybe a rock.

"What can the matter be?" Randolph said.

He took another step forward. The chief squeaked and stood his ground. Randolph had to stop or bump into him. Randolph stopped.

The chief squeaked, looking right into the bore of Randolph's gun.

"Hold still," Allenby told Randolph, "till we know what's up."

Allenby made an interrogative sound at the chief. The chief squeaked and pointed at the ground. We looked. He was pointing at his shadow.

Randolph stirred uncomfortably.

"Hold still," Allenby warned him, and again he made the questioning sound.

The chief pointed up the street. Then he pointed down the street. He bent to touch his shadow, thumping it with thin fingers. Then he pointed at the wall of a house nearby.

We all looked.

Straight lines had been painted on the curved brick-colored wall, up and down and across, to form many small squares about four inches across. In each square was a bit of squiggly writing, in blackish paint, and a small wooden peg jutting out from the wall.

Burton said, "Looks like a damn crossword puzzle."

"Look," said Janus. "In the lower right corner—a metal ring hanging from one of the pegs."

And that was all we saw on the wall. Hundreds of squares with figures in them—a small peg set in each—and a ring hanging on one of the pegs.

"You know what?" Allenby said slowly. "I think it's a calendar! Just a second—thirty squares wide by twenty-two high—that's six hundred and sixty. And that bottom line has twenty six—twenty-*seven* squares. Six hundred and eighty-seven squares in all. That's how many days there are in the Martian year!"

He looked thoughtfully at the metal ring. "I'll bet that ring is hanging from the peg in the square that represents *today*. They must move it along every day, to keep track. . ."

"What's a calendar got to do with my crossing the street?" Randolph asked in a pained tone.

He started to take another step. The chief squeaked as if it were a matter of desperate concern that he make us understand. Randolph stopped again and swore.

Allenby made his questioning sound again.

The chief pointed emphatically at his shadow, then at the communal calendar—and we could see now that he was pointing at the metal ring.

Burton said slowly, "I think he's trying to tell us that this is *today*. And such-and-such a *time* of day. I bet he's using his shadow as a sundial."

"Perhaps," Allenby granted.

Randolph said, "If this monkey doesn't let me go in another minute—"

The chief squeaked, eyes concerned.

"Stand still," Allenby ordered. "He's trying to warn you of some danger."

The chief pointed down the street again and, instead of squealing, revealed that there was another sound at his command. He said, "Whoooooooosh!"

We all stared at the end of the street.

Nothing! Just the wide avenue between the houses, and the high sand dune down at the end of it, from which we had first looked upon the village.

The chief described a large circle with one hand, sweeping the hand above his head, down to his knees, up again, as fast as he could. He pursed his monkey-lips and said, "Whoooooosh!" And made the circle again.

A Martian emerged from the door in the side of a house across the avenue and blinked at the Sun, as if he had just awakened. Then he saw what was going on below and blinked again, this time in interest. He made his way down around the winding ramp and started to cross the street.

About halfway, he paused, eyed the calendar on the house wall, glanced at his shadow. Then he got down on his hands and knees and *crawled* across the middle of the street. Once past the middle, he rose, walked the rest of the way to join one of the groups and calmly stared at us along with the rest of them.

"They're all crazy," Randolph said disgustedly. "I'm going to cross that street!"

"Shut up. So it's a certain time of a certain day," Allenby mused. "And from the way the chief is acting, he's afraid for you to cross the street. And that other one just *crawled*. By God, do you know what this might tie in with?"

We were silent for a moment. Then Gonzales said, "Of course!"

And Burton said, "The *holes!*"

"Exactly," said Allenby. "Maybe whatever made—or makes—the holes comes right down the center of the street here. Maybe that's why they built the village this way—to make room for—"

"For what?" Randolph asked unhappily, shifting his feet.

"I don't know," Allenby said. He looked thoughtfully at the chief. "That circular motion he made—could he have been describing something that went around and around the planet? Something like—oh, no!" Allenby's eyes glazed. "I wouldn't believe it in a million years."

His gaze went to the far end of the street, to the high sand dune that rose there. The chief seemed to be waiting for something to happen.

"I'm going to crawl," Randolph stated. He got to his hands and knees and began to creep across the center of the avenue.

The chief let him go.

The sand dune at the end of the street suddenly erupted. A forty-foot spout of dust shot straight out from the sloping side, as if a bullet had emerged. Powdered sand hazed the air, yellowed it almost the full length of the avenue. Grains of sand stung the skin and rattled minutely on the houses.

WhoooSSSHHHHH!

Randolph dropped flat on his belly. He didn't have to continue his trip. He had made other arrangements.

That night in the ship, while we all sat around, still shaking our heads every once in a while, Allenby talked with Earth. He sat there, wearing the headphones, trying to make himself understood above the godawful static.

". . . an exceedingly small body," he repeated wearily to his unbelieving audience, "about four inches in diameter. It travels at a mean distance of four feet above the surface of the planet, at a velocity yet to be calculated. Its unique nature results in many hitherto unobserved—I might say even unimagined—phenomena." He stared blankly in front of him for a moment, then delivered the understatement of his life. "The discovery may necessitate a re-examination of many of our basic postulates in the physical sciences."

The headphones squawked.

Patiently, Allenby assured Earth that he was entirely serious, and reiterated the results of his observations. I suppose that he, an astronomer, was twice as flabbergasted as the rest of us. On the other hand, perhaps he was better equipped to adjust to the evidence.

"Evidently," he said, "when the body was formed,

it traveled at such fantastic velocity as to enable it to—" his voice was almost a whisper—"to punch holes in things."

The headphones squawked.

"In rocks," Allenby said, "in mountains, in anything that got in its way. And now the holes form a large portion of its fixed orbit."

Squawk.

"Its mass must be on the order of—"

Squawk.

"—process of making the holes slowed it, so that now it travels just fast enough—"

Squawk.

"—maintain its orbit and penetrate occasional objects such as—"

Squawk.

"—and sand dunes—"

Squawk.

"My God, I *know* it's a mathematical monstrosity," Allenby snarled. "*I* didn't put it there!"

Squawk.

Allenby was silent for a moment. Then he said slowly, "A name?"

Squawk.

"H'm," said Allenby. "Well, well." He appeared to brighten just a little. "So it's up to me, as leader of the expedition, to name it?"

Squawk.

"Well, well," he said.

That chop-licking tone was in his voice. We'd heard it all too often before. We shuddered, waiting.

"Inasmuch as Mars' outermost moon is called Deimos, and the next Phobos," he said, "I think I shall name the third moon of Mars—*Bottomos*."

RAY BRADBURY

KALEIDOSCOPE

*It would be indecent and insulting to
both the author and the reader for me
to make any extended comment on this
story. Only one is needed: no victories—
even against outer space—have ever
been or ever will be won wholly without losses...*

THE FIRST CONCUSSION cut the ship up the side like a
giant can opener. The men were thrown into space
like a dozen wriggling silverfish. They were scattered
into a dark sea; and the ship, in a million pieces, went
on like a meteor swarm seeking a lost sun.

"Barkley, Barkley, where are you?"

The sound of voices calling like lost children on a
cold night.

"Woode, Woode!"

"Captain!"

"Hollis, Hollis, this is Stone."

"Stone, this is Hollis. Where are you?"

"I don't know, how can I? Which way is up? I'm
falling. Good gosh, I'm falling."

They fell. They fell as pebbles fall in the long
autumns of childhood, silver and thin. They were scattered as jackstones are scattered from a gigantic throw.
And now instead of men there were only voices—all
kinds of voices. Disembodied and impassioned, in vary-
ing degrees of terror and resignation.

"We're going away from each other."

This was true. Hollis, swinging head over heels,

knew this was true. He knew it with a vague accept-
ance. They were parting to go their separate ways,
and nothing could bring them back. They were wearing their sealed-tight space suits with the glass tubes
over their pale faces, but they hadn't had time to lock
on their force units. With them, they could be small
lifeboats in space, saving themselves, saving others,
collecting together, finding each other until they were
an island of men with some plan. But without the force
units snapped to their shoulders they were meteors,
senseless, each going to a separate and irrevocable fate.

A period of perhaps ten minutes elapsed while the
first terror died and a metallic calm took its place.
Space began to weave their strange voices in and out,
on a great dark loom, crossing, recrossing, making a
final pattern.

"Stone to Hollis. How long can we talk by phone?"

"It depends on how fast you're going your way and
I'm going mine."

"An hour, I make it."

"That should do it," said Hollis, abstracted and quiet.

"What happened?" said Hollis, a minute later.

"The rocket blew up, that's all. Rockets do blow
up."

"Which way are you going?"

"It looks like I'll hit the sun."

"It's Earth for me. Back to old Mother Earth at ten
thousand miles per hour. I'll burn like a match." Hollis
thought of it with a queer abstraction of mind. He
seemed to be removed from his body, watching it fall
down and down through space, as objective as he had
been in regard to the first falling snowflakes of a winter
season long gone.

The others were silent, thinking of the destiny that
had brought them to this, falling, falling, and nothing
they could do to change it. Even the captain was quiet,
for there was no command or plan he knew that could
put things back together again.

"Oh, it's a long way down, oh, it's a long way down,

a long, long, long way down," said a voice. "I don't want to die, I don't want to die, it's a long way down."

"Who's that?"

"I don't know."

"Stimson, I think. Stimson, is that you?"

"It's a long way and I don't like it, oh God, I don't like it."

"Stimson, this is Hollis, Stimson, you hear me?"

A pause while they fell separate from one another. "Stimson?"

"Yes." He replied at last.

"Stimson, take it easy, we're all in the same fix."

"I don't want to be here, I want to be somewhere else."

"There's a chance we'll be found."

"I must be, I must be," said Stimson. "I don't believe this, I don't believe any of this is happening."

"It's a bad dream," said someone.

"Shut up!" said Hollis.

"Come and make me," said the voice. It was Applegate. He laughed noisily, with a similar objectivity. "Come and shut me up."

Hollis for the first time felt the impossibility of his position. A great anger filled him, for he wanted more than anything in existence at this moment to be able to do something to Applegate. He had wanted for many years to do something and now it was too late. Applegate was only a telephonic voice.

Falling, falling, falling!

Now, as if they had discovered the horror, two of the men began to scream. In a nightmare, Hollis saw one of them float by, very near, screaming and screaming.

"Stop it!" The man was almost at his fingertips, screaming insanely. He would never stop. He would go on screaming for a million miles, as long as he was in radio range, disturbing all of them, making it impossible for them to talk to one another.

Hollis reached out. It was best this way. He made

the extra effort and touched the man. He grasped the man's ankle and pulled himself up along the body until he reached the head. The man screamed and clawed frantically, like a drowning swimmer. The screaming filled the universe.

One way or the other, thought Hollis. The sun or Earth or meteors will kill him, so why not now?

He smashed the man's glass mask with his iron fist. The screaming stopped. He pushed off from the body and let it spin away on its own course, falling, falling.

Falling, falling down space went Hollis and the rest of them in the long, endless dropping and whirling of silent terror.

"Hollis, you still there?"

Hollis did not speak, but felt the rush of heat in his face.

"This is Applegate again."

"All right, Applegate."

"Let's talk. We haven't anything else to do."

The captain cut in. "That's enough of that. We've got to figure a way out of this."

"Captain, why don't you shut up?" said Applegate.

"What!"

"You heard me, Captain. Don't pull your rank on me, you're ten thousand miles away by now, and let's not kid ourselves. As Stimson puts it, it's a long way down."

"See here, Applegate!"

"Can it. This is a mutiny of one. I haven't a dang thing to lose. Your ship was a bad ship and you were a bad captain and I hope you roast when you hit the sun."

"I'm ordering you to stop!"

"Go on, order me again!" Applegate smiled across ten thousand miles. The captain was silent. Applegate continued, "Where were we, Hollis? Oh, yes, I remember. I hate you, too. But you know that. You've known it for a long time."

Hollis clenched his fists, hopelessly.

"I want to tell you something," said Applegate. "Make you happy I was the one who blackballed you with the Rocket Company five years ago."

A meteor flashed by. Hollis looked down and his left hand was gone. Blood spurted. Suddenly there was no air in his suit. He had enough air in his lungs to move his right hand over and twist a knob at his left elbow, tightening the joint and sealing the leak. It had happened so quickly that he was not surprised. Nothing surprised him any more. The air in the suit came back to normal in an instant now that the leak was sealed. And the blood that had flowed so swiftly was pressured as he fastened the knob yet tighter, until it made a tourniquet.

All of this took place in a terrible silence on his part. And the other men chatted. That one man, Lespere, went on and on with his talk about his wife on Mars, his wife on Venus, his wife on Jupiter, his money, his wondrous times, his drunkenness, his gambling, his happiness. On and on, while they all fell, fell. Lespere reminisced on the past, happy, while he fell to his death.

It was so very odd. Space, thousands of miles of space, and these voices vibrating in the center of it. No one visible at all, and only the radio waves quivering and trying to quicken other men into emotion.

"Are you angry, Hollis?"

"No." And he was not. The abstraction had returned and he was a thing of dull concrete, forever falling nowhere.

"You wanted to get to the top all your life, Hollis. And I ruined it for you. You always wondered what happened. I put the black mark on you just before I was tossed out myself."

"That isn't important," said Hollis. And it was not. It was gone. When life is over it is like a flicker of bright film, an instant on the screen, all of its prejudices and passions condensed and illumined for an instant on space, and before you could cry out. There was a happy day, there a bad one, there an evil face, there a good one, the film burned to a cinder, the screen was dark.

From this outer edge of his life, looking back, there was only one remorse, and that was only that he wished to go on living. Did all dying people feel this way, as if they had never lived? Does life seem that short, indeed, over and down before you took a breath? Did it seem this abrupt and impossible to everyone, or only to himself, here, now with a few hours left to him for thought and deliberation?

One of the other men was talking. "Well, I had me a good life. I had a wife on Mars and one on Venus and one on Earth and one on Jupiter. Each of them had money and they treated me swell. I had a wonderful time. I got drunk and once I gambled away twenty thousand dollars."

"But you're here now," thought Hollis. "I didn't have any of those things. When I was living I was jealous of you, Lespere, when I had another day ahead of me I envied you your women and your good times. Women frightened me and I went into space, always wanting them, and jealous of you for having them, and money, and as much happiness as you could have in your own wild way. But now, falling here, with everything over, I'm not jealous of you any more, because it's over for you as it is over for me, and right now it's like it never was." Hollis craned his face forward and shouted into the telephone.

"It's all over, Lespere!"

Silence.

"It's just as if it never was, Lespere!"

"Who's that?" Lespere's faltering voice.

"This is Hollis."

He was being mean. He felt the meanness, the senseless meanness of dying. Applegate had hurt him, now he wanted to hurt another. Applegate and space had both wounded him.

"You're out here, Lespere. It's all over. It's just as if it had never happened, isn't it?"

"No."

"When anything's over, it's just like it never happened. Where's your life any better than mine, now? While it was happening, yes, but now? Now is what counts. Is it any better, is it?"

"Yes, it's better!"

"How!"

"Because I got my thoughts; I remember!" cried Lespere, far away, indignant, holding his memories to his chest with both hands.

And he was right. With a feeling of cold water gushing through his head and his body, Hollis knew he was right. There were differences between memories and dreams. He had only dreams of things he had wanted to do, while Lespere had memories of things done and accomplished. And this knowledge began to pull Hollis apart, with a slow, quivering precision.

"What good does it do you?" he cried to Lespere. "Now? When a thing's over it's not good any more. You're no better off than me."

"I'm resting easy," said Lespere. "I've had my turn. I'm not getting mean at the end, like you."

"Mean?" Hollis turned the word on his tongue. He had never been mean, as long as he could remember, in his life. He had never dared to be mean. He must have saved it all of these years for such a time as this. "Mean." He rolled the word into the back of his mind. He felt tears start in his eyes and roll down his face. Someone must have heard his gasping voice.

"Take it easy, Hollis."

It was, of course, ridiculous. Only a minute before he had been giving advice to others, to Stimson, he had felt a braveness which he had thought to be the genuine thing, and now he knew that it had been nothing but shock and the objectivity possible in shock. Now he was trying to pack a lifetime of suppressed emotion into an interval of minutes.

"I know how you feel, Hollis," said Lespere, now twenty thousand miles away, his voice fading. "I don't take it personally."

But aren't we equal, his wild mind wondered. Lespere and I? Here, now? If a good thing's over it's done, and what good is it? You die anyway. But he knew he was rationalizing, for it was like trying to tell the difference between a live man and a corpse. There was a spark in one, and not in the other, an aura, a mysterious element.

So it was with Lespere and himself; Lespere had lived a good full life, and it made him a different man now, and he, Hollis, had been as good as dead for many years. They came to death by separate paths and, in all likelihood, if there were kinds of deaths, their kinds would be as different as night from day. The quality of death, like that of life, must be of infinite variety, and if one has already died once, then what is there to look for in dying for once and all, as he was now?

It was a second later that he discovered his right foot was cut sheer away. It almost made him laugh. The air was gone from his suit again, he bent quickly, and there was blood, and the meteor had taken flesh and suit away to the ankle. Oh, death in space was most humorous, it cut you away, piece by piece, like a black and invisible butcher. He tightened the valve at the knee, his head swirling into pain, fighting to remain aware, and with the valve tightened, the blood retained, the air kept, he straightened up and went on falling, falling, for that was all there was left to do.

"Hollis?"

Hollis nodded sleepily, tired of waiting for death.

"This is Applegate again," said the voice.

"Yes."

"I've had time to think. I listened to you. This isn't good. It makes us mean. This is a bad way to die. It brings all the bile out. You listening, Hollis?"

"Yes."

"I lied. A minute ago. I lied. I didn't blackball you. I don't know why I said that. Guess I wanted to hurt you. You seemed the one to hurt. We've always fought. Guess I'm getting old fast and repenting fast. I guess listening to you be mean made me ashamed. Whatever the reason, I want you to know I was an idiot, too. There's not an ounce of truth in what I said. To heck with you."

Hollis felt his heart began to work again. It seemed as if it hadn't worked for five minutes, but now all of his limbs began to take color and warmth. The shock was over, and the successive shocks of anger and terror and loneliness were passing. He felt like a man emerging from a cold shower in the morning, ready for breakfast and a new day.

"Thanks, Applegate."

"Don't mention it. Up your nose, you slob."

"Where's Stimson, how is he?"

"Stimson?"

They listened.

No answer.

"He must be gone."

"I don't think so. Stimson!"

They listened again.

They could hear a long, slow, hard breathing in their phones.

"That's him. Listen."

"Stimson!"

No reply.

Only the slow, hard breathing.

"He won't answer."

"He's gone insane, God help him."

"That's it. Listen."

The silent breathing, the quiet.

"He's closed up like a clam. He's in himself, making a pearl. Listen to the poet, will you. He's happier than us now, anyway."

They listened to Stimson float away.

"Hey," said Stone.

"What?" Hollis called across space, for Stone, of all of them, was a good friend.

"I've got myself into a meteor swarm, some little asteroids."

"Meteors?"

"I think it's the Myrmidone cluster that goes out past Mars and in toward Earth once every five years. I'm right in the middle. It's like a big kaleidoscope. You get all kinds of colors and shapes and sizes. God, it's beautiful, all the metal."

Silence.

"I'm going with them," said Stone. "They're taking me off with them. I'll be damned." He laughed tightly.

Hollis looked to see, but saw nothing. There were only the great jewelries of space, the diamonds and sapphires and emerald mists and velvet inks of space, with God's voice mingling among the crystal fires. There was a kind of wonder and imagination in the thought of Stone going off in the meteor swarm, out past Mars for years and coming in toward Earth every five years, passing in and out of the planet's ken for the next million years, Stone and the Myrmidone cluster eternal and unending, shifting and shaping like the kaleidoscope colors when you were a child and held the long tube to the sun and gave it a twirl.

"So long, Hollis." Stone's voice, very faint now. "So long."

"Good luck," shouted Hollis across thirty thousand miles.

"Don't be funny," said Stone, and was gone.

The stars closed in.

Now all the voices were fading, each on their own trajectories, some to the sun, others into farthest space.

And Hollis himself. He looked down. He, of all the others, was going back to Earth alone.

"So long."

"Take it easy."

"So long, Hollis." That was Applegate.

The many good-bys. The short farewells. And now the great loose brain was disintegrating. The components of the brain, which had worked so beautifully and efficiently in the skull case of the rocket ship racing through space, were dying off one by one, the meaning of their life together was falling apart. And as a body dies when the brain ceases functioning, so the spirit of the ship and their long time together and what they meant to one another was dying. Applegate was now no more than a finger blown from the parent body, no longer to be despised and worked against. The brain was exploded, and the senseless, useless fragments of it were far-scattered. The voices faded and now all of space was silent. Hollis was alone, falling.

They were all alone. Their voices had died like echoes of the words of God spoken and vibrating in the starred space. There went the captain to the sun; there Stone with the meteor swarm; there Stimson, tightened and unto himself; there Applegate toward Pluto; there Smith and Turner and Underwood and all the rest, the shards of the kaleidoscope that had formed a thinking pattern for so long, now hurled apart.

And I? thought Hollis. What can I do? Is there anything I can do now to make up for a terrible and empty life? If I could do one good thing to make up for the meanness I collected all these years and didn't even know was in me? But there's no one here, but myself, and how can you do good all alone? You can't. Tomorrow night I'll hit Earth's atmosphere.

I'll burn, he thought, and be scattered in ashes all over the continental lands. I'll be put to use. Just a little bit, but ashes are ashes and they'll add to the land.

He fell swiftly, like a bullet, like a pebble, like an iron weight, objective, objective all of the time now, not sad or happy or anything, but only wishing he could do a good thing now that everyone was gone, a good thing for just himself to know about.

When I hit the atmosphere, I'll burn like a meteor.

"I wonder," he said. "If anyone'll see me?"

The small boy on the country road looked up and screamed. "Look, Mom, look! A falling star!"

The blazing white star fell down the sky of dusk in Illinois.

"Make a wish," said his mother. "Make a wish."

JACK VANCE

I'LL BUILD YOUR DREAM CASTLE

*If anyone had told me, back in 1950, that
we would not only have unmanned Tel-
stars but also manned Vostoks and Mer-
cury-Atlases by the beginning of the
1960s, I would have laughed him down.
Impossible! I would have said. Not, I
would hedge, because of basic scientific
reasons, though, even back there in 1950,
but rather from the point of view of specific technology and of cost. So if anyone tells you that the kind of space operation undertaken by the hero of this tale
is unlikely ever to happen, you just laugh
him down . . . Of course, I do doubt that
you or I will witness this particular sort
of "far-out" (pun intended) building
technique in our lifetimes—but then, I
may be wrong again!*

WHEN FARRERO first met Douane Angker, of Marlais
& Angker, Class III Structors, something in his brain
twisted, averted itself; and, looking down at the curl
on Angker's tough mouth, he knew the feeling went
double. Angker, short and solid, had concentrated in
him a heavy unctuous vitality, the same way a cigar
stump holds the strongest juices.

Farrero did not, on this occasion, meet Leon Marlais, the other half of the firm, nor did he during the entire length of his job. He would not have recognized him face to face on the pedestrip—because Marlais had an odd mania for privacy, secluded himself behind a coded door-press, an unlisted telescreen. When he used his private copter stage, a polarizing field jarred the view to dazzle and shimmer.

Angker held to no such aloofness. The panel to his office stood always wide. All day the technicians in the adjoining workroom could look in to see him shouldering, driving, battering through his work; watch him barking orders into the telescreen, flourishing a clenched hand for emphasis.

Farrero stayed pretty well away from the office, appearing only for new assignments, avoiding Angker as much as possible. He assumed his work was satisfactory. If not, he felt sure Angker would have fired him, and with gusto. However, the day he knocked at Angker's door to report on the Westgeller job, he knew he was in for trouble.

"Come in!" called Angker, not looking up, and Farrero sauntered forward—tall, lanky, his face, long, droll, wooden, his manner very casual. He had hair the color of wet sand, the mildest of blue eyes.

"Good morning," said Farrero. Angker, after a brief glance upward, grunted. Farrero dropped two strips of microfilm on the desk. "Ready for execution. I've shown them to Westgeller, got his O.K."

"Westgeller? I suppose he can pay for the place." He tipped the strips down the slot in his desk.

"Your credit office likes him," said Farrero. From where he stood, Angker's lowered and foreshortened face looked like a rudely molded mask, with a glazed shapeless nose, thick lumpy lips, eyes hidden under the thrust of his brow. "He makes heavy glass," said Farrero. "The stuff tourist submarines are built from. He's also got a finger in Moon Mining."

The screen on the far wall glowed, ran with blurred

colors. Angker, slipping on polarizers, saw a three-dimensional picture—a large solid house backed by a gloomy wall of fir trees. It was an old-fashioned house, warm, Earthy-looking, with high gables and many chimneys, as if it were intended to fight year after year of winter snow. Its colors were a dark red, with gray, white, and green trim, and the sun cells of the roof glowed a rich burnished copper. Behind, the great fir trees marched almost up to the house; and the trunks of many others could be seen dwindling off through the dim aisles. At the front a wide lawn, vivid as argon fire, rolled gently down to a coruscation of bright flower beds. It was clearly a Class III house.

"Ah . . . ah," Angker grunted. "Nice piece of work, Farrero. Where's the site?"

"Fifty miles from . . . er, Minusinsk, on the Yenisei." Farrero dropped into a chair, crossed his legs. "Fifty-four degrees latitude, thereabouts."

"Take him hours to get there," commented Angker sourly.

Farrero shrugged. "He says he likes it. Likes the winter—snow—solitude. The untouched forests, wild life, wolves, peasants, things like that. He's got a life-time lease on three hundred acres."

Angker grunted again, leaned back in his chair. "What's the cost estimate?"

Farrero laid his head back, against the support, half-closed his eyes. "Cost us 28,000 munits to build. Plus ten per cent makes 30,800. I gave it to Westgeller as 31,000."

Angker leveled a sudden under-eyebrow glance at Farrero, squared up in his seat. He pressed a button. A cutaway section of the first floor flicked upon the screen. He pressed again. The second floor. Again. Detailed wall plans. He looked up, and the lines from his nostrils down seemed to gather, purse his mouth, pull it out into a hard lump.

"How do you fix on that figure?" he jerked a pencil

toward the screen. "I say that house'll run upwards of 40,000. Ten per cent puts our bid somewhere near 44,000, 45,000."

"I really don't think so," said Farrero politely.

"What is the basis for your estimate?" inquired Angker, as gently.

Farrero clasped his hands around his knee. "Well— look at it from this angle. One of the shortcomings of modern civilization—ancient civilization too, for that matter—is that the average man never gets all he wants of the most desirable products, never makes his life fit his dreams. Very few people can afford space yachts, Venusian fruit, good film libraries, Class III houses. I suppose it could be said that these always unfulfilled ambitions create an incentive to work, to make money, to—"

Angker made a guttural noise. "Less philosophy, Farrero. Leave that for the college professors. I want to know how you're going to build a 40,000 munit house for 20,000 munits."

"Well," said Farrero, "as a matter of fact, I've worked out a construction technique to bring Class III prices closer to Class I and II."

"Ah—you have indeed?" Angker was still polite. "Perhaps you'll explain?"

"What's the reason for the differential between Class III and Class II? It's that Class I and II houses are largely prefabbed, and the Class III's are individually built and fitted. We still use carpenters, glaziers, masons, welders, electricians. So, the problem was to find a structural method that would preserve individuality, but cut construction costs. I found the answer. So far as I know it's completely revolutionary."

There was a short pause. Angker sat staring like a mahogany jinni.

"I've tried it on a small scale," Farrero went on, his voice rather more brittle. "It works. For foundations, instead of concrete sills or piers, we fuse the earth under the house with an atomic torch. Then on this glass, flint, slag—whatever you want to call it—we joint up a frame of hyproberyl tubing, stretch Caltonite fabric over it taut. Then we spray on the wall—quick-dry. Also the partitions. The floors come as standard steel sections. The wiring, plumbing, radiants, ventilation, filters are naturally laid out first. Frame, Caltonite fabric, spray, and there's the house, everything but the finish."

"Windows? Doors?"

"Slice 'em out with a torch, set the sills in with a little more quick-dry."

Angker nodded. "Sounds reasonable. Seems like you'd save a lot of time with the utilities, too." He scratched his chin with the pencil. He leaned abruptly forward. "You shouldn't have given Westgeller the estimate till you checked with the office."

Farrero opened his eyes, raised his eyebrows. "That's my job,"—with a glibness of forethought. "That's what you're paying me for. Designing, estimating, selling."

"This is different. You're not acting for the company's best interests. You've cost us—thirty-one from forty-four—13,000 munits."

Farrero shrugged. "The company's making ten per cent. My instructions were to quote estimated cost plus ten per cent."

When Angker was aroused, his dog-brown eyes glowed with russet lights. Now he put his hands on the edge of the desk, and Farrero, with an inward quiver, gazing deep into Angker's eyes, saw the russet flicker.

"Ten per cent," said Angker thickly, "is a rough basis for operation. However, you're supposed to exercise judgment. This is a money-making concern. We guarantee our customers quality, nothing else. If our price suits 'em, fine. If it doesn't, there's nineteen other outfits with the same kind of license we've got. I could have sold that house for 40,000 and Westgeller would be getting a bargain. You told him 32,000. You're cost-ing us 8,000 munits. I don't like it."

"You forget," said Farrero, getting to his feet, "that what makes this saving is *my* private idea. *I* worked it out."

"On company time."

Farrero flushed. "I built a small scale section with company equipment, for company protection—To check the idea, and see whether it was a lemon or not. The scheme was completely formulated before I even left the Institute. In any event, the patent is in my name."

"Well," said Angker heavily, "you'll have to sign it over to Marlais & Angker."

"*Hah!*" Farrero thrust his hands in his pockets. "You think I'm crazy?"

Angker wrenched off the polarizers. "Farrero, how old are you?"

"Twenty-eight."

"You've put in four years at the Institute, studying Class III technique, right?"

"That's what my license reads."

"So it would be just four years wasted if you couldn't get a job with any Class III outfit?"

Farrero said, "I've got lots of ideas. Maybe I'll start an outfit of my own."

Angker chuckled. "Your license doesn't say that. It gives you authority to plan, to design, to sell. Mar-lais & Angker hold the license to build. Those licenses are hard to come by nowadays. Without it you can't contract to build an igloo at the North Pole."

"Very true," said Farrero dryly. "So?"

"So—any process developed during your employ-ment with us becomes our property. You get a bonus, of course. There's a hundred legal precedents to back me up."

"If," Farrero interposed tautly, "I developed the process working for you—which I did not."

"Can you prove it?"

Farrero met the russet lights. "I wouldn't be sur-prised. I've been talking about it for two years. It's a good idea. It'll bring Class III construction within reach of a lot of Class II incomes."

Angker smiled a glittering hypnotic smile. "Let 'em buy Class II houses—from our affiliate XAB Company. Maybe we'll cut prices in Class II."

Farrero took a half step forward. "What kind of talk is that? Does public welfare mean anything to you, at all? You want to take money without giving anything; you're no better than a pickpocket!"

Angker pushed his knuckles on the desk till they became white buttons. "Get your check from Demp-ster. You're through, Farrero. You're through in the whole construction game. I'll see . . . I'll make it my business to see that you never work for any other outfit in the world."

"You think you'll turn my idea over to your engi-neers," jeered Farrero. "Go ahead, let 'em try it. Think I was fool enough to tell you anything important?"

"What more is there?" asked Angker, leaning back in his chair with a half grin.

"Ever try to spray a right angle onto a building? No? Go ahead, try." And Farrero laughed. He stopped. "Sure. Go ahead, try. I've got the patent. I'll throw so many writs and attachments and subpoenas at you, you'll think it's snowing."

"We'll see," said Angker. "Meantime, go out and herd sheep if you want to eat—because I promise you'll never work construction again."

Farrero looked at his fingernails. "Remember what I said about organizing my own outfit?"

Angker pursed his thick lips into a ridiculous smirk. "Have you forgotten the little detail of the license? You haven't got one. You can't get one. There's none being issued. Without a license you can't build a dog-house to sell, anywhere on Earth, Venus, the Moon."

"Sounds pretty definite, doesn't it?" mocked Far-rero.

"Go back to Tek, Farrero. Put in another four years on something else. Hydroponics. Protolectrics. Because in construction you're done."

"Angker," said Farrero, "you just listened to one of my ideas. I've got others. Better ones. Before I'm done I'll have cost you so much money, you'll wish you'd taken me in as a partner. Remember that, Angker."

He left the office.

Angker sat staring at the screen, where without polarizers, the image was a chaotic blur. He touched a button. A soft voice said "Yes?"

"Did you hear this last interview?"

"No," said Marlais.

"I'll run it off for you—quite a lot in it." He pulled open a drawer, twisted a dial, pulled a knob. The magnowire reeled backward to where Farrero had entered the office; then, pulling its impressions past the detector, it echoed for Marlais' ears the entire interview.

"What do you think?" Angker asked the unseen Marlais.

There was a pause, and Angker waited with an anxiety which might have appeared odd to his subordinates.

"Well, Douane," presently came Marlais' soft voice, "you probably could have handled him more smoothly . . . aggression, stubbornness, overt hostility—" his voice trailed off to a whisper. Then: "We'd have a hard time proving ownership of the patent. However, it may be for the best. The industry is stable and comfortable. We're all making money. No telling where the disruption might take us. Perhaps we'd better call a meeting of the association, lay the cards on the table. I think everyone will contract neither to hire Farrero nor use his process."

Angker made a doubtful noise.

"You see," said Marlais, with a gentle edge to his voice, "there are twenty companies in the association.

The chance of Farrero's approaching any given firm is only one in nineteen. We don't count. Consequently, every operator, to protect himself, will be glad to sign a contract. It might be wise to keep a watch on Farrero, to see what he's up to. He sounded like a young man of determination."

The next day about eleven o'clock Angker called his secretary. "Get me Westgeller."

"Yes, sir . . . there's a call coming in for you right now, Mr. Angker. In fact it's Mr. Westgeller himself."

"Well, put him on."

Laurin Westgeller's face appeared on Angker's screen—fat, friendly, with little twinkling blue eyes. "Mr. Angker," said Westgeller, "I've decided to have you go no further with my job. You can send me a bill for your work to date."

Angker sat glowering at the image. He had been on the point of notifying Westgeller that Marlais & Angker could not build for less than 45,000 munits, had fully expected a cancellation. Westgeller's beating him to the punch left him puzzled, resentful.

"What's the matter? Price too high?" he asked sarcastically.

"No," replied Westgeller, "the price hardly enters into the picture. In fact, I plan to spend 300,000 munits on a house."

Angker's jaw slacked. "300,000 munits? Who . . . I mean, shall I send you out a consultant?"

"No," said Laurin Westgeller. "I've already signed —with one of your late employees, Mr. Farrero, who's going into business for himself."

Angker stared. "Farrero? Why, Farrero has no license to build! The minute he drives a stake into the ground he's liable for a ten thousand munit fine!"

Westgeller nodded. "So he informed me. Thank you, however, for your advice. Good day." The screen blurred, sank through the pink after-image to blank ground glass.

Angker blurted the news through to Marlais.

"There's nothing we can do until Farrero tries to fulfill the contract," said Marlais. "When and if he makes an illegal move, we file charges."

Angker grunted, shook his head. "He's got something up his sleeve. Farrero's not crazy."

"*Nobody* who gets 300,000 munit contracts is crazy," said the soft voice. "But all we can do is wait, see what his plans are. You've got an investigator on him?"

"Yes—Lescovic. He worked for us in that New Zealand deal."

"Yes, I remember. I'll be interested to learn what Farrero has in mind."

Two hours later, Angker's telescreen buzzer sounded.

"Yes?" snarled Angker.

"A Mr. Lescovic, sir."

"Put him on." The face of the investigator appeared —a passive, fat, dark-eyed face, with wide red lips and a button nose.

"Well?"

"Farrero's slipped us."

The spasmodic jerk of Angker's arms shoved him back in the chair. "Where . . . how did this happen?"

"About an hour ago. We dusted his clothes with F-radiant powder, and following him was easy with an F-detector. He walked into the Transport Union, and into a public lavatory. I waited across the lobby, watching the screen. He showed like a big ball of fire. He moved around a little, then was still. When he didn't move after ten minutes, I got suspicious, went to look. His clothes were hung on a hook, but Farrero, no. He gave us the clean slip."

Angker slapped the desk. "Find him, then!"

"There're four operatives on the case right now, sir."

"Call me as soon as you get anything."

Six months later the call came through. The buzzer

sounded late in the afternoon. Angker hardly looked up from a model of a Caribbean island. "Yes?"

"Mr. Lescovic calling."

Angker looked up, rubbed his jaw. "Lescovic?"

"The detective, Mr. Angker."

"Oh yes." Angker pulled the case from its mental pigeonhole. "Put him through."

The fat bland face appeared on the screen. "Farrero's back in town."

"When did he get back?"

"Well, evidently during the week."

"Find out where he's been?"

"No word on that."

"What's he doing now?"

"He's calling on Franklin Kerry, of Kerry Armatures. Been there two hours."

"Kerry! Why, Kerry's one of our clients! At least he's looking over our bid for building his house."

Lescovic let a spark of interest show in his careful dark eyes. "He's got plenty of money—registered at the Gloriana."

Angker said. "Hold on a minute." He flipped a switch, reported to Marlais.

Marlais was noncommittal. "We've nothing to go on. We'll have to wait, see what happens."

Angker brought back Lescovic's placid face. "Watch him. Report everything he does. Find out what he wants with Kerry."

"Yes, sir." The screen faded.

Angker slammed into Marlais' office. "Well, he's done it again."

Marlais had been sitting in half-darkness, gazing through the window, out across the many-tiered city, out to the dusk-hung horizon. He slowly turned his head.

"I presume you mean Farrero."

Angker stamped back and forth. "Glochmeinder this time. Last month it was Crane. Before that, Haggarty." He came to an abrupt halt, cursed Farrero with fluid vindictiveness, resumed his pacing. "He doesn't go near any of the small ones, but just let us get wind of a big account—"

"What did Glochmeinder say?"

"Just what Kerry and Crane and Haggarty and Desplains and Churchward and Klenko and Westgeller said. He's given his contract to Farrero, and that's *all* he'll say."

Marlais rose to his feet, rubbed his chin. "There's a leak in the office. Somewhere."

The muscles roped around Angker's mouth. "I've been trying to find it. When I do—" He slowly clenched and unclenched his hand in the air.

Marlais turned back to the window. "No word from the detective?"—from over his shoulder.

"I gave you his last report. Farrero's been ordering all over the world—construction materials and landscaping supplies. He's got fifteen hundred men working for him, according to the Department of Labor Statistics, but we can't find where—and there's not a job going that isn't a legitimate, licensed affair."

"Clever," mused Marlais, toying with the massive blue spinel he used for a paper weight.

"He's cost us a half million munits," gloomed Angker.

Marlais smiled wanly. "Just as he threatened, just so." And he laughed at Angker's quick glare.

For a moment there was silence. Angker paced the floor heavily. Marlais let the smoke from his cigarette trickle up through his finger, lose itself in the half-darkness of the room.

"Well," said Marlais, tamping out the cigarette, "something must be done."

Farrero found himself an office, a two-room suite in the Atlantica Tower, facing west across Amargosa Park, with the Pylon of All Nations thrusting magnificently high in the distance. He also found himself a receptionist, and this was Miss Flora Gustafsson, who claimed Scandinavian ancestry, and had long birch-blond hair, with eyes blue as Folda Fjord, to prove it. She was hardly bigger than a kitten, but everything about her matched, and she was efficient with the detectives.

The teleview buzzed. Flora reached over, screened the caller. "Oh, good afternoon, Mr. Westgeller. I'll put you through to Mr. Farrero."

"Thank you," said Westgeller. Flora looked sharply at the image, buzzed Farrero.

"Hello, Mr. Westgeller," said Farrero. "What can I do for you?"

"Farrero, an old friend of mine, John Etcheverry, wants to build, and I'm sending him around to see you."

"Oh . . . ah, fine, Mr. Westgeller. I'll try to accommodate him, though we're pretty busy."

"Good day, Farrero," and Westgeller abruptly left the screen. Farrero sat stroking his chin, smiling faintly. Then he went into the outer room, kissed Flora.

John Etcheverry was about sixty, tall, thin, pale as a heron. He had a large egg-shaped head, sparse white hair that disobeyed his scalp in damp unruly tendrils. His eyes, set in dark concavities, never seemed to blink. His cheeks were wan, minutely etched. He had large ears with long pale lobes, and a long pale nose that twitched when he spoke.

"Have a seat," said Farrero. "I understand you're planning to build."

"That's right. May I smoke?"

"Certainly. Cigar? Try one of mine."

Etcheverry lit up.

"What do you have in mind? I might as well warn you that my prices come high. I deliver, but it costs a lot of money."

Etcheverry made a brief gesture with his fingers. "I want a country place, seclusion, quiet. I'm prepared to pay for it."

Farrero tapped the desk with a pencil once or twice, laid it down, sat back, quietly watched Etcheverry.

Etcheverry puffed on the cigar. "Westgeller tells me you've satisfied him very well. In fact, that's all he'll say."

Farrero nodded. "It's in the contract. I needed time to protect myself. Now I hardly care any more. I'm just waiting for a call from Capitol City, and then, so far as I'm concerned, I'll drop all secrecy." He leaned forward, pointed the pencil at Etcheverry's narrow chest. "You see, I've got enemies. Twenty Class III licensed structors want my blood. Marlais & Angker in particular. I've had to take precautions. Like for instance—" he pressed the stud and Flora's arch face looked out from the screen. "Get me Westgeller at his office."

Etcheverry chewed his cigar reflectively.

A moment passed. The buzzer sounded. Flora's face returned to the screen. "Mr. Westgeller hasn't been in his office today."

Farrero nodded. "It's not important." He turned back to Etcheverry. "Excuse me . . . a habit left over from the early stages of the game. Endless caution, endless foresight. It all helped then. You'd be surprised the phonies that Marlais & Angker threw at me."

"You have a license?" Etcheverry delicately inspected the tips of his shoes through the cigar smoke.

"No."

"Then you build illegally?"

"No."

Etcheverry pursed his lips. "You'll have to explain."

Farrero stared thoughtfully out the window. "Um . . . how much time can you spare?"

"You mean—"

"Right now."

"Well . . . there are no important demands on my time."

"If you can give me the rest of the day, I'll do better than explain—I'll demonstrate."

"Fine." Etcheverry put out his cigar. "I'll admit you've aroused my curiosity."

Farrero called an air cab. "Purdy Field," he told the driver.

At Purdy Field, Farrero took Etcheverry into the hangar. "Jump in," and he followed the stooped figure into the two-place space boat.

Etcheverry adjusted himself gingerly to the cushions. "If you haven't a license to build, I hope at least you have a license to fly space."

Farrero grinned. "I have. Check it if you care to. It's under the aerator."

"I'll take your word for it."

They rode up off the seared field on snoring atomic jets, beat up, up, up. A hundred miles, two hundred and earth blurred below. A thousand, five thousand, ten thousand miles—twenty, thirty thousand miles, and Farrero kept a close watch on his radar screen. "Should be about here now—" A pip showed yellow-green. "There it is." He swerved the boat, jetted off in the new direction. After a minute:

"You can see it below, off to the left."

Etcheverry, craning his gaunt neck, saw a small irregular asteroid, perhaps a mile in diameter. Farrero edged down the boat, lowered with hardly a jolt on a patch of white sand.

Etcheverry grabbed Farrero's arm violently. "Are you crazy?" he squealed. "Don't open that port! That's space out there! Vacuum!"

Farrero shook his head. "There's air. Fifteen pounds pressure, twenty per cent oxygen. Good breathing. I'm not crazy. Look at the barometer."

Etcheverry looked, watched numbly as Farrero flung open the port. The air was good.

Farrero jumped out of the boat. Etcheverry followed. "But . . . there's gravity here—"

Farrero climbed to the top of a little hillock, waved an arm to Etcheverry. "Come on up."

Etcheverry stalked slowly up the slope.

"This is Westgeller's estate," said Farrero. "His private world. He paid 300,000 munits for it. Look, there's his house."

Westgeller's house sat on a wide flat field covered with emerald-green turf. Nearby a lake glistened in the warm sunlight, and a white crane stood fishing among the rushes. Trees lined the plain, and Etcheverry heard birds singing across the distance.

The house was a long rambling structure, single-story, built of redwood planking. There were many windows, and below each, a window box overflowing with floral color. Beach umbrellas, green, orange, blue, rose like other, larger flowers from a terrace.

Farrero squinted across the field, smooth and grassy-green as a golf course. "Westgeller is at home. I see his space boat. Like to call on him? Might like to talk things over with your old friend, eh, Mr. Etcheverry?"

Etcheverry gave him a sharp side glance, said slowly: "Perhaps it would be just as well if—"

Farrero laughed. "Save it. It's no good. You probably don't know I read lips. Well, I do. I was stone deaf the first ten years of my life. And when you flashed Westgeller's picture on my screen, his voice saying, 'I'm sending over my dear old friend Etcheverry,' and his lips saying, 'I've decided to have you stop work on my job, Mr. Angker,' I smelled a rat. I suppose you're Marlais. It's a cinch you're not Angker."

The thin man shrugged, gave Farrero a quick side-glance. "I'm Marlais. Nice set-up you've got."

"I like it," said Farrero. "I'm making money."

Marlais looked around the toy world. "You're spending it too." He stamped his long fragile-looking foot on the ground. "You've got me beat. How do you lick gravity? Why doesn't the air all blow away? Seems as if I'm . . . oh, about normal weight."

"You're a little lighter," said Farrero. "Gravity here is three per cent less than on Earth."

"But," and Marlais looked horizon to close horizon, calculated, "call this a half mile in diameter—that'll be a half of a half cubed, approximately—one sixteenth cubic mile. Earth is . . . 512 trillion over two is 256 trillion cubic miles. And the gravity is the same. Why?"

"For one thing," said Farrero, "you're closer to the center of gravity—by almost four thousand miles."

Marlais reached down, plucked a blade of grass, inspected it curiously.

"All new," said Farrero. "The trees brought here at no slight effort, I'll tell you. Lindvist—he's a Danish ecologist—is working with me. He figures out how many bees I need to fertilize the flowers, how many earthworms, how many trees to oxygenate the air."

Marlais nodded his head, darted Farrero a look from shadowed eyes. "Very good, very good!"

"There won't be a millionaire living on Earth in another twenty years," mused Farrero. "I'll have sold them all private planets. Some will want big places. I can furnish them—"

"Incidentally, where did you get this one?"

"Out in space a ways."

Marlais nodded sagely. "That's probably where Marlais & Angker will go to find theirs."

Farrero turned his head slowly, looked the man up and down. Marlais met his gaze blandly.

"So—you think you'll cut in?"

"I'd be a fool if I didn't."

"You think," Farrero went on meditatively, "that you'll cash in on my idea. You've got all the equipment, all the technicians necessary for a quick skim at the cream. Maybe you'll even get some laws enacted, barring non-licensees from the game."

"If I didn't—I'd be a fool."

Farrero shrugged. "Well . . . maybe yes. Maybe no. Like to see another of my jobs? This is Westgeller's. I'll show you Desplains'."

Marlais bowed his head. They re-entered the space boat. Farrero clamped the port, pulsed power through the jets. Westgeller's world fell away beneath them.

They reached Desplains' world half an hour later. "Eventually," said Farrero, "space around Earth will be peppered thick with these little estates. There'll be laws regulating their orbits, minimum distances set for their spacing—" He jerked the controls, threw the power-arm hard over. The space boat fled across Desplains' sky.

Marlais squirmed his long bony shoulder blades, cleared his throat with a sound like a saw cutting a nail, glanced sidewise at Farrero. "Why did you do that?"

Farrero expelled a lung full of taut air. "That was a narrow one. Did you see it slip past?"

"No."

"I forgot that Desplains wanted a moon. It's been installed. We just about rammed it."

He set the boat down on a rocky outcrop. Marlais unsealed the port, angled his skinny legs to the ground. "*Phew*," he grunted, "Desplains must intend to raise orchids—positively dank."

Farrero grinned, loosened his jacket. "He hasn't moved in yet. We're having a little trouble with the atmosphere. He wants clouds, and we're experimenting with the humidity." He looked up. "It's easy to get a muggy high overcast—but Desplains wants big fluffs of cumulus. Well, we'll try. Personally I don't think there's enough total volume of air."

Marlais looked into the sky too, where Earth hung as a huge bright crescent. He licked his pale old lips.

Farrero laughed. "Makes a man feel naked, doesn't it?" He looked across the little world to the queerly close horizon—barely a stone's-throw off, so it seemed —then back to the sweep of sky, with the majestic crescent of Earth dominating a new Moon behind. "Out here," he said, half to himself, "beauty comes a lot at a time."

Marlais gingerly perched himself on a slab of rock. "Exotic place."

"Desplains is an exotic man," said Farrero. "But he's

got the money, and I don't care if he wants the rocks upholstered with rabbit fur." He hopped up beside Marlais. "Desplains wanted something unusual. He's getting it." He indicated a clump of trees. "That's his bayou. Flora from Africa and the Matto Grosso. Fauna from here and there, including a very rare Tasmanian ibis. It's rather pretty, and certainly wild enough—connecting ponds, with overhanging trees. The moss hasn't got a good start yet, and there isn't quite the authentic smell, but give it time. Behind there's a . . . well, call it a swamp—a jungle cut with a lot of waterways. When the flowers all start in blooming it'll be heaven—"

"Individual worlds to suit any conceivable whim," murmured Marlais.

"That's it exactly," said Farrero. "We've got our largest world—about ten miles diameter—sold to a Canadian yachtsman."

"Fred Ableman," said Marlais dryly. "He canceled his contract with us about two months ago."

Farrero nodded. "He wants his world all ocean— blue ocean, plenty of wind to sail his boats. He wants islands here and there, with beaches and coral banks—"

"Coconut palms too, I expect."

"Right—but no sharks. We won't have it completed for another year and a half. It's heavy and unwieldy— difficult to bring out and get established in an orbit. Then there's an awful lot of water needed."

"Where do you get the water? You can't bring it out from Earth?"

Farrero shook his head. "We mine the Hipparchus ice floe, and every time the moon comes in apposition we shoot across a few big chunks. Slow but sure. It costs a lot, but Ableman makes too much money for his own good. Anyway, how could he spend his money better?"

Marlais pursed his lips in agreement. "I expect you get some strange specifications."

Farrero grinned. "There's a man named Klenko,

made his money in fashion design. He's the man responsible for those whirling things women were wearing a year or two ago on their heads. Strange man, strange world. The air is full of thirty-foot glass bubbles, floating loose. Glass bubbles everywhere—topaz, blue, red, violet, green—high and low. It's a hazard trying to land a space boat. He's got a fluorescent forest—activizers in the sap. When he turns ultraviolet on it, the leaves glow ghostly pale colors—silver, pale-green, orange. We built him a big pavilion overhanging a lake. Luminous fish in the lake."

"He evidently plans a lot of night life."

Farrero nodded. "He wants nothing but night. His world won't have any axial spin at all, when we get it trued in its orbit. But he'd better watch his step, or he'll get in trouble with the Anti-Vice League if he goes through with some of his entertainment ideas."

Marlais shrugged, took a cigarette from an onyx case, lit it. "If a man owns his world, I suppose he makes the laws."

"That at least is Klenko's theory."

Marlais blew out a puff of smoke. "One thing has me stumped," and his shadowed eyes calculated Farrero. "How do you beat gravity? So far as I know, artificial gravity has never been discovered."

Farrero nodded. "True."

Marlais made an airy gesture. "Well—whatever the system is, I imagine it will work for Marlais & Angker, too."

"So it would," said Farrero. "Only Marlais & Angker have come to the party late. I don't especially want to drive them into bankruptcy. I don't imagine I could. There'll always be Class III construction on Earth. But Farrero is pulling all the nuggets out of the pan, and he's making an awful dent in that precious twenty."

Marlais shook his head, and a spark appeared back in the depths of his eyes. "You have not quite grasped the idea, my friend. We don't plan to take the back seat.

We have the connections, the equipment, the staff. We can bring the asteroids out here cheaper than you can, undersell you four ways from Sunday. We'll even take losses if we need to. But you won't stay in business long. Whatever, however you handle gravity, our engineers can duplicate the conditions."

"My dear Mr. Marlais," jeered Farrero, "do you think I'm a fool? Do you think I'd leave a loophole for you and the other bandits? Have you ever heard of the Norton Space Claims Act?"

"Certainly. It defines and authorizes mining development of the asteroids."

"That's right. I've filed on eleven hundred and twenty-two asteroids. Of a peculiar nature— You see that little black pebble by your right foot. That shiny one, like flint. Pick it up."

Marlais reached, grasped, strained. His mouth slacked in amazement. He pulled again, till his skinny old arms quivered, creaked. He glanced up at Farrero.

"It weighs close to a ton, I expect," said Farrero. "It's star stuff.* Matter crystallized at tremendous pressure in the heart of a star. It figures out about a ton a cubic inch. A little bit turns on a lot of gravity. Somehow or other, eleven hundred and twenty-two good-sized chunks of the stuff drifted into an orbit around the sun—not too far out from Earth. They're small and dark and not heavy enough to cause any noticeable perturbations. But when you stand on their surface, the center of gravity is close enough to give you fairly close to Earth weight. I've filed on every one of those chunks, Marlais. Some I'll have to lump together, others I'll have to crust over with a few miles of ordinary matter to reduce gravity. It diminishes, you know, as the square of the distance from the center of mass— But I tell you what, Marlais," Farrero opened the port of his space boat, motioned Marlais in, "I know where you can get all this heavy matter you can use."

* See my introduction to the story by Jerome Bixby, page 33. —Ed.

Marlais wordlessly climbed into the boat. He eyed Farrero lambently. "Where?"

Farrero clamped the port, swung the power-arm, and Desplains' world fell off below.

"Here's what you do," Farrero confided. "You go out to Sirius, only ten light-years. It's got a small companion. You can cut chunks off the companion, as big as you want, as many as you want. Bring them back to Earth, and then you'll be in a position to compete with Farrero-Styled Worlds."

Marlais stared ahead at expanding Earth, knees hunched up under his sharp chin. Farrero could not resist a last gibe.

"Of course there'll be the detail of cooling off your acquisitions. I understand they're pretty hot. Twenty or thirty million degrees Centigrade—"

A. E. VAN VOGT

FAR CENTAURUS

*Without question, this is one of the great
tales in the modern literature of space
travel. First published in January, 1944,
more than a year and a half before the
first public demonstration of atomic energy in the form of superbombs, it soars
so far ahead of what we have discovered
in the realms of nuclear and other power
sources that we cannot even conceive of
it. In addition, it involves the space-time
theories of Einstein and many other great
mathematical physicists of our century.
The result is one of the most imagination-
stretching constructions of future possibility to be found in science fiction.*

I WAKENED WITH A start, and thought: How was Renfrew taking it?

I must have moved physically, for blackness edged
with pain closed over me. How long I lay in that
agonized faint, I have no means of knowing. My next
awareness was of the thrusting of the engines that
drove the spaceship.

Slowly this time, consciousness returned. I lay very
quiet, feeling the weight of my years of sleep, determined to follow the routine prescribed so long ago by
Pelham.

I didn't want to faint again.

I lay there, and I thought: It was silly to have worried about Jim Renfrew. He wasn't due to come out of his state of suspended animation for another fifty years.

I began to watch the illuminated face of the clock in the ceiling. It had registered 23:12; now it was 23:22. The ten minutes Pelham had suggested for a time lapse between passivity and initial action was up.

Slowly, I pushed my hand toward the edge of the bed. *Click!* My fingers pressed the button that was there. There was a faint hum. The automatic massager began to fumble gently over my naked form.

First, it rubbed my arms; then it moved to my legs, and so on over my body. As it progressed, I could feel the fine slick of oil that oozed from it working into my dry skin.

A dozen times I could have screamed from the pain of life returning. But in an hour I was able to sit up and turn on the lights.

The small, sparsely furnished, familiar room couldn't hold my attention for more than an instant. I stood up.

The movement must have been too abrupt. I swayed, caught on to the metal column of the bed, and retched discolored stomach juices.

The nausea passed. But it required an effort of will for me to walk to the door, open it, and head along the narrow corridor that led to the control room.

I wasn't supposed to so much as pause there, but a spasm of absolutely dreadful fascination seized me; and I couldn't help it. I leaned over the control chair, and glanced at the chronometer.

It said: 53 years, 7 months, 2 weeks, 0 days, 0 hours and 27 minutes.

Fifty-three years! A little blindly, almost blankly, I thought: Back on Earth, the people we had known, the young men we'd gone to college with, that girl who had kissed me at the party given us the night we left—they were all dead. Or dying of old age.

I remembered the girl very vividly. She was pretty, vivacious, a complete stranger. She had laughed as she offered her red lips, and she had said, "A kiss for the ugly one, too."

She'd be a grandmother now, or in her grave.

Tears came to my eyes. I brushed them away, and began to heat the can of concentrated liquid that was to be my first food. Slowly, my mind calmed.

Fifty-three years and seven and one half months, I thought drably. Nearly four years over my allotted time. I'd have to do some figuring before I took another dose of Eternity drug. Twenty grains had been calculated to preserve my flesh and my life for exactly fifty years.

The stuff was evidently more potent than Pelham had been able to estimate from his short period advance tests.

I sat tense, narrow-eyed, thinking about that. Abruptly, I grew conscious of what I was doing. Laughter spat from my lips. The sound split the silence like a series of pistol shots, startling me.

But it also relieved me. Was I sitting here actually being critical?

A miss of only four years was a bull's-eye across that span of years.

Why, I was alive and still young. Time and space had been conquered. The universe belonged to man.

I ate my "soup," sipping each spoonful deliberately. I made the bowl last every second of thirty minutes. Then, greatly refreshed, I made my way back to the control room.

This time I paused for a long look through the plates. It took only a few moments to locate Sol, a very brightly glowing star in the approximate center of the rear-view plate.

Alpha Centauri required longer to locate. But it shone finally, a glow point in a light sprinkled darkness.

I wasted no time trying to estimate their distances. They *looked* right. In fifty-four years we had covered approximately one tenth of the four and one third light years to the famous nearest star system.

Satisfied, I threaded my way back to the living quarters. Take them in a row, I thought. Pelham first.

As I opened the air-tight door of Pelham's room, a sickening odor of decayed flesh tingled in my nostrils. With a gasp I slammed the door, stood there in the narrow hallway, shuddering.

After a minute, there was still nothing but the reality.

Pelham was dead.

I cannot clearly remember what I did then. I ran; I know that. I flung open Renfrew's door, then Blake's. The clean, sweet smell of their rooms, the sight of their silent bodies on their beds brought back a measure of my sanity.

A great sadness came to me. Poor, brave Pelham. Inventor of the Eternity drug that had made the great plunge into interstellar space possible, he lay dead now from his own invention.

What was it he had said: "The chances are greatly against any of us dying. But there is what I am calling a death factor of about ten percent, a by-product of the first dose. If our bodies survive the initial shock, they will survive additional doses."

The death factor must be greater than ten percent. That extra four years the drug had kept me asleep—

Gloomily, I went to the storeroom, and procured my personal spacesuit and a tarpaulin. But even with their help, it was a horrible business. The drug had preserved the body to some extent, but pieces kept falling off as I lifted it.

At last, I carried the tarpaulin and its contents to the air lock, and shoved it into space.

I felt pressed now for time. These waking periods were to be brief affairs, in which what we called the "current" oxygen was to be used up, but the main reserves were not to be touched. Chemicals in each room slowly refreshed the "current" air over the years, readying it for the next to awaken.

In some curious defensive fashion, we had neglected

to allow for an emergency like the death of one of our members; even as I climbed out of the spacesuit, I could feel the difference in the air I was breathing.

I went first to the radio. It had been calculated that half a light year was the limit of radio reception, and we were approaching that limit now.

Hurriedly, though carefully, I wrote my report out, then read it into a transcription record, and started sending. I set the record to repeat a hundred times.

In a little more than five months hence, headlines would be flaring on Earth.

I clamped my written report into the ship log book, and added a note for Renfrew at the bottom. It was a brief tribute to Pelham. My praise was heartfelt, but there was another reason behind my note. They had been pals, Renfrew, the engineering genius who built the ship, and Pelham, the great chemist-doctor, whose Eternity drug had made it possible for men to take this fantastic journey into vastness.

It seemed to me that Renfrew, waking up into the great silence of the hurtling ship, would need my tribute to his friend and colleague. It was little enough for me to do, who loved them both.

The note written, I hastily examined the glowing engines, made notations of several instrument readings, and then counted out fifty-five grains of Eternity drug. That was as close as I could get to the amount I felt would be required for one hundred and fifty years.

For a long moment before sleep came, I thought of Renfrew and the terrible shock that was coming to him on top of all the natural reactions to his situation, that would strike deep into his peculiar sensitive nature—

I stirred uneasily at the picture.

The worry was still in my mind when darkness came.

Almost instantly, I opened my eyes. I lay thinking. The drug! It hadn't worked.

The draggy feel of my body warned me of the

truth. I lay very still watching the clock overhead. This time it was easier to follow the routine except that, once more, I could not refrain from examining the chronometer as I passed through the galley.

It read: 201 years, 1 month, 3 weeks, 5 days, 7 hours, 8 minutes.

I sipped my bowl of that super soup, then went eagerly to the big log book.

It is utterly impossible for me to describe the thrill that coursed through me, as I saw the familiar handwriting of Blake, and then, as I turned back the pages, of Renfrew.

My excitement drained slowly, as I read what Renfrew had written. It was a report; nothing more; gravitometric readings, a careful calculation of the distance covered, a detailed report on the performance of the engines, and finally, an estimate of our speed variations, based on the seven consistent factors.

It was a splendid mathematical job, a first-rate scientific analysis. But that was all there was. No mention of Pelham, not a word of comment on what I had written or on what had happened.

Renfrew had awakened; and, if his report was any criterion, he might as well have been a robot.

I knew better than that.

So—I saw as I began to read Blake's report—did Blake.

Bill:

TEAR THIS SHEET OUT WHEN YOU'VE READ IT!

Well, the worst has happened. We couldn't have asked fate to give us an unkindlier kick in the pants. I hate to think of Pelham being dead. What a man he was, what a friend! But we all knew the risk we were taking, he more than any of us. So all we can say is, "Sleep well, good friend. We'll never forget you."

But Renfrew's case is now serious. After all, we

were worried, wondering how he'd take his first awakening, let alone a bang between the eyes like Pelham's death. And I think that the first anxiety was justified.

As you and I have always known, Renfrew was one of Earth's fair-haired boys. Just imagine any one human being born with his combination of looks, money and intelligence. His great fault was that he never let the future trouble him. With that dazzling personality of his, and the crew of worshipping women and yes-men around him, he didn't have much time for anything but the present.

Realities always struck him like a thunderbolt. He could leave those three ex-wives of his—and they weren't so ex, if you ask me—without grasping that it was forever.

That good-by party was enough to put anyone into a sort of mental haze when it came to realities. To wake up a hundred years later, and realize that those he loved had withered, died, and been eaten by worms—well-l-l!

(I deliberately put it as baldly as that, because the human mind thinks of awfully strange angles, no matter how it censures speech.)

I personally counted on Pelham acting as a sort of psychological support to Renfrew; and we both know that Pelham recognized the extent of his influence over Renfrew. That influence must be replaced. Try to think of something, Bill, while you're charging around doing the routine work. We've got to live with that guy after we all wake up at the end of five hundred years.

Tear out this sheet. What follows is routine.

                                        Ned

I burned the letter in the incinerator, examined the two sleeping bodies—how deathly quiet they lay!— and then returned to the control room.

In the plate, the sun was a very bright star, a jewel set in black velvet, a gorgeous, shining brilliant.

Alpha Centauri was brighter. It was a radiant light in that panoply of black and glitter. It was still impossible to make out the separate suns of Alpha A, B, C, and Proxima, but their combined light brought a sense of awe and majesty.

Excitement blazed inside me; and consciousness came of the glory of this trip we were making, the first men to head for far Centaurus, the first men to dare aspire to the stars.

Even the thought of Earth failed to dim that surging tide of wonder; the thought that seven, possibly eight generations, had been born since our departure; the thought that the girl who had given me the sweet remembrance of her red lips, was now known to her descendants as their great-great-great-great grandmother—if she were remembered at all.

The immense time involved, the whole idea, was too meaningless for emotion.

I did my work, took my third dose of the drug, and went to bed. The sleep found me still without a plan about Renfrew.

When I woke up, alarm bells were ringing.

I lay still. There was nothing else to do. If I had moved, consciousness would have slid from me. Though it was mental torture even to think it, I realized that, no matter what the danger, the quickest way was to follow my routine to the second and in every detail.

Somehow I did it. The bells clanged and *brrred*, but I lay there until it was time to get up. The clamor was hideous, as I passed through the control room. But I *passed* through and sat for half an hour sipping my soup.

The conviction came to me that if that sound continued much longer, Blake and Renfrew would surely waken from their sleep.

At last, I felt free to cope with the emergency.

Breathing hard, I eased myself into the control chair, cut off the mind-wrecking alarms, and switched on the plates.

A fire glowed at me from the rear-view plate. It was a colossal *white* fire, longer than it was wide, and filling nearly a quarter of the whole sky. The hideous thought came to me that we must be within a few million miles of some monstrous sun that had recently roared into this part of space.

Frantically, I manipulated the distance estimators—and then for a moment stared in blank disbelief at the answers that clicked metallically onto the product plate.

Seven miles! *Only* seven miles! Curious is the human mind. A moment before, when I had thought of it as an abnormally shaped sun, it hadn't resembled anything but an incandescent mass. Abruptly, now, I saw that it had a solid outline, an unmistakable material shape.

Stunned, I leaped to my feet because—

It was a spaceship! An enormous, mile-long ship. Rather—I sank back into my seat, subdued by the catastrophe I was witnessing, and consciously adjusting my mind—the flaming hell of what had been a spaceship. Nothing that had been alive could possibly still be conscious in that horror of ravenous fire. The only possibility was that the crew had succeeded in launching lifeboats.

Like a madman, I searched the heavens for a light, a glint of metal that would show the presence of survivors.

There was nothing but the night and the stars and the hell of burning ship.

After a long time, I noticed that it was farther away, and seemed to be receding. Whatever drive forces had matched its velocity to ours must be yielding to the fury of the energies that were consuming the ship.

I began to take pictures, and I felt justified in turning on the oxygen reserves. As it withdrew into distance, the miniature nova that had been a torpedo-shaped space liner began to change color, to lose its white intensity. It became a red fire silhouetted against darkness. My last glimpse showed it as a long, dull glow that looked like nothing else than a cherry colored nebula seen edge on, like a blaze reflecting from the night beyond a far horizon.

I had already, in between observations, done everything else required of me; and now, I re-connected the alarm system and, very reluctantly, my mind seething with speculation, returned to bed.

As I lay waiting for my final dosage of the trip to take effect, I thought: the great star system of Alpha Centauri must have inhabited planets. If my calculations were correct, we were only one point six light years from the main Alpha group of suns, slightly nearer than that to red Proxima.

Here was proof that the universe had at least one other supremely intelligent race. Wonders beyond our wildest expectations were in store for us. Thrill on thrill of anticipation raced through me.

It was only at the last instant, as sleep was already grasping at my brain that the realization struck that I had forgotten about the problem of Renfrew.

I felt no alarm. Surely, even Renfrew would come alive in that great fashion of his when confronted by a complex alien civilization.

Our troubles were over.

Excitement must have bridged that final one hundred fifty years of time. Because, when I wakened, I thought:

"We're here! It's over, the long night, the incredible journey. We'll all be waking, seeing each other, as well as the civilization out there. Seeing, too, the great Centauri suns."

The strange thing, it struck me as I lay there exulting, was that the time seemed long. And yet . . . yet I had been awake only three times, and only once for the equivalent of a full day.

In the truest sense of meaning, I had seen Blake and Renfrew—and Pelham—not more than a day and a half ago. I had had only thirty-six hours of consciousness since a pair of soft lips had set themselves against mine, and clung in the sweetest kiss of my life.

Then why this feeling that millenniums had ticked by, second on slow second? Why this eerie, empty awareness of a journey through fathomless, unending night?

Was the human mind so easily fooled?

It seemed to me, finally, that the answer was that I had been alive for those five hundred years, all my cells and my organs had existed, and it was not even impossible that some part of my brain had been horrendously aware throughout the entire unthinkable period.

And there was, of course, the additional psychological fact that I knew now that five hundred years had gone by, and that—

I saw with a mental start, that my ten minutes were up. Cautiously, I turned on the massager.

The gentle, padded hands had been working on me for about fifteen minutes when my door opened; the light clicked on, and there stood Blake.

The too-sharp movement of turning my head to look at him made me dizzy. I closed my eyes, and heard him walk across the room toward me.

After a minute, I was able to look at him again without seeing blurs. I saw then that he was carrying a bowl of the soup. He stood staring down at me with a strangely grim expression on his face.

At last, his long, thin countenance relaxed into a wan grin.

" 'Lo, Bill," he said. "*Ssshh!*" he hissed immediately. "Now, don't try to speak. I'm going to start feeding you this soup while you're still lying down. The sooner you're up, the better I'll like it."

He was grim again, as he finished almost as if it were an afterthought: "I've been up for two weeks."

He sat down on the edge of the bed, and ladled out a spoonful of soup. There was silence, then, except for the rustling sound of the massager. Slowly, the strength flowed through my body; and with each passing second, I became more aware of the grimness of Blake.

"What about Renfrew?" I managed finally, hoarsely. "He awake?"

Blake hesitated, then nodded. His expression darkened with frown; he said simply:

"He's mad, Bill, stark, staring mad. I had to tie him up. I've got him now in his room. He's quieter now, but at the beginning he was a gibbering maniac."

"Are you crazy?" I whispered at last. "Renfrew was never so sensitive as that. Depressed and sick, yes; but the mere passage of time, abrupt awareness that all his friends are dead, couldn't make him insane."

Blake was shaking his head. "It isn't only that. Bill—"

He paused, then: "Bill, I want you to prepare your mind for the greatest shock it's ever had."

I stared up at him with an empty feeling inside me. "What do you mean?"

He went on grimacing: "I know you'll be able to take it. So don't get scared. You and I, Bill, are just a couple of lugs. We're along because we went to U with Renfrew and Pelham. Basically, it wouldn't matter to insensitives like us whether we landed in 1,000,000 B. C. or A. D. We'd just look around and say: 'Fancy seeing you here, mug?' or 'Who was that pterodactyl I saw you with last night? That wasn't no pterodactyl; that was Unthahorsten's bulbous wife.'"

I whispered, "Get to the point, Ned. What's up?"

Blake rose to his feet. "Bill, after I'd read your reports about, and seen the photographs of, that burning ship, I got an idea. The Alpha suns were pretty close two weeks ago, only about six months away at our average speed of five hundred miles a second. I thought to myself: 'I'll see if I can tune in some of their radio stations.'"

"Well," he smiled wryly, "I got hundreds in a few minutes. They came in all over the seven dial waves, with bell-like clarity."

He paused; he stared down at me, and his smile was a sickly thing. "Bill," he groaned, "we're the prize fools in creation. When I told Renfrew the truth, he folded up like ice melting into water."

Once more, he paused; the silence was too much for my straining nerves.

"For heaven's sake, man—" I began. And stopped. And lay there, very still. Just like that the lightning of understanding flashed on me. My blood seemed to thunder through my veins. At last, weakly, I said: "You mean—"

Blake nodded. "Yeah," he said. "That's the way it is. And they've already spotted us with their spy rays and energy screens. A ship's coming out to meet us."

"I only hope," he finished gloomily, "they can do something for Jim."

I was sitting in the control chair an hour later when I saw the glint in the darkness. There was a flash of bright silver, that exploded into size. The next instant an enormous spaceship had matched our velocity less than a mile away.

Blake and I looked at each other. "Did they say," I said shakily, "that that ship left its hangar ten minutes ago?"

Blake nodded. "They can make the trip from Earth to Centauri in three hours," he said.

I hadn't heard that before. Something happened inside my brain. "What!" I shouted. "Why, it's taken us five hund—"

I stopped; I sat there. "Three hours!" I whispered. "How *could* we have forgotten human progress?"

In the silence that fell then, we watched a dark hole open in the clifflike wall that faced us. Into this cavern, I directed our ship.

The rear-view plate showed that the cave entrance was closing. Ahead of us lights flashed on, and focused on a door. As I eased our craft to the metal floor, a face flickered onto our radio plate.

"Cassellahat!" Blake whispered in my ear. "The only chap who's talked direct to me so far."

It was a distinguished, a scholarly looking head and face that peered at us. Cassellahat smiled, and said:

"You may leave your ship, and go through the door you see."

I had a sense of empty spaces around us, as we climbed gingerly out into the vast receptor chamber. Interplanetary spaceship hangars were like that, I reminded myself. Only this one had an alien quality that—

"Nerves!" I thought sharply.

But I could see that Blake felt it, too. A silent duo, we filed through the doorway into a hallway, that opened into a very large, luxurious room.

It was such a room as a king or a movie actress on set might have walked into without blinking. It was all hung with gorgeous tapestries—that is, for a moment, I thought they were tapestries; then I saw they weren't. They were—I couldn't decide.

I had seen expensive furniture in some of the apartments Renfrew maintained. But these settees, chairs, and tables glittered at us, as if they were made of a matching design of differently colored fires. No, that was wrong; they didn't glitter at all. They—

Once more I couldn't decide.

I had no time for more detailed examination. For a man arrayed very much as we were, was rising from one of the chairs. I recognized Cassellahat.

He came forward, smiling. Then he slowed, his nose wrinkling. A moment later, he hastily shook our hands, then swiftly retreated to a chair ten feet away, and sat down rather primly.

It was an astoundingly ungracious performance. But I was glad that he had drawn back that way. Because, as he shook my hand so briefly, I had caught a faint whiff of perfume from him. It was a vaguely unpleasant odor; and, besides—a man using perfume in quantities!

I shuddered. What kind of foppish nonsense had the human race gone in for?

He was motioning us to sit down. I did so, wondering: Was this our reception? The erstwhile radio operator began:

"About your friend, I must caution you. He is a schizoid type, and our psychologists will be able to effect a temporary recovery only for the moment. A permanent cure will require a longer period, and your fullest co-operation. Fall in readily with all Mr. Renfrew's plans, unless, of course, he takes a dangerous turn.

"But now"—he squirted us a smile—"permit me to welcome you to the four planets of Centauri. It is a great moment for me, personally. From early childhood, I have been trained for the sole purpose of being your mentor and guide; and naturally I am overjoyed that the time has come when my exhaustive studies of the middle period American language and customs can be put to the practical use for which they were intended."

He didn't look overjoyed. He was wrinkling his nose in that funny way I had already noticed, and there was a generally pained expression on his face. But it was his words that shocked me.

"What do you mean," I asked, "studies in American? Don't people speak the universal language any more?"

"Of course"—he smiled—"but the language has developed to a point where—I might as well be frank— you would have difficulty understanding such a simple word as 'yeih.'"

"Yeih?" Blake echoed.

"Meaning 'yes.'"

"Oh!"

We sat silent, Blake chewing his lower lip. It was Blake who finally said:

"What kind of places are the Centauri planets? You said something on the radio about the population centers having reverted to the city structure again."

"I shall be happy," said Cassellahat, "to show you as many of our great cities as you care to see. You are our guests, and several million credits have been placed to your separate accounts for you to use as you see fit."

"Gee!" said Blake.

"I must, however," Cassellahat went on, "give you a warning. It is important that you do not disillusion our peoples about yourselves. Therefore, you must never wander around the streets, or mingle with the crowds in any way. Always, your contact should be via newsreels, radio, or from the *inside* of a closed machine. If you have any plan to marry, you must now finally give up the idea."

"I don't get it!" Blake said wonderingly; and he spoke for us both.

Cassellahat finished firmly: "It is important that no one becomes aware that you have an offensive physical odor. It might damage your financial prospects considerably.

"And now"—he stood up—"for the time being, I shall leave you. I hope you don't mind if I wear a mask in the future in your presence. I wish you well, gentlemen, and—"

He pushed, glanced past us, said: "Ah, here is your friend."

I whirled, and I could see Blake twisting, staring—

"Hi, there, fellows," Renfrew said cheerfully from the door, then wryly: "Have we ever been a bunch of suckers?"

I felt choked. I raced up to him, caught his hand, hugged him. Blake was trying to do the same.

When we finally released Renfrew, and looked around, Cassellahat was gone.

Which was just as well. I had been wanting to punch him in the nose for his final remarks.

"Well, here goes!" Renfrew said.

He looked at Blake and me, grinned, rubbed his hands together gleefully, and added:

"For a week I've been watching, thinking up questions to ask this cluck and—"

He faced Cassellahat. "What," he began, "makes the speed of light constant?"

Cassellahat did not even blink. "Velocity equals the cube of the cube root of gd," he said, "d being the depth of the space time continuum, g the total tolerance or gravity, as you would say, of all the matter in that continuum."

"How are planets formed?"

"A sun must balance itself in the space that it is in. It throws out matter as a sea vessel does anchors. That's a very rough description. I could give it to you in mathematical formula, but I'd have to write it down. After all, I'm not a scientist. These are merely facts that I've known from childhood, or so it seems."

"Just a minute," said Renfrew, puzzled. "A sun throws this matter out without any pressure other than its—desire—to balance itself?"

Cassellahat stared at him. "Of course not. The reason, the pressure involved, is very potent, I assure you. Without such a balance, the sun would fall out of this space. Only a few bachelor suns have learned how to maintain stability without planets."

"A few what?" echoed Renfrew.

I could see that he had been jarred into forgetting the questions he had been intending to ask one by swift one. Cassellahat's words cut across my thought; he said:

"A bachelor sun is a very old, cooled class M star. The hottest one known has a temperature of one hundred ninety degrees F., the coldest forty-eight. Literally, a bachelor is a rogue, crotchety with age. Its main feature is that it permits no matter, no planets, not even gases in its vicinity."

Renfrew sat silent, frowning, thoughtful. I seized the opportunity to carry on a train of idea.

"This business," I said, "of knowing all this stuff without being a scientist, interests me. For instance, back home every kid understood the atomic-rocket principle practically from the day he was born. Boys of eight and ten rode around in specially made toys, took them apart and put them together again. They *thought* rocket-atomic, and any new development in the field was just pie for them to absorb.

"Now, here's what I'd like to know: what is the parallel here to that particular angle?"

"The adeledicnander force," said Cassellahat. "I've already tried to explain it to Mr. Renfrew, but his mind seems to balk at some of the most simple aspects."

Renfrew roused himself, grimaced. "He's been trying to tell me that electrons think; and I won't swallow it."

Cassellahat shook his head. "Not think; they don't think. But they have a psychology."

"Electronic psychology!" I said.

"Simply adeledicnander," Cassellahat replied. "Any child—"

Renfrew groaned: "I know. Any child of six could tell me."

He turned to us. "That's why I lined up a lot of questions. I figured that if we got a good intermediate grounding, we might be able to slip into this adeledicnander stuff the way their kids do."

He faced Cassellahat. "Next question," he said. "What—"

Cassellahat had been looking at his watch. "I'm afraid, Mr. Renfrew," he interrupted, "that if you and I are going to be on the ferry to the Pelham planet, we'd better leave now. You can ask your questions on the way."

"What's all this?" I chimed in.

Renfrew explained: "He's taking me to the great engineering laboratories in the European mountains of Pelham. Want to come along?"

"Not me," I said.

Blake shrugged. "I don't fancy getting into one of those suits Cassellahat has provided for us, designed to keep our odor in, but not theirs out."

He finished: "Bill and I will stay here and play poker for some of that five million credits worth of dough we've got in the State bank."

Cassellahat turned at the door; there was a distinct frown on the flesh mask he wore. "You treat our government gift very lightly."

"Yeih!" said Blake.

"So we stink," said Blake.

It was nine days since Cassellahat had taken Renfrew to the planet Pelham; and our only contact had been a radio telephone call from Renfrew on the third day, telling us not to worry.

Blake was standing at the window of our penthouse apartment in the city of Newmerica; and I was on my back on a couch, in my mind a mixture of thoughts involving Renfrew's potential insanity and all the things I had heard and seen about the history of the past five hundred years.

I roused myself. "Quit it," I said. "We're faced with a change in the metabolism of the human body, probably due to the many different foods from remote stars that they eat. They must be able to smell better, too, because just being near us is agony to Cassellahat, whereas we only notice an unpleasantness from him. It's a case of three of us against billions of them. Frankly, I don't see an early victory over the problem, so let's just take it quietly."

There was no answer; so I returned to my reverie. My first radio message to Earth had been picked up; and so, when the interstellar drive was invented in 2320 A. D., less than one hundred forty years after our departure, it was realized what would eventually happen.

In our honor, the four habitable planets of the Alpha A and B suns were called Renfrew, Pelham, Blake, and

Endicott. Since 2320, the populations of the four planets had become so dense that a total of nineteen billion people now dwelt on their narrowing land spaces. This in spite of migrations to the planets of more distant stars.

The space liner I had seen burning in 2511 A. D. was the only ship ever lost on the Earth-Centauri lane. Traveling at full speed, its screens must have reacted against our spaceship. All the automatics would instantly have flashed on; and, as those defenses were not able at that time to stop a ship that had gone Minus Infinity, every recoil engine aboard had probably blown up.

Such a thing could not happen again. So enormous had been the progress in the adeledicnander field of power, that the greatest liners could stop dead in the full fury of midflight.

We had been told not to feel any sense of blame for that one disaster, as many of the most important advances in adeledicnander electronic psychology had been made as the result of theoretical analyses of that great catastrophe.

I grew aware that Blake had flung himself disgustedly into a nearby chair.

"Boy, oh, boy," he said, "this is going to be some life for us. We can all anticipate about fifty more years of being pariahs in a civilization where we can't even understand how the simplest machines work."

I stirred uneasily. I had had similar thoughts. But I said nothing. Blake went on:

"I must admit, after I first discovered the Centauri planets had been colonized, I had pictures of myself bowling over some dame, and marrying her."

Involuntarily my mind leaped to the memory of a pair of lips lifting up to mine. I shook myself. I said:

"I wonder how Renfrew is taking all this. He—"

A familiar voice from the door cut off my words. "Renfrew," it said, "is taking things beautifully now that the first shock has yielded to resignation, and resignation to purpose."

We had turned to face him by the time he finished. Renfrew walked slowly toward us, grinning. Watching him, I felt uncertain as to just how to take his built-up sanity.

He was at his best. His dark, wavy hair was perfectly combed. His startlingly blue eyes made his whole face come alive. He was a natural physical wonder; and at his normal he had all the shine and swagger of an actor in a carefully tailored picture.

He wore that shine and swagger now. He said:

"I've bought a spaceship, fellows. Took all my money and part of yours, too. But I knew you'd back me up. Am I right?"

"Why, sure," Blake and I echoed.

Blake went on alone: "What's the idea?"

"I get it," I chimed in. "We'll cruise all over the universe, live our life span exploring new worlds. Jim, you've got something there. Blake and I were just going to enter a suicide pact."

Renfrew was smiling, "We'll cruise for a while anyway."

Two days later, Cassellahat having offered no objection and no advice about Renfrew, we were in space.

It was a curious three months that followed. For a while I felt a sense of awe at the vastness of the cosmos. Silent planets swung into our viewing plates, and faded into remoteness behind us, leaving nostalgic memory of uninhabited, windlashed forests and plains, deserted, swollen seas and nameless suns.

The sight and the remembrance brought loneliness like an ache, and the knowledge, the slow knowledge, that this journeying was not lifting the weight of strangeness that had settled upon us ever since our arrival at Alpha Centauri.

There was nothing here for our souls to feed on,

nothing that would satisfactorily fill one year of our life, let alone fifty.

I watched the realization grow on Blake, and I waited for a sign from Renfrew that he felt it, too. The sign didn't come. That of itself worried me; then I grew aware of something else. Renfrew was watching us. Watching us with a hint in his manner of secret knowledge, a suggestion of secret purpose.

My alarm grew; and Renfrew's perpetual cheerfulness didn't help any. I was lying on my bunk at the end of the third month, thinking uneasily about the whole unsatisfactory situation, when my door opened and Renfrew came in.

He carried a paralyzer gun and a rope. He pointed the gun at me and said:

"Sorry, Bill. Cassellahat told me to take no chances, so just lie quiet while I tie you up."

"Blake!" I bellowed.

Renfrew shook his head gently. "No use," he said. "I was in his room first."

The gun was steady in his fingers, his blue eyes were steely. All I could do was tense my muscles against the ropes as he tied me, and trust to the fact that I was twice as strong, at least, as he was.

I thought in dismay: Surely I could prevent him from tying me too tightly.

He stepped back finally, said again. "Sorry, Bill." He added: "I hate to tell you this, but both of you went off the deep end mentally when we arrived at Centauri; and this is the cure prescribed by the psychologists whom Cassellahat consulted. You're supposed to get a shock as big as the one that knocked you for a loop."

The first time I'd paid no attention to his mention of Cassellahat's name. Now my mind flared with understanding.

Incredibly, Renfrew had been told that Blake and I were mad. All these months he had been held steady by a sense of responsibility toward us. It was a beautiful psychological scheme. The only thing was: *what* shock was going to be administered?

Renfrew's voice cut off my thought. He said:

"It won't be long now. We're already entering the field of the bachelor sun."

"Bachelor sun!" I yelled.

He made no reply. The instant the door closed behind him, I began to work on my bonds; all the time I was thinking:

What was it Cassellahat had said? Bachelor suns maintained themselves in this space by a precarious balancing.

In *this* space! The sweat poured down my face, as I pictured ourselves being precipitated into another plane of the space-time continuum—I could feel the ship falling when I finally worked my hands free of the rope.

I hadn't been tied long enough for the cords to interfere with my circulation. I headed for Blake's room. In two minutes we were on our way to the control cabin.

Renfrew didn't see us till we had him. Blake grabbed his gun; I hauled him out of the control chair with one mighty heave and dumped him onto the floor.

He lay there, unresisting, grinning up at us. "Too late," he taunted. "We're approaching the first point of intolerance, and there's nothing you can do except prepare for the shock."

I scarcely heard him. I plumped myself into the chair, and glared into the viewing plates. Nothing showed. That stumped me for a second. Then I saw the recorder instruments. They were trembling furiously, registering a body of INFINITE size.

For a long moment I stared crazily at those incredible figures. Then I plunged the decelerator far over. Before that pressure of full-driven adeledicnander, the machine grew rigid; I had a sudden fantastic picture of two irresistible forces in full collision. Gasping, I jerked the power out of gear.

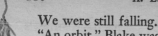

We were still falling.

"An orbit," Blake was saying. "Get us into an orbit."

With shaking fingers, I pounded one out on the keyboard basing my figures on a sun of Sol-ish size, gravity, and mass.

The bachelor wouldn't let us have it.

I tried another orbit, and a third, and more—finally one that would have given us an orbit around mighty Antares itself. But the deadly reality remained. The ship plunged on, down and down.

And there was nothing visible on the plates, not a real shadow of substance. It seemed to me once that I could make out a vague blur of greater darkness against the black reaches of space. But the stars were few in every direction and it was impossible to be sure.

Finally, in despair, I whirled out of the seat, and knelt beside Renfrew, who was still making no effort to get up.

"Listen, Jim," I pleaded, "what did you do this for? What's going to happen?"

He was smiling easily. "Think," he said, "of an old, crusty, human bachelor. He maintains a relationship with his fellows, but the association is as remote as that which exists between a bachelor sun and the stars in the galaxy of which it is a part."

He added: "Any second now we'll strike the first period of intolerance. It works in jumps like quantum, each period being four hundred ninety-eight years, seven months and eight days plus a few hours."

It sounded like gibberish. "But what's going to happen?" I urged. "For Heaven's sake, man!"

He gazed up at me blandly; and, looking up at him, I had the sudden, wondering realization that he was sane, the old completely rational Jim Renfrew, made better somehow, stronger. He said quietly:

"Why, it'll just knock us out of its toleration area; and in doing so will put us back—"

JERK!

The lurch was immensely violent. With a bang, I

struck the floor, skidded, and then a hand—Renfrew's —caught me. And it was all over.

I stood up, conscious that we were no longer falling. I looked at the instrument board. All the lights were dim, untroubled, the needles firmly at zero. I turned and stared at Renfrew, and at Blake, who was ruefully picking himself from the floor.

Renfrew said persuasively: "Let me at the control board, Bill. I want to set our course for Earth."

For a long minute, I gazed at him; and then, slowly, I stepped aside. I stood by as he set the controls and pulled the accelerator over. Renfrew looked up.

"We'll reach Earth in about eight hours," he said, "and it'll be about a year and a half after we left five hundred years ago."

Something began to tug at the roof of my cranium. It took several seconds before I decided that it was probably my brain jumping with the tremendous understanding that suddenly flowed in upon me.

The bachelor sun, I thought dazedly. In easing us out of its field of toleration, it had simply precipitated us into a period of time beyond its field. Renfrew had said . . . had said it worked in jumps of . . . four hundred ninety-eight years and some seven months and—

But what about the ship? Wouldn't twenty-seventh century adeledicnander brought to the twenty-second century change the course of history?

Renfrew shook his head. "Do *we* understand it? Do we even dare monkey with the raw power inside those engines? I'll say not. As for the ship, we'll keep it for our own private use."

"B-but—" I began.

He cut me off. "Look, Bill," he said, "here's the situation: that girl who kissed you—don't think I didn't see you falling like a ton of bricks—is going to be sitting beside you fifty years from now, when *your* voice from space reports to Earth that you had wakened on your first lap of the first trip to Centaurus."

That's exactly what happened.

MURRAY LEINSTER

PROPAGANDIST

*When you stop to think of it, no other
life form on Earth, other than Man, ever
calculatedly, using intelligence rather
than instinct, sets out to deceive another
life form. Other than Man, all animals
that trap other animals (like spiders) or
hunt other animals (like wolves, hawks,
or sharks), or trick other animals (like
some snakes and some birds, I am told),
do so because it is their natural, instinctive way of getting essential food. Only
men do these things not only for necessary food but also for power, or revenge,
or sadism, or whatever other nasty motives men may have for hurting or en-
slaving other animals or men. And that
is why there is so much immediate point
to this story of the first meeting of two
alien races, one ours, the other from a far
star. How could one successfully achieve
communication between such races and
be absolutely certain one was not being
tricked? Only an animal can be trusted
in a situation such as this—for* NO ANI-
MAL CAN BE DISHONEST!

YOU REMEMBER the Space Assassins, of course. They
were that race of which no human being ever saw a
living member, and escaped to tell about it afterward.
You also remember the deadly, far-flung search that

was made for their base, their home. They'd been sniping our ships for a long time. But then a squadron of their space fleet raided the Earth colony on Capella Three and without warning or provocation or alternative slaughtered every one of the colony's half million human population. Then the hunt for them began.

This is the story of one of the incidents of that hunt —and also it's the story of a dog named Buck.

Buck trailed his master sedately into the control room of the light cruiser *Kennessee*. He waited patiently until the skipper looked up from the electron telescope. Then Buck's master—Holden—sat down with the sheaf of wave records he'd brought from the communications room. Buck blinked wisely at the skipper and lay down on the floor with an audible, loose-jointed thump. He put his nose between his paws and sighed heavily. But the sigh was not of unhappiness. Buck was a simple dog. He was friendly with everybody on the *Kennessee*, from the skipper himself to the lowliest mess boy, but his master and private deity was Junior Lieutenant Holden. Whithersoever Holden went, there Buck went also—regulations permitting—and waited until Holden wanted to go somewhere else.

Now he lay on the foamite flooring. He heard his master's voice, and the skipper's in reply. They were concerned and uneasy. Buck dozed. Little, half-formed dreams ran through his slumber. Memory dreams, mostly, of himself racing gloriously through tall grass on the green fields of Earth, with Holden always somewhere near. The voices of the two men formed a half-heard background to his dozing.

The men were troubled. The *Kennessee* rode a comet's orbit through the solar system of Masa Gamma, her drive off and giving no sign of life. She was impersonating a barren visitor from the void, spying out the ground for what would be—if she was successful—the monstrous destruction of an entire race by planet-smasher guided missiles and the merciless weapons of an Earth fleet. The men did not like it. They'd hoped that some other ship would be the one to meet with success in its search. But they had their orders.

Some weeks back the ship had dropped from overdrive to less-than-light speed far beyond the outermost of the Masa Gamma planets. She'd decelerated to an appropriate speed and course for a wanderer, and she'd begun her ride along a comet's path through the eleven-planet system. And almost immediately her receptors had picked up evidence of civilization here. Space radio signals. They were unintelligible, of course, but they told that here was a civilization comparable to human culture on a technical basis. And that was what the *Kennessee*, with every other light ship of Earth's space navy, was hunting for. There was a race which, without known contact with Earthmen, was the deadly enemy of humanity. For years past, exploring ships from Earth had dropped out of sight with ominous frequency. There had been suspicions, but no proof of an inimical race which destroyed humans wherever it came upon them. But six months ago the Earth colony on Capella Three had been wiped out, terribly, by raiders of whom nothing was known except that they were not human. So somewhere there was a race which held Earth to be its enemy. It had to be found. If it could not be negotiated with, it must be destroyed before it grew strong enough to wipe out all of humankind. And the men on the *Kennessee* knew that they might have found it on the planets of Masa Gamma. This system had never been explored before, and this civilization which had space radio might be the one—

Buck, the dog, dozed lightly on the control-room floor. Little fragments of dreams ran through his half-slumbering consciousness: the smells in the engine room; an irrelevant fragment of chasing a cat; a moment or two in which he sniffed elaborately at a tree . . . A slightly louder comment made him open his eyes.

"They've interplanetary travel, sir, at least"—that was Holden. "We've picked up space-radio messages from definitely between planets. It looks like this is the race we were sent to find."

The skipper nodded.

"It could be. But if they're to be smashed on our report, we need to make sure. That's orders, too. Can they smash the *Kennessee?* That's the test for the enemy. If this race can't kill us, they're not the enemy we're looking for. If they can, they are. We've got to find out."

"But interplanetary travel is good evidence—"

"It's not interstellar travel," said the skipper. "We'll send a torp back immediately with all the data to date. But you've picked up no whango waves, Holden. We've no proof that these folk can travel between the stars. The enemy can."

"They might be concealing the fact," said Holden. "They'd have picked up our whango wave on arrival. They might be laying for us, waiting for us to walk into their parlor where they can smash us without a chance to fight back or report. That would be typical."

He stood up and Buck got immediately to his four paws and wagged his tail. His master, Holden, was going to go somewhere. So Buck was going with him. He waited contently. To Buck, happiness was going where Holden went, being wherever Holden was, simply soaking in the sensation of being with Holden. It was a very simple pleasure, but it was all he asked of fate or chance. When Holden petted him or played roughly with him, Buck was filled with ecstatic happiness, but now he waited contentedly enough simply to follow Holden.

"What you say is true enough," agreed the skipper. "They could be laying for us. We'll see. A message torp will make sure that if we don't get back our fleet will know where to come and who to smash. Then we'll make a landing in a lifeboat. Our enemy couldn't resist smashing that! And if it gets away, we'll know something about their weapons, anyhow."

"I volunteer, sir, for the lifeboat," said Holden quickly.

"We'll see," said the skipper. "You get your data ready for the torp. You're sure this record is a scanning beam? Like the old-fashioned radar? And it's being kept on us from this fourth planet?"

"Quite sure, sir," said Holden. "We can't know how detailed the information may be that it takes back. Of course, it would be logical enough to scan a supposed comet—"

"Let's hope," said the skipper, twinkling, "that the echo from our hull says, 'Nobody out here but us comets, boss.' Get your stuff ready for half an hour from now, Holden."

Holden saluted and went out of the control room. Buck went sedately after him, a large brown dog who did not bother his head over such trivia as interstellar travel or nonhuman races that massacred half a million humans with an insensate ferocity.

Buck was a very contented dog. He was with his master.

The Planetary Council of Masa Four was in session. It was not a happy gathering. Scanning beams had reported that a supposed new comet, driving in on a perfectly convincing orbit, was actually an artifact— a spaceship. It used no drive and seemed empty of life. But it had come in through the gravitation field of the outermost planets—and it showed no sign of rotation. Which was impossible unless gyroscopes or some similar device were running within it.

"We have had one visitor from space, before," said the Moderator of the Planetary Council. He looked very weary. "Our histories tell us of the consequences. If this is another ship of the same race, we must destroy it. Since it is attempting secrecy, such action is justified, I think. But that secrecy suggests suspicion of us—a suspicion that we may have destroyed the last visitor. If we destroy this ship also, we may be sure that suspicion will become certainty and a third visit will be made in overwhelming force. That means that we will have to convert our whole civilization for war. We will have somehow to develop an interstellar drive, and we will have to spend the rest of the time in battle for our very survival. We will have to change from a peaceful race to one with a psychology adapted only to war."

The Spokesman for the First Continent said hopefully:

"Is it certain that this is a ship of the same race as the first? It is not of the same form. Is it certain that this race is of a not-possibly-friendly type, like the first?"

"It is not certain," said the Moderator tiredly. "The psychological factors implied by its outer design suggest a different race. But can we risk an attempt at peaceful contact? The crew of one ship would be at our mercy. Might they not pretend friendship in order to escape with information leading to our destruction? Could we trust the friendship of any race at all which sent a single ship to spy?"

There was silence. Two centuries before, another ship had entered the Masan system. Half a planet devastated, and millions upon millions of lives, had been the cost of the destruction of that one ship. But its destruction had been necessary. Its crew made no response to peaceful overtures. Wherever they landed they destroyed, ferociously, everything savoring of a rival civilization. Especially the inhabitants. They could not be treated with—only killed.

"If," said the Spokesman for the Third Continent wistfully, "we could capture a single member of this spaceship's crew, we could make sure that friendship was hopeless. It is a pity we cannot make sure before—"

"It is a great pity," said the Moderator bleakly. "To convert not only our civilization but our people to endless war, for all time, is the greatest of pities. But I do not think there is anything else to do. Will you vote upon preparations for the destruction of this ship?"

The vote was reluctant but unanimous. For war.

The *Kennessee* sent off the torp from the aft communications room. It was not an impressive device, the torp, merely a cigar-shaped object some six feet long. After leaving the *Kennessee* it would drive away at thirty-five gravities' acceleration for fifteen minutes and then go into overdrive—when it would cease to exist, as far as normal space was concerned. Its disappearance would be marked by the emission of a monstrous surge of energy—a "whango wave"—which could be detected at hundreds of millions of miles. Near home base it would come out of overdrive with the emission of another, similar, wave. The second wave was useful. From Masa Gamma to the *Kennessee's* home base was some eighty light-years. A space-radio message transmitted by tight beam would reach home base only in time to be of interest to the crew's great-grandchildren. But the torp would arrive within days, its reappearance wave would be picked up by a far-flung net of communications ships, and they would receive and forward the torp's automatically transmitted messages, and later pick it up for the recovery of written data and physical specimens.

Buck was not allowed to be present at the launching. He was a large dog, and the aft communications room was in the tapering, slender tail of the *Kennessee*. It would be crowded. Holden ordered him out. And Buck was far too well assured, both of Holden's affection for him and of his own worth, to be sensitive about such a matter. He knew there were times when he couldn't be underfoot. But he also knew that he was welcome anywhere else on the ship. He went trotting sedately in search of inferior, but still human, company until his master could allow him around again.

He found crew members stocking a lifeboat for its special mission. He went companionably into the lifeboat with the working party. He wriggled into the control cubicle with the man sent to remove its records —and observed. Presently other men arrived, the work party left, and there were sundry heaving movements of the lifeboat. Buck blinked from where he lay more or less curled up on the floor. Stars shone in the lifeboat portholes. There was a glaring bright light. Unshielded sunshine from Masa Gamma came in a forward port and made a patch of incandescence on the back wall. Junior Lieutenant Maynard walked into the control cubicle and flipped the phone switch.

"Lifeboat in launching position, blister removed, ready to take off," he said briskly.

"All right," said Holden's voice from the speaker. It sounded gloomy. "Take off when the whango wave hits. It may jam their scanner and get you out of the beam unobserved. Luck."

Buck knew loud-speakers. But also he knew his master's voice. He wagged his tail. It thumped. Maynard jerked his head around and yelled: "Buck! Here's Buck! Behind me!"

An instant's silence. Then Holden's voice, more gloomy still.

"No time to get him back on board. He'll have to go along. Sorry, Maynard."

"No harm," said Maynard cheerfully. "Maybe he'll mascot us. How much time?"

"Twenty seconds," said Holden's voice. "You have all the luck! I was high man for this job until you drew that ace!"

Maynard chuckled. The *Kennessee* rode into a very probably hostile solar system. If it was the home of the race that had been sniping off Earth ships and had massacred the colonists of Capella Three, there was not much chance that the cruiser would ever get away again. But its junior officers had played a hand of stud poker for the privilege of making a dare-landing on the system's largest planet.

The speaker suddenly emitted a sound so savage and so loud that the diaphragm jangled musically only once, and then made strangled, rasping noises. That was the whango wave of the message torp. It was a blast of untuned and untunable radiation which would jam every receiver in range while it lasted.

There was a crushing feeling of weight. Buck slid back against the back rest of the seat on which he now lay. He was pressed hard against the upholstery. He wriggled and panted. His eyes grew plaintive. Buck did not like acceleration. In fact, he did not like life-boat travel. But he had his fill of it in the next eighteen hours, anyhow.

A message arrived at the hastily improvised Department of War on Masa Four. The Department of War was being feverishly organized to coordinate every erg of energy in the entire solar system into synchrophased power beams which at a given moment would stab out from four planets at once—all of them on the same side of the local sun—and converge terribly upon the pseudo comet. There would be no material weapon for the ship's detectors to note in time for any maneuver of escape. This weapon would strike at the speed of light. An object in the focus of the combined beams would experience the interior temperature of a sun. It was unthinkable that any possible relay could operate before it was volatilized. The weapon was irresistible—as against a single ship. But the computation of phase relationships for the moving planetary projectors, so that the separate beams would reinforce instead of partially canceling one another, was a matter of terrifying complexity. This weapon could destroy one ship of known course and speed, or one ship on the ground, if enough time could be had for calculations. But it would be useless against a fleet. Days or weeks were required for the adjustment of the multitude of beams for a hit on a predetermined spot. Against ships of changing course and speed, the weapon was useless.

A message arrived at the Department of War.

SMALL SPACE CRAFT DETACHED ITSELF FROM INVADING VESSEL AT INSTANT OF STRONG UNTUNED WAVE DISTURBANCE. SMALL CRAFT MAKING GUIDED FLIGHT TOWARD PLANET FOUR. WILL LAND ON DARK SIDE NORTHERN AREA FIRST CONTINENT. REQUEST ORDERS.

The Department of War was newly organized and had not time to acquire traditions of pomposity and bureaucratic delay. Within minutes its orders went back:

EVACUATE ALL POPULATION FROM AREA IN QUESTION. HAVE GROUND VEHICLES ATMOSPHERE FLIERS READY TO TEST ARMAMENT OF CRAFT. BROADCAST APPEAL FOR VOLUNTEERS, GIVING DUE WARNING OF PROBABLE DEATH. NO SPACE CRAFT TO BE USED. NO HINT OF ADEQUATE DEFENSES MUST BE GIVEN TO ENEMY UNTIL FULL-SCALE OPERATION BY ENTIRE SYSTEM.

The population of the Masa Four had had one experience of invaders from beyond. Some twenty-five million citizens began a swift, orderly evacuation—as a precaution against the landing of an unarmed lifeboat.

Buck waked from an uneasy doze when the lifeboat descended to the planet's dark side. Every observation device known to man was at work to gather information, but Buck was not interested in technicalities. He yawned elaborately, even as scanner beams were noted. He stretched as the scanner beams cut off abruptly. He shook himself comfortably as the analyzers reported the atmosphere to be Earth-type, with a considerable excess of the inert gases but well inside the comfort range of oxygen-nitrogen mixtures.

The lifeboat went down carefully, feeling for dangers. Infrared equipment reported the shore of a sea and oddities that could be the equipment of a harbor. Maynard sheered the tiny craft away. He actually neared ground only a hundred-odd miles away. It was his job to get himself killed if the local population could manage it, but it was not his job to make them. If they knew the seeming comet out in space was a spaceship, they'd be on the alert. If they were the race that had murdered the Capellan colonists, they'd try to keep him from getting back to his ship. If they weren't—

The lifeboat grounded with infinite caution in what the scanners declared was a jungle of feathery-leaved vegetation. For long, long minutes Maynard sat tense, prepared to fling the little craft skyward at any sign of action against it. Nothing happened. The outside microphones transmitted noises, to be sure, but they were the random sounds of wild jungle life. After a long time Maynard cracked a port. Still nothing.

"If anybody wants to volunteer to get biological specimens," said Maynard, "he can step out. In case of alarm, though, I'm going to take this boat up and try to wriggle back—to find out what they'll try to use to stop us."

Voices answered. There was the clanking of an unlocking door. Buck trotted back to it. Fascinating smells came in the opening. Men stepped out—armed and cautious. The exit door stayed open. One man stood by to shut and dog it if the lifeboat shot skyward.

It took courage for men to venture out, knowing that they might have to be abandoned so the lifeboat's mission of drawing enemy fire—if this race was inimical—could be carried out. But Buck was fascinated by the smells. He would have liked to get back to Holden, of course, but these men were his friends, too. If they went out into this place of innumerable novel smells—

He jumped lightly to the ground. His nose was in-

stantly busy. The ground had a different smell from
that of Earth. The plants were new. There were scents
which must be animals, but not any animals Buck had
ever scented before. He heard a man moving nearby,
taking samples of vegetation. Very much could be in-
ferred from the types of starch and cellulose this
planet's vegetation contained. But Buck could have
told much more, from what his nose discovered. Here
a little carnivore had trailed a skittering small thing
which periodically darted up into overhanging vegetation, and as periodically darted down again. There a
small herbivore had made a vast, terrified leap for no
apparent reason—which meant that a flying thing had
made a swoop at it, and missed. And here a thing
which had almost the smell of a snake moved in
distinctive hops, while there was a definite smell of a
warm-blooded animal in something which left a completely continuous trail by traveling on its belly.

Buck explored, utterly absorbed in this world of
literally new smells. From time to time he heard the
sounds made by the men, and was reassured. But he
strayed farther and farther from the grounded lifeboat—only sometimes he stopped and listened to it—
and he had found the burrow of some living creature
and was sniffing absorbedly at its entrance when the
really significant noises began.

One noise began at the horizon and swept toward
the zenith. It was a dull, humming rumble, like the
motors of atmosphere fliers Buck had heard back
on Earth. It was mechanical and, therefore, of man,
and, therefore, not to be feared or suspected. At the
same time there came distant clankings. And they were
like bulldozers and other machines of men, and they
were not to be feared, either. Buck sniffed fascinatedly
at the burrow.

Men's voices called sharply. Had Holden called him,
Buck would have gone bounding instantly. But he
owed a lesser obedience to other men. He sniffed again
and again, lingeringly. Then, as he trotted unhurriedly

in response to the call, he heard the zooming roar of a lifeboat drive in atmosphere. It shot toward the sky. It did not occur to Buck that he might have had to be left behind—as a man would have been abandoned under like circumstances—because the lifeboat had to test out the deadliness of armaments on this planet, but had to be aloft to test them fully.

When he got back to the place where the lifeboat had been, though, it was gone.

Buck was simply bewildered. The droning above grew to a thunderous, circling roar. There were many flying things overhead, and they cruised back and forth in the darkness in a pattern which would have made it difficult indeed for the lifeboat to have escaped without coming under radar-aimed fire. At the same time, the clanking mechanical noises came closer from at least three directions.

Buck smelled incredulously at the place where the lifeboat had been but where it was no longer. He ran uneasily along the scent trails left by the men who had gathered biological specimens. It was completely unthinkable that the men had deserted him. He came back again and again to the place where the lifeboat had rested. He was unhappy, of course, but it was not possible for him to imagine himself abandoned. He waited uncomfortably for the men to notice that he'd been left behind and to come back after him.

Roarings circled in the overcast sky above him. Clankings approached in the encircling dark. Those were things of men—not his men, perhaps, but certainly men who would be friendly to a large, brown, well-mannered dog with a collar around his neck which said he belonged to Holden. They might even help him get back to Holden. But meantime he trotted uneasily about the place to which the lifeboat had not returned. The noises and clankings grew louder.

When the noises were very near, a blindingly bright white light abruptly shone down from a low-flying plane which spun in dizzy tight circles overhead. The light showed everything with a pitiless clarity, and Buck blinked dazedly. But he was not alarmed. Machines and bright lights and flying things meant men. And a self-respecting dog has a perfectly comfortable relationship with all men, though it is a special relationship with the crew of his ship, and his tie to his master is unique.

Buck moved prudently out of the way as machines with glaring lights came clanking through the jungle, thrusting aside the feathery trees with a powerful violence. He moved out of their path, but he did not dodge into the shadows. He blinked and wagged his tail abstractedly and prepared to greet the men in the machines with due courtesy. Of course they would help him get back to Holden!

A machine stopped, and something got out of it. But the figure was not a man. Buck sniffed incredulously. Then his hackles rose. It was not possible! Machines were handled by men! Only by men! The Masan moved toward him. Buck growled warningly. Unbearable light smote upon him. He growled again, bristling, a big brown dog growling in warning that members of a mere race which might have been sniping Earth ships and massacring Earth colonies had better not bother him! Buck, of course, knew nothing of missing ships or massacres. He was a dog, a man's dog, and he could imagine no creature which was not inferior to man and which a man's dog could not reasonably defy.

It was an extraordinary picture. Alien and unlikely jungle trees rising toward an overcast sky in which a bright white light whirled in dizzying circles. Huge, gleaming machines with lights—very bright lights— stabbing through the jungle's feathery leafage and casting innumerable sharp shadows. The Masans, inhabitants of the fourth planet of Masa Gamma—not too much unlike men, to be sure—staring at a place in the jungle where a ship's lifeboat had landed and where a big brown dog stood warningly at bay and growled at them of the wrath of his masters.

There was a pause. A race which has space radios, and interplanetary ships, and radar, is not likely to be altogether stupid. And there were scanners in the ground vehicles, too, which carried back to record rooms everything the machines saw. The best brains of the race watched this meeting. And perhaps it was back where the scanned picture of the event was seen that someone realized that Buck's paws were not made for the handling of machinery or the making of space-ships. Or perhaps something more subtle—

There were sounds which Buck somehow knew were language, though he could not understand them as words. He turned sedately from the first figure, which had halted at his growl. He blinked dignifiedly at the surrounding lights. None advanced toward him. Buck emitted sundry small, confident, admonitory rumblings. His men had been here. They had gone away. They would come back for him. Of course. He was going to wait for them. He was not arbitrary about it. He would allow the machines to pass as they pleased. Men probably wished the machines to do thus and so, and he would not interfere. But he would wait here.

He deliberately turned himself around twice and lay down on the ground. But his head stayed erect and he blinked at the lights. He calmly and confidently settled down for men to notice that he'd been left behind and to come back for him.

But he hoped desperately that Holden would be with them.

A report went to the Department of War on Planet Four. It was a highly accurate report, covering the landing of a small space craft on the northern area of the First Continent. The footprints of men were accurately transmitted, as well as the impression left by the spaceboat in the soil. There were motion pictures of Buck. Most of the report, naturally, was about him.

". . . Limited but definite intelligence," said the report. "Is aware of social relationships neither hostile nor friendly, but tolerant. Is familiar with machines and regards them without fear but without interest. Has an extraordinary air of self-confidence and seems justified in opposing the wishes of more intelligent beings, though offering no hostility unless an attempt is made to force it to comply . . . Appears to be a member of a subject species to the makers of the space craft, though its utility is not clear, since it has neither prehensile claws nor any apparent technical aptitude for the supervision of machines . . . We are setting up psychoscanning devices to attempt to extract information from its memories, of course without its awareness of the process. Meanwhile we are making every effort to leave it emotionally undisturbed. . . ."

A later report:
" . . . Psychoscanners have been able to secure excellent pictures and sound memories from the animal. It is of a species which lives in symbiosis with the creatures operating the space craft. Its utility to the superior race is not yet clear, but its subservience to them—they are not much unlike us—is proven by the records forwarded with this report. The animal's vision appears to be comparatively poor, but its hearing and smell are excellent. Its memories of smells, in particular, are especially vivid. We have vision-memory records of various members of the spaceship's crew, but smell-memories of every individual. Apparently, however, little or no technical information can be had from the animal because of the disinterest of the 'Buck'—this is the auditory memory of the animal's name for itself—in such matters. Memories of the naval base and of the presumed home planet of the invaders are concerned almost exclusively with smells. It is extremely concerned with trees and posts and the smells associated with them. . . . We regret that no useful technical information can be had. . . ."

An order from the Department of War:

URGENT. FIRST ATTENTION. THIS ORDER SUPERSEDES ALL OTHERS WHATSOEVER AND CLAIMS THE OBEDIENCE OF EVERY CITIZEN BEFORE ANY OTHER ACTIVITY WHATEVER.

The Planetary Council has decided that information obtained from the Buck will determine our attitude toward the invaders. The fullest data must be secured concerning the relative loyalty of superior and inferior. Subject races can be psychologically conditioned to loyalty to tyrannical superiors. To what extent was this done to the Buck, and how? To what extent are rights conceded to the inferior race? What punishments are inflicted for mistakes of the race of inferior intelligence? What social stigma attaches to them? To what degree does the Buck expect loyalty to his kind from the superior race? What is the nature of the compact between the two—explicit or implied—and to what extent is it observed by the superior? What . . .

The order continued in exhausting detail. It was based upon the realization that Buck—as a domestic animal—contained within his skull an absolutely objective picture of the human race. Buck would not be unbiased in his contemplation of his memories, but his memories would be right. A dog's-eye view of humanity would be, within its limits, an extraordinarily revealing view.

The Planetary Council accepted the conclusion that no technical or military information could be had from Buck. But what information it could obtain would be priceless. No man could be truthful about his own race, talking to an alien entity. But a dog—

The Planetary Council pushed its preparations for war. It had very little hope of anything but never-ending battle through all the centuries of the future. But what hopes it had were centered in Buck.

Buck himself found life confusing. The place where

the lifeboat had landed was fenced in now, and he was inside the fence. The things which were not men treated him with respect, and he treated them with the self-respecting courtesy of a well-mannered dog. They pointed things at him, and he was bored. But presently they had a loud-speaker which made noises. Once it barked at him in exact similitude of another dog—in fact, Buck remembered a dog at the Rigel base whose bark had sounded exactly like that. He barked back angrily. But the loud-speaker did not bark again. Another time, Holden's voice came out of it. And Buck leaped in frenzied joy, his tail wagging until it was almost a blur, and gave tongue in such howlings of heartbroken joy as a dog does give when his master returns after many days. When he realized that it was the loud-speaker, he could not accept the disappointment. He went whimpering about the enclosure, searching for Holden.

There were other stimuli applied to Buck, too. One of the Masans brought him food. At first Buck sniffed at it gingerly. If he must eat of unfamiliar things, he preferred food of his own killing. But ultimately he tolerated the Masan and ate. The Masan had a loud-speaker attached to his body, and it said "Buck" on various occasions, and at first Buck's tail wagged joyously at the familiar syllable. But even when the Masan himself mastered the articulation of the name, Buck did not accept him fully. He wanted men. Especially, he wanted Holden. He dozed, and dreamed of Holden. He slept, and sometimes his dreams were such as to make his paws make tiny, jerking, frustrated movements, and sometimes he barked or whimpered or whined in his sleep. But the whinings were of the desperate joy he felt when in his dreams he saw Holden.

He had no idea that the things pointed at him by the Masans made records of his memories as they were evoked by the increasing stock of stimuli the Masans were able to apply. Buck had understood the mean-

ing of well over a hundred words, when combined
with certain tones of voice. These words invariably
provoked similar responses as the loud-speaker uttered
them from the record of Buck's memories.

While the preparations for the destruction of the
Kennessee went on, the Masans studied Buck inten-
sively. With their increasing comprehension of his
brain, they tried to win his friendship. The one Masan
assigned to the task tried painstakingly to fill the part
of Holden. He used the memory-recordings of Holden's voice. He tried to reproduce the strokings that
Buck's memories said caused quiverings of ecstasy.
Once he tried to tussle with Buck, as Holden did. And
that took courage, because Buck was a big and powerful dog and the Masan was slight and relatively frail.

But Buck would not play. He was polite and he was
amiable within the limits a dog sets for himself toward other animals also useful to man—horses, for
example, and cows and sheep and very occasionally a
cat. But a dog will not play with a gamboling lamb
nor run with a freed colt. Buck was reserved. His
loyalty to man, and especially to Holden, could not
be broken. And though he did eat, and condescend-
ingly tolerated the Masan scientist—considered to
have one of the two or three best brains in the system
—who tried to replace Holden in his affections, he
began to pine away as days and days passed by and
began to stretch into weeks. He grew thin, though he
was abstractedly aware that the people who were not
men had begun very definitely to like him.

After all, a man's dog doesn't thrive when he's
separated from the man.

The *Kennessee* rode on in the orbit it had chosen.
Maynard had made an unhappy, abject apology to
Holden for the desertion of Buck, and Holden accepted it, and neither of them felt at all better afterward. A man would have been left behind under
exactly the same circumstances, but a dog is some-

how different. He can't take care of himself. His abandonment couldn't be helped, but it rankled.

The material brought back from Masa Four was duly examined. The space-radio records piled up, and electron-telescope examination of the planets continued, and evidences of a highly developed civilization accumulated—while scanner-beam observation of the *Kennessee* from Masa Four went on unendingly.

It was a dubious situation extended almost to the breaking point. The lifeboat voyage had produced a reaction of ground vehicles and atmosphere fliers. It gave an impression of limited offensive power. But, on the other hand, there was interplanetary travel here. And the scanner beam on the *Kennessee* and the instant detection of the lifeboat was proof that the people of this system knew exactly what the *Kennessee* was.

A civilization without defense weapons but with interplanetary ships and space radio should have tried to make contact with the *Kennessee*. If only to placate invaders, some attempt to open communication should have been made. Absence of such efforts was ominous. The appearance was that of a race which played possum until it could strike an overwhelming blow. So the *Kennessee* stayed in a state of nerve-racking alertness, with detectors out all around, and relays set to throw on overdrive should a high-velocity guided missile seem to draw near.

"It looks bad," admitted the skipper to Holden. "We'd have tried to make contact, in their shoes. But whoever raided the Capella colony simply rode in and started killing. Maybe these people are that sort. Anyhow, if they do get us, our fleet will know who did it and come take them apart with planet-smasher bombs."

Holden said dourly:

"I wish I'd been in that lifeboat. When do we send back another message torp?"

"We make no more landings," said the skipper. He

added, "You'd never be able to find where the other
boat landed, and anyhow Buck—"

"Was probably blasted the instant they saw him,"
said Holden.

He couldn't blame anybody, but he was angry. He
missed Buck.

On the twelfth day after Buck's landing, an interplanetary ship took off from Masa Four. The *Kennessee* had now ridden in beyond that planet and was
headed for a perihelion point on the other side of Masa
Gamma. If she survived to get there, it was the skipper's intention to put on overdrive and go back to
base with all his records. But this interplanetary ship
changed all plans. It appeared to be a rocket, in that
it left behind a trailing cloud of vapor which looked
like ejected gases. The spectroscopes, though, showed
it to be merely hydrocarbon—smoke particles. And
it altogether lacked the backward velocity which
would have proved it a means of propulsion. It was
simply a trail of vapor, as if for advertisement.

In two days it had climbed well away from the
planet and changed direction in a long smooth curve.
The Navigation Officer came to the control room
shortly after, to report that it was on an interception
course, with interception speed, and would draw gradually closer to the *Kennessee* until contact was made.
Then its trail of vapor broke, and swelled, and broke,
and swelled, as if unmistakably to draw attention from
the cruiser.

The control-room loud-speaker boomed shortly.
Holden's voice:

"Sir!" he said harshly. "That phony rocket is beam-
ing signals at us, running up and down the spectrum
and trying frequency and amplitude modulation and
everything else. Listen!"

The speaker said resonantly: "*Woof!*" It was Buck's
joyous bark. An instant later came the word "Buck" in
a distorted but definitely recognizable version of Holden's own voice. And then, quite insanely, "*Lie down,*

sir!" "*Come get it boy!*" "*Fetch it, Buck,*" and all the other phrases to which the dog Buck had been trained to respond. As a means of opening communication between alien and mutually suspicious races, the vocabulary known to a big brown dog named Buck lacked dignity, but nothing could have been much more informative.

"You see what it means, sir!" said Holden in a strained voice. "They got the stuff out of Buck's brain, somehow! They read his memories! They must have, somehow! They want to make contact!" Then he said thickly, "But if they killed him to rummage in his brain—"

"Mr. Holden," said the skipper, "answer them, please. Speak as if to Buck himself, and see what happens."

In the speaker in the control room he heard Holden's voice as he spoke into another microphone.

"Buck!" said Holden hoarsely. "If you hear me, speak up boy! Buck! Do you hear me?"

And then the loud-speaker bellowed with the joyous uproar with which Buck replied to his master. He barked and bayed and yelped and whined all at once, and then barked crazily like a creature gone quite mad with joy.

"He . . . he heard me, sir," said Holden unsteadily. "They didn't hurt him! I . . . I think, sir—"

"Quite so, Mr. Holden," said the skipper sedately. "I was about to order you to take a lifeboat and take another chance to learn something of these people. Suppose you go over and make contact with them? A race which knows a good dog when it sees one, and is honest enough to return him to his master, can't be the race that massacred half a million people on Capella Three!"

The Masan scientist who'd tried to replace Holden in Buck's affections nevertheless grew rather friendly with Holden after the *Kennessee* landed on Masa Four.

A message torp, sent back to base, had explained the situation and the reason for friendly contact with the Masan civilization. Of course, if the *Kennessee* vanished, the Masans would be known to be definitely responsible, but that did not seem to bother them. And it did not bother the humans, either.

The Masan scientist explained to Holden:

"It has worked out very well. With your atomic power, you can put any amount of energy into the power beam we've showed you, for battle with our common enemy. It is odd that we made power beams to fuel our interplanetary ships because we didn't have atomic energy, and you made atomic energy because you didn't have power beams!"

"There'll be a lot of stuff that will fit together like that," said Holden. "Our civilization will mesh nicely, as long as we trust each other."

"Yes," said the Masan, somehow ruefully. "We intended to blast you to atoms, because we were afraid, and you intended to destroy our planets, because you were, also. I think both our races owe much to Buck."

"I still," said Holden uncomfortably, "can't see how you were able to trust us so completely. I don't think we'd have trusted strangers as you do us. Just because of Buck—"

"But it is because of Buck," said the Masan wisely. "We could extract all of his memories. All of them. His kind adores men. He would accept any cruelty from you. But you are not cruel. He would give his life gladly, but no man would ask it. He is yours, unreservedly, but you do not accept from him without giving in return. Do you know when the policy of the Planetary Council, to trust men without limit, was finally decided?"

"Why . . . no," said Holden.

"When you entered the airlock of our ship," said the Masan, smiling, "and Buck met you. He had told us every secret he could impart. He had been almost a traitor, without knowing it. He had told us everything he knew of men. But when you entered our ship he leaped joyfully at you and you rolled on the floor together—you hugged him! You did not think of possible harm he had done. You were as glad to see him as he was to see you. That was when our policy was decided. Then we knew that men will always repay trust with loyalty." Then the Masan added, "That is, most men."

Holden said uncomfortably:

"Well—that's something that has worried the skipper. You people act as if all of us were as decent as our dogs think us. We aren't. You'll have to be . . . well . . . a little cagey, sometimes . . ."

"So," said the Masan, "we learned from Buck. But also we learned that there will always be men to trust."

Buck came dashing madly up the dark-green lawn. Holden and the Masan scientist sat on a sort of terrace of the Masan's home. Buck came racing up, panting happily, and thrust his muzzle into Holden's hand. He gave the Masan a brief tail-wag and went dashing off again.

"That," said the Masan, "is something he would never do to me, though I . . . yes . . . I think I like him as much as you do."

"That's because he's my dog," said Holden. "But he treats you like a man. Didn't you notice?"

"True! I had not realized! But it is true! Listen! We must have dogs, we Masans! Dogs to like us as they like men! And then no man who likes dogs can ever distrust a Masan who likes them also, and no Masan—" The Masan laughed. "We could not despise a man an honest dog had for a master! Our two races will be brothers!"

That is all of the story about this one part of the hunt for the Space Assassins. Everybody knows that their home system was found, and everybody knows that when we tried to open negotiations with them

their ships attacked us in a raging ferocity, and that
there was no possible end to it but the extermination
of men—and Masans—or of the Assassins. The battle
was the first that was ever fought with power beams
in Earth ships with Masan gunners. That's history that
everybody knows.

But not everybody knows that there is a statue of
Buck before the Planetary Council building on Masa
Four. The Masans think it quite natural. They like
dogs enormously, and dogs like them, too. The Masans
already have a proverb that a dog is a Masan's best
friend. There's no statue of Buck on Earth, though.
But he doesn't mind. Buck is a very happy dog.

He's with Holden. He follows him everywhere.

DAMON KNIGHT

CABIN BOY

*First we ran into the problem of Future
Man meeting Ancient Man (i.e., us) in
Van Vogt's story. Next we encountered
Murray Leinster's other-star race of humanoid people, enough like us to be able
to communicate, after some rather extraordinary difficulties. And now we
meet a totally, impossibly alien type of
living and obviously thinking protoplasm,
and find ourselves at a stand-off. For the
most part we have, in this delightful tale,
the opportunity of seeing the aliens from
their own point of view. (Or, rather,
their point of view as we understand it,
through Damon Knight's vivid interpre-
tation. Maybe he has it all wrong—who
knows?) Whether the point of view is
accurate or not, no one can deny that
the result, in this tale, is thoroughly delightful.*

I

THE CABIN BOY's name was unspeakable, and even its
meaning would be difficult to convey in any human
tongue. For convenience, we may as well call him
Tommy Loy.

Please bear in mind that all these terms are approximations. Tommy was not exactly a cabin boy, and
even the spaceship he served was not exactly a spaceship, nor was the Captain exactly a captain. But if you

think of Tommy as a freckled, scowling, red-haired, willful, prank-playing, thoroughly abhorrent brat, and of the Captain as a crusty, ponderous old man, you may be able to understand their relationship.

A word about Tommy will serve to explain why these approximations have to be made, and just how much they mean. Tommy, to a human being, would have looked like a six-foot egg made of greenish gelatin. Suspended in this were certain dark or radiant shapes which were Tommy's nerve centers and digestive organs, and scattered about its surface were star-shaped and oval markings which were his sensory organs and gripping mechanisms—his "hands." At the lesser end was an orifice which expelled a stream of glowing vapor—Tommy's means of propulsion. It should be clear that if instead of saying, "Tommy ate his lunch," or, "Tommy said to the Captain . . ." we reported what really happens, some pretty complicated explanations would have to be made.

Similarly, the term "cabin boy" is used because it is the closest in human meaning. Some vocations, like sea-faring, are so demanding and so complex that they simply cannot be taught in classrooms; they have to be lived. A cabin boy is one who is learning such a vocation and paying for his instruction by performing certain menial, degrading, and unimportant tasks.

That describes Tommy, with one more similarity —the cabin boy of the sailing vessel was traditionally occupied after each whipping with preparing the mischief, or the stupidity, that earned him the next one.

Tommy, at the moment, had a whipping coming to him and was fighting a delaying action. He knew he couldn't escape eventual punishment, but he planned to hold it off as long as he could.

Floating alertly in one of the innumerable corridors of the ship, he watched as a dark wave sprang into being upon the glowing corridor wall and sped toward him. Instantly, Tommy was moving away from it, and at the same rate of speed.

The wave rumbled: "Tommy! Tommy Loy! Where *is* that obscenity boy?"

The wave moved on, rumbling wordlessly, and Tommy moved with it. Ahead of him was another wave, and another beyond that, and it was the same throughout all the corridors of the ship. Abruptly the waves reversed their direction. So did Tommy, barely in time. The waves not only carried the Captain's orders but scanned every corridor and compartment of the ten-mile ship. But as long as Tommy kept between the waves, the Captain could not see him.

The trouble was that Tommy could not keep this up forever, and he was being searched for by other lowly members of the crew. It took a long time to traverse all of those winding, interlaced passages, but it was a mathematical certainty that he would be caught eventually.

Tommy shuddered, and at the same time he squirmed with delight. He had interrupted the Old Man's sleep by a stench of a particularly noisome variety, one of which he had only lately found himself capable. The effect had been beautiful. In human terms, since Tommy's race communicated by odors, it was equivalent to setting off a firecracker beside a sleeper's ear.

Judging by the jerkiness of the scanning waves' motion, the Old Man was still unnerved.

"Tommy!" the waves rumbled. "Come out, you little piece of filth, or I'll smash you into a thousand separate stinks! By Spore, when I get hold of you—"

The corridor intersected another at this point, and Tommy seized his chance to duck into the new one. He had been working his way outward ever since his crime, knowing that the search parties would do the same. When he reached the outermost level of the ship, there would be a slight possibility of slipping back past the hunters—not much of a chance, but better than none.

He kept close to the wall. He was the smallest member of the crew—smaller than any of the other cabin boys, and less than half the size of an Ordinary; it was always possible that when he sighted one of the search party, he could get away before the crewman saw him. He was in a short connecting corridor now, but the scanning waves cycled endlessly, always turning back before he could escape into the next corridor. Tommy followed their movement patiently, while he listened to the torrent of abuse that poured from them. He snickered to himself. When the Old Man was angry, everybody suffered. The ship would be stinking from stem to stern by now.

Eventually the Captain forgot himself and the waves flowed on around the next intersection. Tommy moved on. He was getting close to his goal by now; he could see a faint gleam of starshine up at the end of the corridor.

The next turn took him into it—and what Tommy saw through the semi-transparent skin of the ship nearly made him falter and be caught. Not merely the fiery pinpoints of stars shone there, but a great, furious glow which could only mean that they were passing through a star system. It was the first time this had happened in Tommy's life, but of course it was nothing to the Captain, or even to most of the Ordinaries. Trust them, Tommy thought resentfully, to say nothing to him about it!

Now he knew he was glad he'd tossed that surprise at the Captain. If he hadn't, he wouldn't be here, and if he weren't here . . .

A waste capsule was bumping automatically along the corridor, heading for one of the exit pores in the hull. Tommy let it catch up to him, then englobed it, but it stretched him so tight that he could barely hold it. That was all to the good; the Captain wouldn't be likely to notice that anything had happened.

The hull was sealed, not to keep atmosphere inside, for there was none except by accident, but to prevent loss of liquid by evaporation. Metals and other mineral elements were replaceable; liquids and their constituents, in ordinary circumstances, were not.

Tommy rode the capsule to the exit sphincter, squeezed through, and instantly released it. Being polarized away from the ship's core, it shot into space and was lost. Tommy hugged the outer surface of the hull and gazed at the astonishing panorama that surrounded him.

There was the enormous black half-globe of space—Tommy's sky, the only one he had ever known. It was sprinkled with the familiar yet always changing patterns of the stars. By themselves, these were marvels enough for a child whose normal universe was one of ninety-foot corridors and chambers measuring, at most, three times as much. But Tommy hardly noticed them. Down to his right, reflecting brilliantly from the long, gentle curve of the greenish hull, was a blazing yellow-white glory that he could hardly look at. A star, the first one he had ever seen close at hand. Off to the left was a tiny, milky-blue disk that could only be a planet.

Tommy let go a shout, for the sheer pleasure of its thin, hollow smell. He watched the thin mist of particles spread lazily away from his body, faintly luminous against the jet blackness. He shivered a little, thickening his skin as much as he could. He could not stay long, he knew; he was radiating heat faster than he could absorb it from the sun or the ship's hull.

But he didn't want to go back inside, and not only because it meant being caught and punished. He didn't want to leave that great, dazzling jewel in the sky. For an instant he thought vaguely of the future time when he would be grown, the master of his own vessel, and could see the stars whenever he chose; but the picture was too far away to have any reality. Great Spore, that wouldn't happen for twenty thousand years!

Fifty yards away, an enormous dark spot on the hull, one of the ship's vision devices, swelled and darkened. Tommy looked up with interest. He could see nothing in that direction, but evidently the Captain had spotted something. Tommy watched and waited, growing colder every second, and after a long time he saw a new pinpoint of light spring into being. It grew steadily larger, turned fuzzy at one side, then became two linked dots, one hard and bright, the other misty.

Tommy looked down with sudden understanding, and saw that another wide area of the ship's hull was swollen and protruding. This one showed a pale color under the green and had a dark ring around it: it was a polarizer. The object he had seen must contain metal, and the Captain was bringing it in for fuel. Tommy hoped it was a big one; they had been short of metal ever since he could remember.

When he glanced up again, the object was much larger. He could see now that the bright part was hard and smooth, reflecting the light of the nearby sun. The misty part was a puzzler. It looked like a crewman's voice, seen against space—or the ion trail of a ship in motion. But was it possible for metal to be alive?

II

Leo Roget stared into the rear-view scanner and wiped beads of sweat from his brown, half-bald scalp. Flaming gas from the jets washed up toward him along the hull; he couldn't see much. But the huge dark ovoid they were headed for was still there, and it was getting bigger. He glanced futilely at the control board. The throttle was on full. They were going to crash in a little more than two minutes, and there didn't seem to be a single thing he could do about it.

He looked at Frances McMenamin, strapped into the acceleration harness beside his own. She said, "Try cutting off the jets, why don't you?"

Roget was a short, muscular man with thinning straight black hair and sharp brown eyes. McMenamin was slender and ash-blond, half an inch taller than he was, with one of those pale, exquisitely shaped faces that seem to be distributed equally among the very stupid and the very bright. Roget had never been perfectly sure which she was, although they had been companions for more than three years. That, in a way, was part of the reason they had taken this wild trip: she had made Roget uneasy, and he wanted to break away, and at the same time he didn't. So he had fallen in with her idea of a trip to Mars—"to get off by ourselves and think"—and here, Roget thought, they were, not thinking particularly.

He said, "You want us to crash quicker?"

"How do you know we will?" she countered. "It's the only thing we haven't tried. Anyhow, we'd be able to see where we're going, and that's more than we can do now."

"All right," said Roget, "all *right*." She was perfectly capable of giving him six more reasons, each screwier than the last, and then turning out to be right. He pulled the throttle back to zero, and the half-heard, half-felt roar of the jets died.

The ship jerked backward suddenly, yanking them against the couch straps, and then slowed.

Roget looked into the scanner again. They were approaching the huge object, whatever it was, at about the same rate as before. Maybe, he admitted unwillingly, a little slower. Damn the woman! How could she possibly have figured that one out in advance?

"And," McMenamin added reasonably, "we'll save fuel for the takeoff."

Roget scowled at her. "If there is a takeoff," he said. "Whatever is pulling us down there isn't doing it to show off. What do we do—tell them that was a very impressive trick and we enjoyed it, but we've got to be leaving now?"

"We'll find out what's doing it," said McMenamin, "and stop it if we can. If we can't, the fuel won't do us any good anyway."

That was, if not Frances' most exasperating trick, at least high on the list. She had a habit of introducing your own argument as if it were not only a telling point on her side, but something you had been too dense to see. Arguing with her was like swinging at someone who abruptly disappeared and then sandbagged you from behind.

Roget was fuming, but he said nothing. The greenish surface below was approaching more and more slowly, and now he felt a slight but definite tightening of the couch straps that could only mean deceleration. They were being maneuvered in for a landing as carefully and efficiently as if they were doing it themselves.

A few seconds later, a green horizon line appeared in the direct-view ports, and they touched. Roget's and McMenamin's couches swung on their gimbals as the ship tilted slowly, bounced and came to rest.

Frances reached inside the wide collar of her pressure suit to smooth a ruffle that had got crumpled between the volcanic swell of her bosom and the front of the transparent suit. Watching her, Roget felt a sudden irrational flow of affection and—as usually happened—a simultaneous notification that his body disagreed with his mind's opinion of her. This trip, it had been tacitly agreed, was to be a kind of final trial period. At the end of it, either they would split up or decide to make it permanent, and up to now, Roget had been silently determined that it was going to be a split. Now he was just as sure that, providing they ever got to Mars or back to Earth, he was going to nail her for good.

He glanced at her face. She knew, all right, just as she'd known when he'd felt the other way. It should have irritated him, but he felt oddly pleased and comforted. He unstrapped himself, fastened down his helmet, and moved toward the airlock.

He stood on a pale-green, almost featureless surface that curved gently away in every direction. Where he stood, it was brilliantly lighted by the sun, and his shadow was sharp and as black as space. About two thirds of the way to the horizon, looking across the short axis of the ship, the sunlight stopped with knife-edge sharpness, and he could make out the rest only as a ghostly reflection of starlight.

Their ship was lying on its side, with the pointed stern apparently sunk a few inches into the green surface of the alien ship. He took a cautious step in that direction, and nearly floated past it before he could catch himself. His boot magnets had failed to grip. The metal of this hull—if it *was* metal—must be something that contained no iron.

The green hull was shot through with other colors here, and it rose in a curious, almost rectangular mound. At the center, just at the tip of the earth vessel's jets, there was a pale area; around that was a dark ring which lapped up over the side of the ship. He bent to examine it. It was in shadow, and he used his helmet light.

The light shone through the mottled green substance; he could see the skin of his own ship. It was pitted, corroding. As he watched, another pinpoint of corruption appeared on the shiny surface, and slowly grew.

Roget straightened up with an exclamation. His helmet phones asked, "What is it, Leo?"

He said, "Acid or something eating the hull. Wait a minute." He looked again at the pale and dark mottlings under the green surface. The center area was not attacking the ship's metal; that might be the muzzle of whatever instrument had been used to pull them down out of their orbit and hold them there. But if it was turned off now . . . He had to get the ship away from the dark ring that was destroying it. He couldn't fire the jets otherwise, because they were half buried; he'd blow the tubes if he tried.

He said, "You still strapped in?"

"Yes."

"All right, hold on." He stepped back to the center of the little ship, braced his corrugated boot soles against the hard green surface, and shoved.

The ship rolled. But it rolled like a top, around the axis of its pointed end. The dark area gave way before it, as if it were jelly-soft. The jets still pointed to the middle of the pale area, and the dark ring still lapped over them. Roget moved farther down and tried again, with the same result. The ship would move freely in every direction but the right one. The attracting power, clearly enough, was still on.

He straightened dejectedly and looked around. A few hundred yards away, he saw something he had noticed before, without attaching any significance to it; a six-foot egg, of some lighter, more translucent substance than the one on which it lay. He leaped toward it. It moved sluggishly away, trailing a cloud of luminous gas. A few seconds later he had it between his gloved hands. It squirmed, then ejected a thin spurt of vapor from its forward end. It was alive.

McMenamin's head was silhouetted in one of the forward ports. He said, "See this?"

"Yes! What is it?"

"One of the crew, I think. I'm going to bring it in. You work the airlock—it won't hold both of us."

". . . All right."

The huge egg crowded the cabin uncomfortably. It was pressed up against the rear wall, where it had rolled as soon as Frances had pulled it into the ship. The two human beings stood at the other side of the room, against the control panel, and watched it.

"No features," said Roget, "unless you count those markings on the surface. This thing isn't from anywhere in the solar system, Frances—it isn't even any order of evolution we ever heard of."

"I know," she said abstractedly. "Leo, is he wearing any protection against space that you can see?"

"No," said Roget. "That's *him*, not a spacesuit. Look, you can see halfway into him. But—"

Frances turned to look at him. "That's it," she said. "It means this is his natural element—space!"

Roget looked thoughtfully at the egg. "It makes sense," he said. "He's adapted for it, anyhow—ovoid, for a high volume-to-surface ratio. Tough outer shell. Moves by jet propulsion. It's hard to believe, because we've never run into a creature like him before, but I don't see why not. On earth there are organisms, plants, that can live and reproduce in boiling water, and others that can stand near-zero temperatures."

"He's a plant, too, you know," Frances put in.

Roget stared at her, then back at the egg. "That color, you mean? Chlorophyll. It could be."

"Must be," she corrected firmly. "How else would he live in a vacuum?" And then, distressedly, "Oh, what a smell!"

They looked at each other. It *had* been something monumental in the way of smells, though it had only lasted a fraction of a second. There had been a series of separate odors, all unfamiliar and all overpoweringly strong. At least a dozen of them, Roget thought; they had gone past too quickly to count.

"He did it before, outside, and I saw the vapor." He closed his helmet abruptly and motioned McMenamin to do the same. She frowned and shook her head. He opened his helmet again. "It might be poisonous!"

"I don't think so," said McMenamin. "Anyway, we've got to try something." She walked toward the green egg. It rolled away from her, and she went past it into the bedroom.

In a minute she reappeared, carrying an armload of plastic boxes and bottles. She came back to Roget and knelt on the floor, lining up the containers with their nipples toward the egg.

"What's this for?" Roget demanded. "Listen, we've got to figure some way of getting out of here. The ship's being eaten up—"

"Wait," said McMenamin. She reached down and squeezed three of the nipples quickly, one after the

other. There was a tiny spray of face powder, then
one of cologne (Nuit Jupitérienne), followed by a jet
of good Scotch.

Then she waited. Roget was about to open his mouth
when another blast of unfamiliar odors came from the
egg. This time there were only three: two sweet ones
and one sharp.

McMenamin smiled. "I'm going to name him Stinky,"
she said. She pressed the nipples again, in a different
order. Scotch, face powder, Nuit Jupitérienne. The
egg replied: sharp, sweet, sweet.

She gave him the remaining combination, and he
echoed it; then she put a record cylinder on the floor
and squirted the face powder. She added another cylinder and squeezed the cologne. She went along the line
that way, releasing a smell for each cylinder until there
were ten. The egg had responded, recognizably in
some cases, to each one. Then she took away seven of
the cylinders and looked expectantly at the egg.

The egg released a sharp odor.

"If ever we tell anybody," said Roget in an awed
tone, "that you taught a six-foot Easter egg to count to
ten by selective flatulence—"

"Hush, fool," she said. "This is a tough one."

She lined up three cylinders, waited for the sharp
odor, then added six more to make three rows of three.
The egg obliged with a penetrating smell which was a
good imitation of citron extract, Frances' number nine.
He followed it immediately with another of his own
rapid, complicated series of smells.

"He gets it," said McMenamin. "I think he just told
us that three times three are nine." She stood up. "You
go out first, Leo. I'll put him out after you and then
follow. There's something more we've got to show him
before we let him go."

Roget followed orders. When the egg came out and
kept on going, he stepped in its path and held it back.
Then he moved away, hoping the thing would get the
idea that they weren't trying to force it but wanted it

to stay. The egg wobbled indecisively for a moment and then stayed where it was. Frances came out the next minute, carrying one of the plastic boxes and a flashlight.

"My nicest powder," she said regretfully, "but it was the only thing I could find enough of." She clapped her gloved hands together sharply, with the box between them. It burst, and a haze of particles spread around them, glowing faintly in the sunlight.

The egg was still waiting, somehow giving the impression that it was watching them alertly. McMenamin flicked on the flashlight and pointed it at Roget. It made a clear, narrow path in the haze of dispersed particles. Then she turned it on herself, on the ship, and finally upward, toward the tiny blue disk that was Earth. She did it twice more, then stepped back toward the airlock, and Roget followed her.

They stood watching as Tommy scurried off across the hull, squeezed himself into it and disappeared.

"That was impressive," Roget said. "But I wonder just how much good it's going to do us."

"He knows we're alive, intelligent, friendly, and that we come from Earth," said McMenamin thoughtfully. "Or, anyhow, we did our best to tell him. That's all we can do. Maybe he won't want to help us; maybe he can't. But it's up to him now."

III

The mental state of Tommy, as he dived through the hull of the ship and into the nearest radial corridor, would be difficult to describe fully to any human being. He was the equivalent of a very small boy—that approximation still holds good—and he had the obvious reactions to novelty and adventure. But there was a good deal more. He had seen living, intelligent beings of an unfamiliar shape and substance, who lived in metal and had some connection with one of those enormous, enigmatic ships called planets, which no captain of his own race dared approach.

And yet Tommy *knew*, with all the weight of knowledge accumulated, codified and transmitted over a span measured in billions of years, that there was no other intelligent race than his own in the entire universe, that metal, though life-giving, could not itself be alive, and that no living creature, having the ill luck to be spawned aboard a planet, could ever hope to escape so tremendous a gravitational field.

The final result of all this was that Tommy desperately wanted to go somewhere by himself and think. But he couldn't; he had to keep moving, in time with the scanning waves along the corridor, and he had to give all his mental energy to the problem of slipping past the search party.

The question was—how long had he been gone? If they had reached the hull while he was inside the metal thing, they might have looked for him outside and concluded that he had somehow slipped past them, back to the center of the ship. In that case, they would probably be working their way back, and he had only to follow them to the axis and hide in a chamber as soon as they left it. But if they were still working outward, his chances of escape were almost nil. And now it seemed more important to escape than it had before.

There was one possibility which Tommy, who, in most circumstances, would try anything, hated to think about. Fuel lines—tubes carrying the rushing, radiant ion vapor that powered the ship—adjoined many of these corridors, and it was certain that if he dared to enter one, he would be perfectly safe from detection as long as he remained in it. But, for one thing, these lines radiated from the ship's axis and none of them would take him where he wanted to go. For another, they were the most dangerous places aboard ship. Older crew members sometimes entered them to make emergency repairs, but they got out as quickly as they could. Tommy did not know how long he could survive there; he had an unpleasant conviction that it would not be long.

Only a few yards up the corridor was the sealed sphincter which gave entrance to such a tube. Tommy looked at it indecisively as the motion of the scanning waves brought him nearer. He had still not made up his mind when he caught a flicker reflected around the curve of the corridor behind him.

Tommy squeezed himself closer to the wall and watched the other end of the corridor approach with agonizing slowness. If he could only get around that corner . . .

The flicker of motion was repeated, and then he saw a thin rind of green poke into view. There was no more time to consider entering the fuel line, no time to let the scanning waves' movement carry him around the corner. Tommy put on full speed, cutting across the next wave and down the cross-corridor ahead.

Instantly the Captain's voice shouted from the wall, "Ah! Was that him, the dirty scut? After him, lads!"

Tommy glanced behind as he turned another corner, and his heart sank. It was no cabin boy who was behind him, or even an Ordinary, but a Third Mate—so huge that he filled nearly half the width of the corridor, and so powerful that Tommy, in comparison, was like a boy on a bicycle racing an express train.

He turned another corner, realizing in that instant that he was as good as caught: the new corridor ahead of him stretched straight and without a break for three hundred yards. As he flashed down it, the hulk of the Mate appeared around the bend behind.

The Mate was coming up with terrifying speed, and Tommy had time for only one last desperate spurt. Then the other body slammed with stunning force against his, and he was held fast.

As they coasted to a halt, the Captain's voice rumbled from the wall, "*That's* it, Mister. Hold him where I can see him!"

The scanning areas were stationary now. The Mate moved Tommy forward until he was squarely in range of the nearest.

Tommy squirmed futilely. The Captain said, "*There's* our little jokester. It's a pure pleasure to see you again, Tommy. What—no witty remarks? Your humor all dried up?"

Tommy gasped, "Hope you enjoyed your nap, Captain."

"Very good," said the Captain with heavy sarcasm. "Oh, *very* entertaining, Tommy. Now would you have anything more to say, before I put the whips to you?"

Tommy was silent.

The Captain said to the Mate, "Nice work, Mister. You'll get extra rations for this."

The Mate spoke for the first time, and Tommy recognized his high, affected voice. It was George Adkins, who had recently spored and was so proud of the new life inside his body that there was no living with him. George said prissily, "Thank you, sir, I'm sure. Of course, I really shouldn't have exerted myself the way I just did, in my state."

"Well, you'll be compensated for it," the Captain said testily. "Now take the humorist down to Assembly Five. We'll have a little ceremony there."

"Yes, sir," said the Mate distantly. He moved off, shoving Tommy ahead of him, and dived into the first turning that led downward.

They moved along in silence for the better part of a mile, crossing from one lesser passage to another until they reached a main artery that led directly to the center of the ship. The scanning waves were still stationary, and they were moving so swiftly that there was no danger of being overheard. Tommy said politely, "You won't let them be too hard on me, will you, sir?"

The Mate did not reply for a moment. He had been baited by Tommy's mock courtesy before, and he was as wary as his limited intelligence allowed. Finally he said, "You'll get no more than what's coming to you, young Tom."

"Yes, sir. I know that, sir. I'm sorry I made you exert yourself, sir, in your condition and all."

"You should be," said the Mate stiffly, but his voice betrayed his pleasure. It was seldom enough that even a cabin boy showed a decent interest in the Mate's prospective parenthood. "They're moving about, you know," he added, unbending a little.

"Are they, sir? Oh, you must be careful of yourself, sir. How many are there, please, sir?"

"Twenty-eight," said the Mate, as he had on every possible occasion for the past two weeks. "Strong and healthy—so far."

"That's remarkable, sir!" cried Tommy. "Twenty-eight! If I might be so bold, sir, you ought to be careful of what you eat. Is the Captain going to give you your extra rations out of that mass he just brought in topside, sir?"

"I'm sure *I* don't know."

"Gosh!" exclaimed Tommy. "I wish I could be sure . . ."

He let the pause grow. Finally the Mate said querulously, "What do you mean? Is there anything wrong with the metal?"

"I don't really know, sir, but it isn't like any we ever had before. That is," Tommy added, "since I was spored, sir."

"Naturally," said the Mate. "*I've* eaten all kinds myself, you know."

"Yes, sir. But doesn't it usually come in ragged shapes, sir, and darkish?"

"Of course it does. Everybody knows that. Metal is nonliving, and only living things have regular shapes."

"Yes, sir. But I was topside, sir, while I was trying to get away, and I saw this metal. It's quite regular, except for some knobs at one end, sir, and it's as smooth as you are, sir, and shiny. If you'll forgive me, sir, it didn't look at all appetizing to me."

"Nonsense," said the Mate uncertainly. "Nonsense," he repeated, in a stronger tone. "You must have been mistaken. Metal can't be alive."

"That's just what I thought, sir," said Tommy excitedly. "But there are live things in this metal, sir. I saw them. And the metal wasn't just floating along the way it's supposed to, sir. I saw it when the Captain brought it down, and . . . But I'm afraid you'll think I'm lying, sir, if I tell you what it was doing."

"Well, what was it doing?"

"I swear I saw it, sir," Tommy went on. "The Captain will tell you the same thing, sir, if you ask him—he must have noticed."

"Sterilize it all, what *was* it doing?"

Tommy lowered his voice. "There was an ion trail shooting from it, sir. It was trying to get away!"

While the Mate was trying to absorb that, they reached the bottom of the corridor and entered the vast globular space of Assembly Five, lined with crewmen waiting to witness the punishment of Tommy Loy.

This was not going to be any fun at all, thought Tommy, but at least he had paid back the Third Mate in full measure. The Mate, for the moment, at any rate, was not taking any joy in his promised extra rations.

When it was over, Tommy huddled in a corner of the crew compartment where they had tossed him, bruised and smarting in every nerve, shaken by the beating he had undergone. The pain was still rolling through him in faint, uncontrollable waves, and he winced at each one, in spite of himself, as though it were the original blow.

In the back of his mind, the puzzle of the metal ship was still calling, but the other experience was too fresh, the remembered images too vivid.

The Captain had begun, as always, by reciting the Creed.

In the beginning was the Spore, and the Spore was alone.

(And the crew: *Praised be the Spore!*)

Next there was light, and the light was good. Yea, good for the Spore and the Spore's First Children.

(Praised be they!)

But the light grew evil in the days of the Spore's Second Children.

(Woe unto them!)

And the light cast them out. Yea, exiled were they, into the darkness and the Great Deep.

(Pity for the outcasts in the Great Deep!)

Tommy had mumbled his responses with the rest of them, thinking rebellious thoughts. There was nothing evil about light; they lived by it still. What must have happened—the Captain himself admitted as much when he taught history and natural science classes—was that the earliest ancestors of the race, spawned in the flaming heart of the Galaxy, had grown too efficient for their own good.

They had specialized, more and more, in extracting energy from starlight and the random metal and other elements they encountered in space; and at last they absorbed, willy-nilly, more than they could use. So they had moved, gradually and naturally, over many generations, out from that intensely radiating region into the "Great Deep"—the universe of thinly scattered stars. And the process had continued, inevitably; as the level of available energy fell, their absorption of it grew more and more efficient.

Now, not only could they never return to their birthplace, but they could not even approach a single sun as closely as some planets did. Therefore the planets, and the stars themselves, were objects of fear. That was natural and sensible. But why did they have to continue this silly ritual, invented by some half-evolved, superstitious ancestor, of "outcasts" and "evil"?

The Captain finished:

Save us from the Death that lies in the Great Deep . . .

(The creeping Death that lies in the Great Deep!)

And keep our minds pure . . .

(As pure as the light in the days of the Spore, blessed be He!)

And our course straight . . .
(As straight as the light, brothers!)
That we may meet our lost brothers again in the Day
of Reuniting.
(Speed that day!)

Then the pause, the silence that grew until it was like the silence of space. At last the Captain spoke again, pronouncing judgment against Tommy, ending, "Let him be whipped!"

Tommy tensed himself, thickening his skin, drawing his body into the smallest possible compass. Two husky Ordinaries seized him and tossed him at a third. As Tommy floated across the room, the crewman pressed himself tightly against the wall, drawing power from it until he could contain no more. And as Tommy neared him, he discharged it in a crackling arc that filled Tommy's body with the pure essence of pain, and sent him hurtling across the chamber to the next shock, and the next, and the next.

Until the Captain had boomed, "Enough!" and they had carried him out and left him here alone.

He heard the voices of crewmen as they drew their rations. One of them was grumbling about the taste, and another, sounding happily bloated, was telling him to shut up and eat, that metal was metal.

That would be the new metal, however much of it had been absorbed by now, mingled with the old in the reservoir. Tommy wondered briefly how much of it there was, and whether the alien ship—if it *was* a ship—could repair even a little damage to itself. But that assumed life in the metal, and in spite of what he had seen, Tommy couldn't believe in it. It seemed beyond question, though, that there were living things inside the metal; and when the metal was gone, how would they live?

Tommy imagined himself set adrift from the ship, alone in space, radiating more heat than his tiny volume could absorb. He shuddered.

He thought again of the problem that had obsessed him ever since he had seen the alien, five-pointed creatures in the metal ship. Intelligent life was supposed to be sacred. That was part of the Creed, and it was stated in a sloppy, poetic way like the rest of it, but it made a certain kind of sense. No crewman or captain had the right to destroy another for his benefit, because the same heredity was in them all. They were all potentially the same, none better than another.

And you ate metal, because metal was nonliving and certainly not intelligent. But if that stopped being true . . .

Tommy felt he was missing something. Then he had it: In the alien ship, trying to talk to the creatures that lived in metal, he had been scared almost scentless—but underneath the fright and the excitement, he had felt wonderful. It had been, he realized suddenly, like the mystic completion that was supposed to come when all the straight lines met, in the "Day of Reuniting"— when all the far-flung ships, parted for all the billions of years of their flight, came together at last. It was talking to someone different from yourself.

He wanted to talk again to the aliens, teach them to form their uncouth sounds into words, learn from them . . . Vague images swirled in his mind. They were products of an utterly different line of evolution. Who knew what they might be able to teach him?

And now the dilemma took shape. If his own ship absorbed the metal of theirs, they would die; therefore he would have to make the Captain let them go. But if he somehow managed to set them free, they would leave and he would never see them again.

A petty officer looked into the cubicle and said, "All right, Loy, out of it. You're on garbage detail. You eat after you work, if there's anything left. Lively, now!"

Tommy moved thoughtfully out into the corridor, his pain almost forgotten. The philosophical problems presented by the alien ship, too, having no apparent solution, were receding from his mind. A new thought was taking their place, one that made him glow inside with the pure rapture of the devoted practical jokester.

The whipping he was certainly going to get—and, so soon after the last offense, it would be a beauty—scarcely entered his mind.

IV

Roget climbed in, opening his helmet, and sat down warily in the acceleration couch. He didn't look at the woman.

McMenamin said quietly, "Bad?"

"Not good. The outer skin's gone all across that area, and it's eating into the lead sheathing. The tubes are holding up pretty well, but they'll be next."

"We've done as much as we can, by rolling the ship around?"

"Just about. I'll keep at it, but I don't see how it can be more than a few hours before the tubes go. Then we're cooked, whatever your fragrant little friend does."

He stood up abruptly and climbed over the slanting wall which was now their floor, to peer out the direct-view port. He swore, slowly and bitterly. "You try the radio again while I was out?" he asked.

"Yes." She did not bother to add that there had been no response. Here, almost halfway between the orbits of earth and Mars, they were hopelessly out of touch. A ship as small as theirs couldn't carry equipment enough to bridge the distance.

Roget turned around, said, "By God—" and then clenched his jaw and strode out of the room. Mc-Menamin heard him walk through the bedroom and clatter around in the storage compartment behind.

In a few moments he was back with a welding torch in his hand. "Should have thought of this before," he said. "I don't know what'll happen if I cut into that hull—damn thing may explode, for all I know—but it's better than sitting doing nothing." He put his helmet down with a bang and his voice came tinnily in her helmet receiver. "Be back in a minute."

"Be careful," McMenamin said again.

Roget closed the outer lock door behind him and looked at the ravished hull of the ship. The metal had been eaten away in a broad band all around the ship, just above the tail, as if a child had bitten around the small end of a pear. In places the clustered rocket tubes showed through. He felt a renewed surge of anger, with fear deep under it.

A hundred years ago, he reminded himself, the earliest space voyagers had encountered situations as bad as this one, maybe worse. But Roget was a city man, bred for city virtues. He didn't, he decided, know quite how to feel or act. What were you supposed to do when you were about to die, fifteen million miles from home? Try to calm McMenamin—who was dangerously calm already—or show your true nobility by making one of those deathbed speeches you read in the popular histories? What about suggesting a little suicide pact? There was nothing in the ship that would give them a cleaner death than the one ahead of them. About all he could do would be to stab Frances, then himself, with a screwdriver.

Her voice said in the earphones, "You all right?"

He said, "Sure. Just going to try it." He lowered himself to the green surface, careful not to let his knees touch the dark, corrosive area. The torch was a small, easily manageable tool. He pointed the snout at the dark area where it lapped up over the hull, turned the switch on and pressed the button. Flame leaped out, washing over the dark surface. Roget felt the heat through his suit. He turned off the torch to see what effect it had had.

There was a deep, charred pit in the dark stuff, and it seemed to him that it had pulled back a little from the area it was attacking. It was more than he had expected. Encouraged, he tried again.

There was a sudden tremor under him and he leaped

nervously to his feet, just in time to avoid the corrosive wave as it rolled under him. For a moment he was only conscious of the thick metal of his boot soles and the thinness of the fabric that covered his knees; then, as he was about to step back out of the way, he realized that it was not only the dark ring that had expanded, that was still expanding.

He moved jerkily—too late—as the pale center area swept toward and under him. Then he felt as if he had been struck by a mighty hammer.

His ears rang, and there was a mist in front of his eyes. He blinked, tried to raise an arm. It seemed to be stuck fast at the wrist and elbow. Panicked, he tried to push himself away and couldn't. As his vision cleared, he saw that he was spread-eagled on the pale disk that had spread out under him. The metal collars of his wrist and elbow joints, all the metal parts of his suit, were held immovably. The torch lay a few inches away from his right hand.

For a few moments, incredulously, Roget still tried to move. Then he stopped and lay in the prison of his suit, looking at the greenish-cream surface under his helmet.

Frances' voice said abruptly, "Leo, is anything wrong?"

Roget felt an instant relief that left him shaken and weak. His forehead was cold. He said after a moment, "Pulled a damn fool trick, Frances. Come out and help me if you can."

He heard a click as her helmet went down. He added anxiously, "But don't come near the pale part, or you'll get caught too."

After a while she said, "Darling, I can't think of anything to do."

Roget was feeling calmer, somehow not much afraid any more. He wondered how much oxygen was left in his suit. Not more than an hour, he thought. He said, "I know. I can't, either."

Later he called, "Frances?"

"Yes?"

"Roll the ship once in a while, will you? Might get through to the wiring or something, otherwise."

". . . All right."

After that, they didn't talk. There was a great deal to be said, but it was too late to say it.

v

Tommy was on garbage detail with nine other unfortunates. It was a messy, hard, unpleasant business, fit only for a cabin boy—collecting waste from the compartment and corridor receptacles and pressing it into standard capsule shapes, then hauling it to the nearest polarizer. But Tommy, under the suspicious eye of the petty officer in charge, worked with an apparent total absorption until they had cleaned out their section of the six inmost levels and were well into the seventh.

This was the best strategic place for Tommy's departure, since it was about midway from axis to hull, and the field of operations of any pursuit was correspondingly broadened. Also, the volume in which they labored had expanded wedgewise as they climbed, and the petty officer, though still determined to watch Tommy, could no longer keep him constantly in view.

Tommy saw the officer disappear around the curve of the corridor, and kept on working busily. He was still at it, with every appearance of innocence and industry, when the officer abruptly popped into sight again about three seconds later.

The officer stared at him with baffled disapproval and said unreasonably, "Come on, come on, Loy. Don't slack."

"Right," said Tommy, and scurried faster.

A moment later Third Mate Adkins hove majestically into view. The petty officer turned respectfully to face him.

"Keeping young Tom well occupied, I see," said the Mate.

"Yes, sir," said the officer. "Appears to be a re-formed character, now, sir. Must have learned a lesson, one way or another."

"Ha!" said the Mate. "Very good. Oh, Loy, you might be interested in this—the Captain himself has told me that the new metal is perfectly all right. Un-usually rich, in fact. I've had my first ration already—very good it was, too—and I'm going to get my extras in half an hour or so. Well, good appetite, all." And, while the lesser crewmen clustered against the walls to give him room, he moved haughtily off down the cor-ridor.

Tommy kept on working as fast as he could. He was draining energy he might need later, but it was neces-sary to quiet the petty officer's suspicions entirely, in order to give himself a decent start. In addition, his artist's soul demanded it. Tommy, in his own way, was a perfectionist.

Third Mate Adkins was due to get his extras in about half an hour, and if Tommy knew the Captain's habits, the Captain would be taking his first meal from the newly replenished reservoir at about the same time. That set the deadline. Before the half hour was up, Tommy would have to cut off the flow of the new metal, so that stomachs which had been gurgling in anticipation would remain desolately void until the next windfall.

The Mate, in spite of his hypochondria, was a glut-ton. With any luck, this would make him bitter for a month. And the Old Man—but it was better not to dwell on that.

The petty officer hung around irresolutely for an-other ten minutes, then dashed off down the corridor to attend to the rest of his detail. Without wasting a moment, Tommy dropped the capsule he had just col-lected and shot away in the other direction.

The rest of the cabin boys, as fearful of Tommy as they were of constituted authority, would not dare to raise an outcry until they spotted the officer coming back. The officer, because of the time he had wasted in watching Tommy, would have to administer a thorough lecture on slackness to the rest of the detail before he returned.

Tommy had calculated his probable margin to a nicety, and it was enough, barring accidents, to get him safely away. Nevertheless, he turned and twisted from one system of corridors to another, carefully confusing his trail, before he set himself to put as much vertical distance behind him as he could.

This part of the game had to be accomplished in a fury of action, for he was free to move in the corridors only until the Captain was informed that he was loose again. After that, he had to play hounds and hares with the moving strips through which the Captain could see him.

When the time he had estimated was three quarters gone, Tommy slowed and came to a halt. He inspected the corridor wall minutely, and found the almost imperceptible trace that showed where the scanning wave nearest him had stopped. He jockeyed his body clear of it, and then waited. He still had a good distance to cover before he dared play his trump, but it was not safe to move now; he had to wait for the Captain's move.

It came soon enough: the scanning waves erupted into simultaneous motion and anger. "Tommy!" they bellowed. "Tommy Loy! Come back, you unmentionable excrescence, or by Spore you'll regret it! Tommy!"

Moving between waves, Tommy waited patiently until their motion carried him from one corridor to another. The Captain's control over the waves was not complete: in some corridors they moved two steps upward for one down, in others the reverse. When he got into a downward corridor, Tommy scrambled out of it again as soon as he could and started over.

Gradually, with many false starts, he worked his way up to the thirteenth level, one level short of the hull.

Now came the hard part. This time he had to enter the fuel lines, not only for sure escape, but to gather the force he needed. And for the first time in his life, Tommy hesitated before something that he had set himself to do.

Death was a phenomenon that normally touched each member of Tommy's race only once—only captains died, and they died alone. For lesser members of the crew, there was almost no mortal danger; the ship protected them. But Tommy knew what death was, and as the sealed entrance to the fuel line swung into view, he knew that he faced it.

He made himself small, as he had under the lash. He broke the seal. Quickly, before the following wave could catch him, he thrust himself through the sphincter.

The blast of ions gripped him, flung him forward, hurting him like a hundred whips. Desperately he held himself together, thickening his insulating shell against that deadly flux of energy; but still his body absorbed it, till he felt a horrid fullness.

The walls of the tube fled past him, barely perceptible in the rush of glowing haze. Tommy held in that growing tautness with his last strength, meanwhile looking for an exit. He neither knew nor cared whether he had reached his goal; he had to get out or die.

He saw a dim oval on the wall ahead, hurled himself at it, clung, and forced his body through.

He was in a horizontal corridor, just under the hull. He drank the blessed coolness of it for an instant, before moving to the nearest sphincter. Then he was out, under the velvet-black sky and the diamond blaze of stars.

He looked around. The pain was fading now; he felt only an atrocious bloatedness that tightened his skin and made all his movements halting. Forward of him, up the long shallow curve of the hull, he could see the alien ship, and the two five-pointed creatures beside it.

Carefully, keeping a few feet between himself and the hull, he headed toward it.

One of the creatures was sprawled flat on the polarizer that had brought its ship down. The other, standing beside it, turned as Tommy came near, and two of its upper three points moved in an insane fashion that made Tommy feel ill. He looked away quickly and moved past them, till he was directly over the center of the polarizer and only a few inches away.

Then, with a sob of relief, he released the energy his body had stored. In one thick, white bolt, it sparked to the polarizer's center.

Shaken and spent, Tommy floated upward and surveyed what he had done. The muzzle of the polarizer was contracting, puckering at the center, the dark corrosive ring following it in. So much energy, applied in one jolt, must have shorted and paralyzed it all the way back to the ship's nerve center. The Captain, Tommy thought wryly, would be jumping now!

And he wasn't done yet. Tommy took one last look at the aliens and their ship. The sprawled one was up now, and the two of them had their upper points twined around each other in a nauseating fashion. Then they parted suddenly, and, facing Tommy, wiggled their free points. Tommy moved purposefully off across the width of the ship, heading for the three heavy-duty polarizers.

He had to go in again through that hell not once more, but twice. Though his nerves shrank from the necessity, there was no way of avoiding it. For the ship could not alter its course, except by allowing itself to be attracted by a sun or other large body—which was unthinkable—but it could rotate at the Captain's will. The aliens were free now, but the Captain had only to spin ship in order to snare them again.

Four miles away, Tommy found the second polarizer. He backed away a carefully calculated distance before he re-entered the hull. At least he could know in advance how far he had to go—and he knew now, too, that the energy he had stored the first time had been adequate twice over. He rested a few moments; then, like a diver plunging into a torrent, he thrust himself into the fuel line.

He came out again, shuddering with pain, and pushed himself through the exit. He felt as bloated as he had before. The charge of energy was not as great, but Tommy knew that he was weakening. This time, when he discharged over the polarizer and watched it contract into a tiny, puckered mass, he felt as if he could never move again, let alone expose himself once more to that tunnel of flame.

The stars, he realized dully, were moving in slow, ponderous arcs over his head. The Captain was spinning ship. Tommy sank to the hull and lay motionless, watching half attentively for a sight of the alien ship.

There it was, a bright dot haloed by the flame of its exhaust. It swung around slowly, gradually, with the rest of the firmament, growing smaller slowly.

"He'll get them before they're out of range," Tommy thought. He watched as the bright dot climbed overhead, began to fall on the other side.

The Captain had one polarizer left. It would be enough.

Wearily Tommy rose and followed the bright star. It was not a joke any longer. He would willingly have gone inside to the bright, warm, familiar corridors that led downward to safety and deserved punishment. But somehow he could not bear to think of those fascinating creatures—those wonderful playthings—going to fill the Captain's fat belly.

Tommy followed the ship until he could see the pale gleam of the functioning polarizer. Then he crawled through the hull once more, and again he found a sealed entrance to the fuel tube. He did not let himself think about it. His mind was numb already; and he pushed himself through uncaring.

This time it was worse than ever before; he had not

dreamed that it could be so bad. His vision dimmed and he could barely see the exit, or feel its pressure, when he dragged himself out. Lurching drunkenly, he passed a scanning wave on his way to the hull sphincter, and heard the Captain's voice explode.

Outside, ragged black patches obscured his vision of the stars. The pressure inside him pressed painfully outward, again and again, and each time he held it back. Then he felt rather than saw that he was over the pale disk, and, as he let go the bolt, he lost consciousness.

When his vision cleared, the alien ship was still above him, alarmingly close. The Captain must have had it almost reeled in again, he thought, when he had let go that last charge.

Flaming, it receded into the Great Deep, and he watched it go until it disappeared.

He felt a great peace and a great weariness. The tiny blue disk that was a planet had moved its apparent position a little nearer its star. The aliens were going back there, to their unimaginable home, and Tommy's ship was forging onward into new depths of darkness—toward the edge of the Galaxy and the greatest Deep.

He moved to the nearest sphincter as the cold bit at him. His spirits lifted suddenly as he thought of those three stabs of energy, equally spaced around the twelve-mile perimeter of the ship. The Captain would be utterly speechless with rage, he thought, like an aged martinet who had had his hands painfully slapped by a small boy.

For, as we warned you, the Captain was not precisely a captain, nor the ship precisely a ship. Ship and captain were one and the same, hive and queen bee, castle and lord.

In effect, Tommy had circumnavigated the skipper.

ARTHUR C. CLARKE

A WALK IN THE DARK

*In the previous three stories, we have en-
countered life in three different guises—
including our own in a moderately distant
future. In the horrifying little tale that
follows, we meet up with something entirely different—fear of a "life form"
that possibly does not even exist. (It may,
on the other hand—and that provides the
gruesomeness of the story!)*

ROBERT ARMSTRONG had walked just over two miles, as
far as he could judge, when his torch failed. He stood
still for a moment, unable to believe that such a misfortune could really have befallen him. Then, half mad-
dened with rage, he hurled the useless instrument
away. It landed somewhere in the darkness, disturbing
the silence of this little world. A metallic echo came
ringing back from the low hills. Then all was quiet
again.

This, thought Armstrong, was the ultimate misfortune. Nothing more could happen to him now. He was
even able to laugh bitterly at his luck, and resolved
never again to imagine that the fickle goddess had ever
favored him. Who would have believed that the only
tractor at Camp IV would have broken down when he
was just setting off for Port Sanderson? He recalled the
frenzied repair work, the relief when the second start
had been made—and the final debacle when the caterpillar track had jammed hopelessly.

It was no use then regretting the lateness of his departure: he could not have foreseen these accidents,

and it was still a good four hours before the *Canopus* took off. He *had* to catch her, whatever happened: no other ship would be touching at this world for another month. Apart from the urgency of his business, four more weeks on this out-of-the-way planet were unthinkable.

There had been only one thing to do. It was lucky that Port Sanderson was little more than six miles from the camp—not a great distance, even on foot. He had been forced to leave all his equipment behind, but it could follow on the next ship and he could manage without it. The road was poor, merely stamped out of the rock by one of the Board's hundred-ton crushers, but there was no fear of going astray.

Even now he was in no real danger, though he might well be too late to catch the ship. Progress would be slow, for he dare not risk losing the road in this region of canyons and enigmatic tunnels that had never been explored. It was, of course, pitch dark. Here at the edge of the Galaxy the stars were so few and scattered that their light was negligible. The strange crimson sun of this lonely world would not rise for many hours, and although five of the little moons were in the sky, they could barely be seen by the unaided eye. Not one of them could even cast a shadow.

Armstrong was not the man to bewail his luck for long. He began to walk slowly along the road, feeling its texture with his feet. It was, he knew, fairly straight except where it wound through Carver's Pass. He wished he had a stick or something to probe the way before him, but he would have to rely for guidance on the feel of the ground.

It was terribly slow at first, until he gained confidence. He had never known how difficult it was to walk in a straight line. Although the feeble stars gave him his bearings, again and again he found himself stumbling among the virgin rocks at the edge of the crude roadway. He was traveling in long zigzags that took him to alternate sides of the road. Then he would stub his toes against the bare rock and grope his way back onto the hard-packed surface once again.

Presently it settled down to a routine. It was impossible to estimate his speed; he could only struggle along and hope for the best. It should be easy enough unless he lost his way. But he dared not think of that.

Once he had mastered the technique, he could afford the luxury of thought. He could not pretend that he was enjoying the experience, but he had been in much worse positions before. As long as he remained on the road he was perfectly safe. He had been hoping that as his eyes became adapted to the starlight he would be able to see the way, but he now knew that the whole journey would be blind. The discovery gave him a vivid sense of his remoteness from the heart of the Galaxy. On a night as clear as this, the skies of almost any other planet would have been blazing with stars. Here at this outpost of the Universe the sky held perhaps a hundred faintly gleaming points of lights, as useless as the five ridiculous moons on which no one had ever bothered to land.

A slight change in the road interrupted his thoughts. Was there a curve here, or had he veered off to the right again? He moved very slowly along the invisible and ill-defined border. Yes, there was no mistake: the road was bending to the left. He tried to remember its appearance in the daytime, but he had seen it only once before. Did this mean that he was nearing the Pass? He hoped so, for the journey would then be half completed.

He peered ahead into the blackness, but the ragged line of the horizon told him nothing. Presently he found that the road had straightened itself again, and his spirits sank. The entrance to the Pass must still be some way ahead: there were at least four more miles to go.

Four miles! How ridiculous the distance seemed! How long would it take the *Canopus* to travel four miles? He doubted if man could measure so short an interval of time. And how many trillions of miles had he, Robert Armstrong, traveled in his life? It must have reached a staggering total by now, for in the last twenty years he had scarcely stayed more than a month at a time on any single world. This very year he had twice made the crossing of the Galaxy, and that was a notable journey even in these days of the phantom drive.

He tripped over a loose stone, and the jolt brought him back to reality. It was no use, here, thinking of ships that could eat up the light-years. He was facing Nature, with no weapons but his own strength and skill.

It was strange that it took him so long to identify the real cause of his uneasiness. The last four weeks had been very full, and the rush of his departure, coupled with the annoyance and anxiety caused by the tractor's breakdowns, had driven everything else from his mind. Moreover, he had always prided himself on his hard-headedness and lack of imagination. Until now, he had forgotten all about that first evening at the base when the crews had regaled him with the usual tall yarns concocted for the benefit of newcomers.

It was then that the old base clerk had told the story of his walk by night from Port Sanderson to the camp, and of what had trailed him through Carver's Pass, keeping always beyond the limit of his torchlight.

Armstrong, who had heard such tales on a score of worlds, had paid it little attention at the time. This planet, after all, was known to be uninhabited. But logic could not dispose of the matter as easily as that. Suppose, after all, there was some truth in the old man's fantastic tale?

It was not a pleasant thought, and Armstrong did not intend to brood upon it. But he knew that if he dismissed it out of hand, it would continue to prey on his mind. The only way to conquer imaginary fears was to face them boldly: he would have to do that now.

His strongest argument was the complete barrenness of this world, and its utter desolation, though against that one could set many counterarguments, as indeed the old clerk had done. Man had lived on this planet for only twenty years, and much of it was still unexplored. No one could deny that the tunnels out in the wasteland were rather puzzling, but everyone believed them to be volcanic vents. Though, of course, life often crept into such places. With a shudder he remembered the giant polyps that had snared the first explorers of Vargon III.

It was all very inconclusive. Suppose, for the sake of argument, one granted the existence of life here. What of that?

The vast majority of life forms in the Universe were completely indifferent to man. Some, of course, like the gas-beings of Alcoran or the roving wave-lattices of Shandaloon, could not even detect him, but passed through or around him as if he did not exist. Others were merely inquisitive, some embarrassingly friendly. There were few that would attack unless provoked.

Nevertheless, it was a grim picture that the old stores clerk had painted. Back in the warm, well-lighted smoking room, with the drinks going round, it had been easy enough to laugh at it. But here in the darkness, miles from any human settlement, it was very different.

It was almost a relief when he stumbled off the road again and had to grope with his hands until he found it once more. This seemed a very rough patch, and the road was scarcely distinguishable from the rocks around. In a few minutes, however, he was safely on his way again.

It was unpleasant to see how quickly his thoughts returned to the same disquieting subject. Clearly it was worrying him more than he cared to admit.

He drew consolation from one fact: it had been quite obvious that no one at the base had believed the old fellow's story. Their questions and banter had proved that. At the time he had laughed as loudly as any of them. After all, what *was* the evidence? A dim shape, just seen in the darkness, that might well have been an oddly formed rock. Anyone could imagine such shapes at night if he were sufficiently overwrought. If it had been hostile, why hadn't the creature come any closer?

"Because it was afraid of my light," the old chap had said.

Well, that was plausible enough; it would explain why nothing had ever been seen in the daytime. Such a creature might live underground, only emerging at night. Hang it, why was he taking the old idiot's ravings so seriously! Armstrong got control of his thoughts again. If he went on this way, he told himself angrily, he would soon be seeing and hearing a whole menagerie of monsters.

There was, of course, one factor that disposed of the ridiculous story at once. It was really very simple; he felt sorry he hadn't thought of it before. What would such a creature live on? There was not even a trace of vegetation on the whole of the planet. He laughed to think that the bogy could be disposed of so easily— and in the same instant felt annoyed with himself for not laughing aloud. If he was so sure of his reasoning, why not whistle, or sing, or do anything to keep up his spirits? He put the question fairly to himself as a test of his manhood. Half ashamed, he had to admit that he was still afraid—afraid because "there *might* be something in it, after all." But at least his analysis had done him some good.

It would have been better if he had left it there and remained half convinced by his argument. But a part of his mind was still busily trying to break down his careful reasoning. It succeeded only too well, and when he remembered the plant-beings of Xantil Major, the shock was so unpleasant that he stopped dead in his tracks.

Now, the plant-beings of Xantil were not in any way

horrible; they were, in fact, extremely beautiful creatures. But what made them appear so distressing now was the knowledge that they could live for indefinite periods with no food whatsoever. All the energy they needed for their strange lives they extracted from cosmic radiation—and that was almost as intense here as anywhere else in the Universe.

He had scarcely thought of one example before others crowded into his mind and he remembered the life form on Trantor Beta, which was the only one known capable of directly utilizing atomic energy. That, too, had lived on an utterly barren world very much like this. . . .

Armstrong's mind was rapidly splitting into two distinct portions, one half trying to convince the other and neither wholly succeeding. He did not realize how far his morale had gone until he found himself holding his breath lest it conceal any sound in the darkness about him. Angrily he cleared his mind of the rubbish that had been gathering there and turned once more to the immediate problem.

There was no doubt that the road was slowly rising, and the silhouette of the horizon seemed much higher in the sky. The road began to twist, and suddenly he was aware of great rocks on either side of him. Soon only a narrow ribbon of sky was still visible, and darkness became, if possible, even more intense.

Somehow, he felt safer with the rock walls surrounding him. It meant that he was protected except in two directions. Also, the road had been leveled more carefully and it was easy to keep to it. Best of all, he knew that the trip was more than half completed.

For a moment his spirits began to rise. Then, with maddening perversity, his mind went back into the old grooves again. He remembered that it was on the far side of Carver's Pass that the old clerk's adventure had taken place, if it had ever happened at all.

In half a mile he would be out in the open again, out of the protection of these sheltering rocks. The thought seemed doubly horrible now, and he felt already a sense of nakedness. He could be attacked from any direction, and he would be utterly helpless.

Until now, he had still retained some self-control. Very resolutely he had kept his mind away from the one fact that gave some color to the old man's tale—the single piece of evidence that had stopped the banter in the crowded room back at the camp and brought a sudden hush upon the company. Now, as Armstrong's will weakened, he recalled again the words that had struck a momentary chill even in the warm comfort of the base building.

The little clerk had been very insistent on one point. He had never heard any sound of pursuit from the dim shape sensed, rather than seen, at the limit of his light. There was no scuffling of claws or hooves on rock, nor even the clatter of displaced stones. It was as if, so the old man had declared in that solemn manner of his, "as if the thing that was following could see perfectly in the darkness, and had many small legs or pads so that it could move swiftly and easily over the rock, like a giant caterpillar or one of the carpet-things of Kralkor II."

Yet although there had been no noise of pursuit, there had been one sound that the old man had caught several times. It was so unusual that its very strangeness made it doubly ominous. It was a faint but horribly persistent *clicking*.

The old fellow had been able to describe it very vividly—much too vividly for Armstrong's liking now.

"Have you ever listened to a large insect crunching its prey?" he said. "Well, it was just like that. I imagine that a crab makes exactly the same noise with its claws when it clashes them together. It was a—what's the word? A *chitinous* sound."

At this point, Armstrong remembered laughing loudly. (Strange, how it was all coming back to him now.) But no one else had laughed, though they had been quick to do so earlier. Sensing the change of tone, he sobered and asked the man to continue his story.

It had been quickly told. The next day a party of skeptical technicians had gone into the no man's land beyond Carver's Pass. They were not skeptical enough to leave their guns behind, but they had no cause to use them, for they found no trace of any living thing. There were the inevitable pits and tunnels, glistening holes down which the light of the torches rebounded endlessly until it was lost in the distance, but the planet was riddled with them.

Though the party found no sign of life, it discovered one thing it did not like at all. Out in the barren and unexplored land beyond the Pass they had come upon a tunnel even larger than the rest. Near the mouth of that tunnel was a massive rock half embedded in the ground. And the sides of that rock had been worn away, as if it had been used as an enormous whetstone!

No less than five of those present had seen this disturbing rock. None of them could explain it satisfactorily as a natural formation, but they still refused to accept the old man's story. Armstrong had asked them if they had ever put it to the test. There had been an uncomfortable silence. Then big Andrew Hargraves had said, "Hell, who'd walk out to the Pass at night just for fun!" and had left it at that.

Indeed, there was no other record of anyone's walking from Port Sanderson to the camp by night, or for that matter by day. During the hours of light, no unprotected human being could live in the open beneath the rays of the enormous, lurid sun that seemed to fill half the sky. And no one would walk six miles, wearing radiation armor, if the tractor was available.

Armstrong felt that he was leaving the Pass. The rocks on either side were falling away, and the road was no longer as firm and well packed as it had been. He was coming out into the open plain once more, and somewhere not far away in the darkness was that enigmatic pillar that might have been used for sharpening monstrous fangs or claws. It was not a reassuring thought.

Feeling distinctly worried now, Armstrong made a great effort to pull himself together. He would try and be rational again: he would think of business, the work he had done at the camp—anything but this infernal place. For a while he succeeded quite well. But presently, with a maddening persistence, every train of thought came back to the same point. He could not get out of his mind the picture of that inexplicable rock and its appalling possibilities.

The ground was quite flat again, and the road drove on straight as an arrow. There was one gleam of consolation: Port Sanderson could not be much more than two miles away. Armstrong had no idea how long he had been on the road. Unfortunately, his watch was not illuminated and he could only guess at the passage of time. With any luck, the *Canopus* should not take off for another two hours at least. But he could not be sure, and now another fear began to enter his mind, the dread that he might see a vast constellation of lights rising swiftly into the sky ahead and know that all this agony of mind had been in vain.

He was not zigzagging so badly now, and seemed to be able to anticipate the edge of the road before stumbling off it. It was probable, he cheered himself by thinking, that he was traveling almost as fast as if he had a light. If all went well, he might be nearing Port Sanderson in thirty minutes, a ridiculously small space of time. How he would laugh at his fears when he strolled into his already reserved stateroom in the *Canopus* and felt that peculiar quiver as the phantom drive hurled the great ship far out of this system, back to the clustered star-clouds near the center of the Galaxy, back toward Earth itself, which he had not seen for so many years.

One day, he told himself, he really must visit Earth again. All his life he had been making the promise, but always there had been the same answer—lack of time.

Strange, wasn't it, that such a tiny planet should have played so enormous a part in the development of the Universe, should even have come to dominate worlds far wiser and more intelligent than itself!

Armstrong's thoughts were harmless again, and he felt calmer. The knowledge that he was nearing Port Sanderson was immensely reassuring, and he deliberately kept his mind on familiar, unimportant matters. Carver's Pass was already far behind, and with it that thing he no longer intended to recall. One day, if he ever returned to this world, he would visit the Pass in the daytime and laugh at his fears. In twenty minutes, they would join the nightmares of childhood.

It was almost a shock, though one of the most pleasant he had ever known, when he saw the lights of Port Sanderson come up over the horizon. The curvature of this little world was very deceptive: it did not seem right that a planet with a gravity almost as great as Earth's should have a horizon so close at hand. One day someone would have to discover what lay at this world's core to give it so great a density.

Perhaps the many tunnels would help. It was an unfortunate turn of thought, but the nearness of his goal had robbed it of terror now. Indeed, the thought that he might really be in danger seemed to give his adventure a certain piquancy and heightened interest. Nothing could happen to him now, with ten minutes to go and the lights of the port in sight.

A few minutes later his feelings changed abruptly when he came to the sudden bend in the road. He had forgotten the chasm that caused this detour and added half a mile to the journey. Well, what of it? An extra half mile would make no difference now—another ten minutes at the most.

It was very disappointing when the lights of the city vanished. Armstrong had not remembered the hill which the road was skirting: perhaps it was only a low ridge, scarcely noticeable in the daytime. But by hiding the lights of the port it had taken away his chief talisman and left him again at the mercy of his fears.

Very unreasonably, his intelligence told him, he began to think how horrible it would be if anything happened now, so near the end of the journey. He kept the worst of his fear at bay for a while, hoping desperately that the lights of the city would soon reappear. But as the minutes dragged on he realized that the ridge must be longer than he imagined. He tried to cheer himself by the thought that the city would be all the nearer when he saw it again, but somehow logic seemed to have failed him now. For presently he found himself doing something he had not stooped to do even out in the waste by Carver's Pass.

He stopped, turned slowly round, and with bated breath listened until his lungs were nearly bursting.

The silence was uncanny, considering how near he must be to the port. There was certainly no sound from behind him. Of course there wouldn't be, he told himself angrily. But he was immensely relieved. The thought of that faint and insistent clicking had been haunting him for the last hour.

So friendly and familiar was the noise that did reach him at last that the anticlimax almost made him laugh aloud. Drifting through the still air from a source clearly not more than a mile away came the sound of a landing-field tractor, perhaps one of the machines loading the *Canopus* itself. In a matter of seconds, thought Armstrong, he would be around this ridge, with the port only a few hundred yards ahead. The journey was nearly ended. In a few moments this evil plain would be no more than a fading nightmare.

It seemed terribly unfair: so little time, such a small fraction of a human life, was all he needed now. But the gods have always been unfair to man, and now they were enjoying their little jest. For there could be no mistaking the rattle of monstrous claws in the darkness *ahead of him*.

ISAAC ASIMOV

BLIND ALLEY

*Practically everybody in the world
spends more time than he should com-
plaining about the inflexibilities, stupidi-
ties, and frustrations of bureaucracies,
governmental and otherwise. Few indeed
are those who have a kind word to say
for them. However, no one who has his
head screwed on properly can deny that
without bureaucracies our complex societies would simply fall apart. And in the
story that follows, it is proved that a
really capable bureaucrat can not only
preserve the society he lives in, but also
achieve some really progressive and, indeed, almost radical actions by working
skillfully within the framework of the
very system that employs him.*

FROM: Bureau for the Outer Provinces

 To: Loodun Antyok, Chief Public Administrator,
 A-8

 Subject: Civilian Supervisor of Cepheus 18, Administrative Position as.

 References:

  (a) Act of Council 2515, of the year 971 of the
Galactic Empire, entitled, "Appointment of Officials
of the Administrative Service, Methods for, Revision
of."

  (b) Imperial Directive, Ja 2374, dated 243/975
G.E.

1. By authorization of reference (a) you are hereby appointed to the subject position. The authority of said position as Civilian Supervisor of Cepheus 18 will extend over non-Human subjects of the Emperor living upon the planet under the terms of autonomy set forth in reference (b).

2. The duties of the subject position shall comprise the general supervision of all non-Human internal affairs, co-ordination of authorized government investigating and reporting committees, and the preparation of semiannual reports on all phases of non-Human affairs.

C. MORILY, Chief, BuOuProv,
12/977 G.E.

LOODUN ANTYOK had listened carefully and now he shook his round head mildly. "Friend, I'd like to help you, but you've grabbed the wrong dog by the ears. You'd better take this up with the Bureau."

Tomor Zammo flung himself back into his chair, rubbed his beak of a nose fiercely, thought better of whatever he was going to say, and answered quietly, "Logical, but not practical. I can't make a trip to Trantor now. You're the Bureau's representative on Cepheus 18. Are you entirely helpless?"

"Well, even as Civilian Supervisor, I've got to work within the limits of Bureau policy."

"Good," Zammo cried, "then tell me what Bureau policy is. I head a scientific investigating committee, under direct Imperial authorization with, supposedly, the widest powers; yet at every angle in the road I am pulled up short by the civilian authorities with only the parrot shriek of 'Bureau policy' to justify themselves. What *is* Bureau policy? I haven't received a decent definition yet."

Antyok's gaze was level and unruffled. He said, "As I see it—and this is not official, so you can't hold me to it—Bureau policy consists in treating the non-Humans as decently as possible."

"Then what authority have they—"

"*Ssh!* No use raising your voice. As a matter of fact, His Imperial Majesty is a humanitarian and a disciple of the philosophy of Aurelion. I can tell you quietly that it is pretty well-known that it is the Emperor himself who first suggested that this world be established. You can bet that Bureau policy will stick pretty close to Imperial notions. And you can bet that I can't paddle my way against *that* sort of current."

"Well, m'boy," the physiologist's fleshy eyelids quivered, "if you take that sort of attitude, you're going to lose your job. No, I won't have you kicked out. That's not what I mean at all. Your job will just fade out from under you, because nothing is going to be accomplished here!"

"Really? Why?" Antyok was short, pink, and pudgy and his plump-cheeked face usually found it difficult to put on display any expression other than one of bland and cheerful politeness—but it looked grave now.

"You haven't been here long. I have." Zammo scowled. "Mind if I smoke?" The cigar in his hand was gnarled and strong and was puffed to life carelessly.

He continued roughly, "There's no place here for humanitarianism, administrator. You're treating non-Humans as if they were Humans and it won't work. In fact, I don't like the word 'non-Human.' They're animals."

"They're intelligent," interjected Antyok, softly.

"Well, intelligent animals, then. I presume the two terms are not mutually exclusive. Alien intelligences mingling in the same space won't work, anyway."

"Do you propose killing them off?"

"Galaxy, no!" He gestured with his cigar. "I propose we look upon them as objects for study, and only that. We could learn a good deal from these animals if we were allowed to. Knowledge, I might point out, that would be used for the immediate benefit of the human race. *There's* humanity for you. *There's* the good of the masses, if it's this spineless cult of Aurelion that interests you."

"What, for instance, do you refer to?"

"To take the most obvious— You have heard of their chemistry, I take it?"

"Yes," Antyok admitted. "I have leafed through most of the reports on the non-Humans published in the last ten years. I expect to go through more."

"Hmp. Well— Then, all I need say is that their chemical therapy is extremely thorough. For instance, I have witnessed personally the healing of a broken bone—what passes for a broken bone with them, I mean—by the use of a pill. The bone was whole in fifteen minutes. Naturally, none of their drugs are any earthly use on Humans. Most would kill quickly. But if we found out how they worked on the non-Humans —on the animals—"

"Yes, yes. I see the significance."

"Oh, you do. Come, that's gratifying. A second point is that these animals communicate in an unknown manner."

"Telepathy!"

The scientist's mouth twisted, as he ground out, "Telepathy! Telepathy! Telepathy! Might as well say by witch brew. Nobody knows anything about telepathy except its name. What is the mechanism of telepathy? What is the physiology and the physics of it? I would like to find out, but I can't. Bureau policy, if I listen to you, forbids."

Antyok's little mouth pursed itself. "But— Pardon me, doctor, but I don't follow you. How are you prevented? Surely the Civil Administration has made no attempt to hamper scientific investigation of these non-Humans. I cannot speak for my predecessor entirely, of course, but I myself—"

"No direct interference has occurred. I don't speak of that. But by the Galaxy, administrator, we're hampered by the spirit of the entire set-up. You're making us deal with non-Humans as if they were Humans.

You allow them their own leader and internal autonomy. You pamper them and give them what Aurelion's philosophy would call 'rights.' I can't deal with their leader."

"Why not?"

"Because he refuses to allow me a free hand. He refuses to allow experiments on any subject without the subject's own consent. The two or three volunteers we get are not too bright. It's an impossible arrangement."

Antyok shrugged helplessly.

Zammo continued, "In addition, it is obviously impossible to learn anything of value concerning the brains, physiology, and chemistry of these animals without dissection, dietary experiments, and drugs. You know, administrator, scientific investigation is a hard game. Humanity hasn't much place in it."

Loodun Antyok tapped his chin with a doubtful finger. "Must it be quite so hard? These are harmless creatures, these non-Humans. Surely, dissection— Perhaps, if you were to approach them a bit differently— I have the idea that you antagonize them. Your attitude might be somewhat overbearing."

"Overbearing! I am not one of these whining social psychologists who are all the fad these days. I don't believe you can solve a problem that requires dissection by approaching it with what is called the 'correct personal attitude' in the cant of the times."

"I'm sorry you think so. Socio-psychological training is required of all administrators above the grade of A-4."

Zammo withdrew his cud of a cigar from his mouth and replaced it after a suitably contemptuous interval. "Then you'd better use a bit of your technique on the Bureau. You know, I *do* have friends at the Imperial court."

"Well, now, I *can't* take the matter up with them, not baldly. Basic policy does not fall within my cognizance and such things can only be initiated by the

Bureau. But, you know, we might try an indirect approach on this." He smiled faintly, "Strategy."

"What sort?"

Antyok pointed a sudden finger, while his other hand fell lightly on the rows of gray-bound reports upon the floor just next his chair. "Now, look, I've gone through most of these. They're dull, but contain *some* facts. For instance, when was the last non-Human infant born on Cepheus 18?"

Zammo spent little time in consideration. "Don't know. Don't care, either."

"But the Bureau would. There's *never* been a non-Human infant born on Cepheus 18—not in the two years the world has been established. Do you know the reason?"

The physiologist shrugged. "Too many possible factors. It would take study."

"All right, then. Suppose you write a report—"

"Reports! I've written twenty."

"Write another. Stress the unsolved problems. Tell them you must change your methods. Harp on the birth-rate problem. The Bureau doesn't dare ignore that. If the non-Humans die out, someone will have to answer to the Emperor. You see—"

Zammo stared, his eyes dark. "That will swing it?"

"I've been working for the Bureau for twenty-seven years. I know its ways."

"I'll think about it." Zammo rose and stalked out of the office. The door slammed behind him.

It was later that Zammo said to a co-worker, "He's a bureaucrat in the first place. He won't abandon the orthodoxies of paper work and he won't risk sticking his neck out. He'll accomplish little by himself, yet maybe more than a little, if we work through him."

From: Administrative Headquarters, Cepheus 18
To: BuOuProv
Subject: Outer Province Project 2563, Part II—

Scientific Investigations of non-Humans of Cepheus
18, Co-ordination of.

References:

(a) BuOuProv letr. Ceph-N-CM/jg, 100132,
dated 302/975 G.E.

(b) AdHQ-Ceph18 letr. AA-LA/mn, dated
140/977 G.E.

Enclosure:

1. SciGroup 10, Physical & Biochemical Division,
Report, entitled, "Physiologic Characteristics of non-
Humans of Cepheus 18, Part XI," dated 172/977 G.E.

1. Enclosure 1, included herewith, is forwarded for
the information of the BuOuProv. It is to be noted
that Section XII, paragraphs 1-16 of Encl. 1, concern
possible changes in present BuOuProv policy with regard to non-Humans with a view to facilitating physical and chemical investigations at present proceeding
under authorization of reference (a).

2. It is brought to the attention of the BuOuProv
that reference (b) has already discussed possible
changes in investigating methods, and that it remains
the opinion of AdHQ-Ceph18 that such changes are
as yet premature. It is nevertheless suggested that the
question of non-Human birth rate be made the subject
of a BuOuProv project assigned to AdHQ-Ceph18, in
view of the importance attached by SciGroup 10 to
the problem, as evidenced in Section V of Enclosure 1.

L. ANTYOK, Superv. AdHQ-Ceph18, 174/977

From: BuOuProv
To: AdHQ-Ceph18
Subject: Outer Province Project 2563—Scientific Investigations of non-Humans of Cepheus 18, Co-ordination of.

Reference:

(a) AdHQ-Ceph18 letr. AA-LA/mn, dated 174/-
977 G.E.

1. In response to the suggestion contained in paragraph 2 of reference (a), it is considered that the

question of the non-Human birth rate does not fall within the cognizance of AdHQ-Ceph18. In view of the fact that SciGroup 10 has reported said sterility to be probably due to a chemical deficiency in the food supply, all investigations in the field are relegated to SciGroup 10 as the proper authority.

2. Investigating procedures by the various Sci-Groups shall continue according to current directives on the subject. No changes in policy are envisaged.

C. MORILY, Chief, BuOuProv, 186/977 G.E.

II

There was a loose-jointed gauntness about the news reporter which made him appear somberly tall. He was Gustiv Bannerd, with whose reputation was combined ability—two things which do not invariably go together despite the maxims of elementary morality.

Loodun Antyok took his measure doubtfully and said, "There's no use denying that you're right. But the SciGroup report was confidential. I don't understand how—"

"It leaked," said Bannerd, callously. "Everything leaks."

Antyok was obviously baffled, and his pink face furrowed slightly. "Then I'll just have to plug the leak here. I can't pass your story. All reference to SciGroup complaints have to come out. You see that, don't you?"

"No." Bannerd was calm enough. "It's important; and I have my rights under the Imperial directive. I think the Empire should know what's going on."

"But it isn't going on," said Antyok, despairingly. "Your claims are all wrong. The Bureau isn't going to change its policy. I showed you the letters."

"You think you can stand up against Zammo when he puts the pressure on?" the newsman asked derisively.

"I will—if I think he's wrong."

"If!" stated Bannerd flatly. Then, in a sudden fervor, "Antyok, the Empire has something great here; something greater by a good deal than the government apparently realizes. They're destroying it. They're treating these creatures like animals."

"Really—" began Antyok, weakly.

"Don't talk about Cepheus 18. It's a zoo. It's a high-class zoo, with your petrified scientists teasing those poor creatures with their sticks poking through the bars. You throw them chunks of meat, but you cage them up. I know! I've been writing about them for two years now. I've almost been living with them."

"Zammo says—"

"Zammo!" This with hard contempt.

"Zammo says," insisted Antyok with worried firmness, "that we treat them too like humans as it is."

The newsman's straight long cheeks were rigid. "Zammo is rather animal-like in his own right. He is a science-worshiper. We can do with less of them. Have you read Aurelion's work?" The last was suddenly posed.

"Umm. Yes. I understand the Emperor—"

"The Emperor tends towards us. That is good—better than the hounding of the last reign."

"I don't see where you're heading."

"These aliens have much to teach us. You understand? It is nothing that Zammo and his SciGroup can use; no chemistry, no telepathy. It's a way of life; a way of thinking. The aliens have no crime, no misfits. What effort is being made to study their philosophy? Or to set them up as a problem in social engineering?"

Antyok grew thoughtful and his plump face smoothed out. "It is an interesting consideration. It would be a matter for psychologists—"

"No good. Most of them are quacks. Psychologists point out problems but their solutions are fallacious. We need men of Aurelion. Men of The Philosophy—"

"But look here, we can't turn Cepheus 18 into . . . into a metaphysical study."

"Why not? It can be done easily."

"How?"

"Forget your puny test-tube peerings. Allow the aliens to set up a society free of Humans. Give them an untrammeled independence and allow an intermingling of philosophies—"

Antyok's nervous response came, "That can't be done in a day."

"We can start in a day."

The administrator said slowly, "Well, I can't prevent you from trying to start." He grew confidential, his mild eyes thoughtful. "You'll ruin your own game, though, if you publish SciGroup 10's report and denounce it on humanitarian grounds. The Scientists are powerful."

"And we of The Philosophy as well."

"Yes, but there's an easy way. You needn't rave. Simply point out that the SciGroup is not solving its problems. Do so unemotionally and let the readers think out your point of view for themselves. Take the birth-rate problem, for instance. *There's* something for you. In a generation, the non-Humans might die out for all science can do. Point out that a more philosophical approach is required. Or pick some other obvious point. Use your judgment, eh?"

Antyok smiled ingratiatingly as he arose. "But for the Galaxy's sake, don't stir up a bad smell."

Bannerd was stiff and unresponsive. "You may be right."

It was later that Bannerd wrote in a capsule message to a friend, "He is not clever, by any means. He is confused and has no guiding-line through life. Certainly utterly incompetent in his job. But he's a cutter and a trimmer, compromises his way around difficulties, and will yield concessions rather than risk a hard stand. He may prove valuable in that. Yours in Aurelion."

From: AdHQ-Ceph18
To: BuOuProv

Subject: Birth rate of non-Humans on Cepheus 18, News Report on.

References:

(a) AdHQ-Ceph18 letr. AA-LA/mn, dated 174/-977 G.E.

(b) Imperial Directive, Ja 2374, dated 243/975 G.E.

Enclosures:

1-G. Bannerd news report, date-lined Cepheus 18, 201/977 G.E.

2-G. Bannerd news report, date-lined Cepheus 18, 203/977 G.E.

1. The sterility of non-Humans on Cepheus 18, reported to the BuOuProv in reference (a) has become the subject of news reports to the galactic press. The news reports in question are submitted herewith for the information of the BuOuProv as Enclosures 1 and 2. Although said reports are based on material considered confidential and closed to the public, the news reporter in question maintained his rights to free expression under the terms of reference (b).

2. In view of the unavoidable publicity and misunderstanding on the part of the general public now inevitable, it is requested that the BuOuProv direct future policy on the problem of non-Human sterility.

L. ANYOK, Superv. AdHQ-Ceph18, 209/977 G.E.

From: BuOuProv
To: AdHQ-Ceph18
Subject: Birth rate of non-Humans on Cepheus 18, Investigation of.

References:

(a) AdHQ-Ceph18 letr. AA-LA/mn, dated 209/-977 G.E.

(b) AdHQ-Ceph18 letr. AA-LA/mn, dated 174/-977 G.E.

1. It is proposed to investigate the causes and the means of precluding the unfavorable birth-rate phenomena mentioned in references (a) and (b). A

project is therefore set up, entitled, "Birth rate of non-Humans on Cepheus 18, Investigation of" to which, in view of the crucial importance of the subject, a priority of AA is given.

2. The number assigned to the subject project is 2910, and all expenses incidental to it shall be assigned to Appropriation number 18/78.

C. MORILY, Chief, BuOuProv, 223/977 G.E.

III

If Tomor Zammo's ill-humor lessened within the grounds of SciGroup 10 Experimental Station, his friendliness had not thereby increased. Antyok found himself standing alone at the viewing window into the main field laboratory.

The main field laboratory was a broad court set at the environmental conditions of Cepheus 18 itself for the discomfort of the experimenters and the convenience of the experimentees. Through the burning sand, and the dry, oxygen-rich air, there sparkled the hard brilliance of hot, white sunlight. And under the blaze, the brick-red non-Humans, wrinkled of skin and wiry of build, huddled in their squatting positions of ease, by ones and twos.

Zammo emerged from the laboratory. He paused to drink water thirstily. He looked up, moisture gleaming on his upper lip. "Like to step in there?"

Antyok shook his head definitely. "No, thank you. What's the temperature right now?"

"A hundred twenty, if there were shade. And they complain of the cold. It's drinking time now. Want to watch them drink?"

A spray of water shot upward from the fountain in the center of the court and the little alien figures swayed to their feet and hopped eagerly forward in a queer springy half-run. They milled about the water, jostling one another. The centers of their faces were suddenly disfigured by the projection of a long and flexible fleshy tube, which thrust forward into the spray and was withdrawn dripping.

It continued for long minutes. The bodies swelled and the wrinkles disappeared. They retreated slowly, backing away, with the drinking tube flicking in and out, before receding finally into a pink, wrinkled mass above a wide, lipless mouth. They went to sleep in groups in the shaded angles, plump and sated.

"Animals!" said Zammo, with contempt.

"How often do they drink?" asked Antyok.

"As often as they want. They can go a week if they have to. We water them every day. They store it under their skin. They eat in the evenings. Vegetarians, you know."

Antyok smiled chubbily. "It's nice to get a bit of firsthand information occasionally. Can't read reports all the time."

"Yes?"—noncommittally. Then, "What's new? What about the lacy-pants boys on Trantor?"

Antyok shrugged dubiously. "You can't get the Bureau to commit itself, unfortunately. With the Emperor sympathetic to the Aurelionists, humanitarianism is the order of the day. You know that."

There was a pause in which the administrator chewed his lip uncertainly. "But there's this birth-rate problem now. It's finally been assigned to AdHQ, you know—and double-A priority, too."

Zammo muttered wordlessly.

Antyok said, "You may not realize it, but that project will now take precedence over all other work proceeding on Cepheus 18. It's important."

He turned back to the viewing window and said thoughtfully, with a bald lack of preamble, "Do you think those creatures might be unhappy?"

"Unhappy!" The word was an explosion.

"Well, then," Antyok corrected hastily, "maladjusted. You understand? It's difficult to adjust an environment to a race we know so little of."

"Did you ever see the world we took them from?"

"I've read the reports—"

"Reports!"—infinite contempt. "I've *seen* it. This may look like desert out there to you, but it's a watery paradise to those devils. They have all the food and water they can get. They have a world to themselves with vegetation and natural water flow, instead of a lump of silica and granite where fungi were force-grown in caves and water had to be steamed out of gypsum rock. In ten years, they would have been dead to the last beast, and we saved them. Unhappy? Ga-a-ah, if they are, they haven't the decency of most animals."

"Well, perhaps. Yet I have a notion."

"A notion? What is your notion?" Zammo reached for one of his cigars.

"It's something that might help you. Why not study the creatures in a more integrated fashion? Let them use their initiative. After all, they did have a highly developed science. Your reports speak of it continually. Give them problems to solve."

"Such as?"

"Oh . . . oh," Antyok waved his hands helplessly. "Whatever you think might help most. For instance, spaceships. Get them into the control room and study their reactions."

"Why?" asked Zammo with dry bluntness.

"Because the reaction of their minds to tools and controls adjusted to the human temperament can teach you a lot. In addition, it will make a more effective bribe, it seems to me, than anything you've yet tried. You'll get more volunteers if they think they'll be doing something interesting."

"That's your psychology coming out. Hm-m-m. Sounds better than it probably is. I'll sleep on it. And where would I get permission in any case to let them handle spaceships? I've none at *my* disposal, and it would take a good deal longer than it was worth to follow down the line of red tape to get one assigned to us."

Antyok pondered and his forehead creased lightly. "It doesn't *have* to be spaceships. But even so— If you would write up another report and make the suggestion yourself—strongly, you understand—I might figure out some way of tying it up with my birth-rate project. A double-A priority can get practically anything, you know, without questions."

Zammo's interest lacked a bit even of mildness. "Well, maybe. Meanwhile, I've some basal metabolism tests in progress, and it's getting late. I'll think about it. It's got its points."

From: AdHQ-Ceph18
To: BuOuProv
Subject: Outer Province Project 2910, Part I—Birth rate of non-Humans on Cepheus 18, Investigation of.
Reference:
(a) BuOuProv letr. Ceph-N-CM/car, 115097, 223/977 G.E.
Enclosure:
1-SciGroup 10, Physical & Biochemical Division Report, Part XV, dated 220/977 G.E.

1. Enclosure 1 is forwarded herewith for the information of the BuOuProv.

2. Special attention is directed to Section V, Paragraph 3 of Enclosure 1 in which it is requested that a spaceship be assigned SciGroup 10 for use in expediting investigations authorized by the BuOuProv. It is considered by AdHQ-Ceph18 that such investigations may be of material use in aiding work now in progress on the subject project, authorized by reference (a). It is suggested, in view of the high priority placed by the BuOuProv upon the subject project, that immediate consideration be given the SciGroup's request.

L. ANTYOK, Superv. AdHQ-Ceph18, 240/977 G.E.

From: BuOuProv
To: AdHQ-Ceph18
Subject: Outer Province Project 2910—Birth rate of non-Humans on Cepheus 18, Investigation of.

Reference:
(a) AdHQ-Ceph18 letr. AA-LA/mn, dated 240/977 G.E.

1. Training Ship *AN-R-2055* is being placed at the disposal of AdHQ-Cept18 for use in investigation of non-Humans on Cepheus 18 with respect to the subject project and other authorized OuProv projects as requested in Enclosure 1 to reference (a).

2. It is urgently requested that work on the subject project be expedited by all available means.

C. MORILY, Head, BuOuProv, 251/977 G.E.

IV

The little bricky creature must have been more uncomfortable than his bearing would admit to. He was carefully wrapped in a temperature already adjusted to the point where his human companions steamed in their open shirts.

His speech was high-pitched and careful. "I find it damp, but not unbearably so at this low temperature."

Antyok smiled. "It was nice of you to come. I had planned to visit you, but a trial run in your atmosphere out there—" The smile had become rueful.

"It doesn't matter. You other-worldlings have done more for us than ever we were able to do for ourselves. It is an obligation that is but imperfectly returned by the endurance on my part of a trifling discomfort." His speech seemed always indirect, as if he approached his thoughts sidelong, or as if it were against all etiquette to be blunt.

Gustiv Bannerd, seated in an angle of the room, with one long leg crossing the other, scrawled nimbly and said, "You don't mind if I record all this?"

The Cepheid non-Human glanced briefly at the journalist. "I have no objection."

Antyok's apologetics persisted. "This is not a purely social affair, sir. I would not have forced discomfort on you for that. There are important questions to be considered, and you are the leader of your people."

The Cepheid nodded. "I am satisfied your purposes are kindly. Please proceed."

The administrator almost wriggled in his difficulty in putting thoughts into words. "It is a subject," he said, "of delicacy, and one I would never bring up if it weren't for the overwhelming importance of the . . . uh . . . question. I am only the spokesman of my government—"

"My people consider the other-world government a kindly one."

"Well, yes, they are kindly. For that reason, they are disturbed over the fact that your people no longer breed."

Antyok paused, and waited with worry for a reaction that did not come. The Cepheid's face was motionless except for the soft, trembling motion of the wrinkled area that was his deflated drinking tube.

Antyok continued, "It is a question we have hesitated to bring up because of its extremely personal angles. Noninterference is my government's prime aim, and we have done our best to investigate the problem quietly and without disturbing your people. But, frankly, we—"

"Have failed?" finished the Cepheid, at the other's pause.

"Yes. Or at least, we have not discovered a concrete failure to reproduce the exact environment of your original world; with, of course, the necessary modification to make it more livable. Naturally, it is thought there is some chemical shortcoming. And so I ask your voluntary help in the matter. Your people are advanced in the study of your own biochemistry. If you do not choose, or would rather not—"

"No, no, I can help." The Cepheid seemed cheerful about it. The smooth flat planes of his loose-skinned, hairless skull wrinkled in an alien response to an uncertain emotion. "It is not a matter that any of us would have thought would have disturbed you otherworldlings. That it does is but another indication of your well-meaning kindness. This world we find congenial, a paradise in comparison to our old. It lacks in nothing. Conditions such as now prevail belong in our legends of the Golden Age."

"Well—"

"But there is a something; a something you may not understand. We cannot expect different intelligences to think alike."

"I shall try to understand."

The Cepheid's voice had grown soft, its liquid undertones more pronounced. "We were dying on our native world; but we were fighting. Our science, developed through a history older than yours, was losing; but it had not yet lost. Perhaps it was because our science was fundamentally biological, rather than physical as yours is. Your people discovered new forms of energy and reached the stars. Our people discovered new truths of psychology and psychiatry and built up a working society free of disease and crime.

"There is no need to question which of the two angles of approach was the more laudable, but there is no uncertainty as to which proved more successful in the end. In our dying world, without the means of life or sources of power, our biological science could but make the dying easier.

"And yet we fought. For centuries past we had been groping toward the elements of atomic power, and slowly the spark of hope had glimmered that we might break through the two-dimensional limits of our planetary surface and reach the stars. There were no other planets in our system to serve as stepping stones. Nothing but some twenty light-years to the nearest star, without the knowledge of the possibility of the existence of other planetary systems, but rather with the supposed near-certainty of the contrary.

"But there is something in all life that insists on striving; even on useless striving. There were only five thousand of us left in the last days. Only five thousand. And our first ship was ready. It was experimental. It would probably have been a failure. But already we had all the principles of propulsion and navigation correctly worked out."

There was a long pause, and the Cepheid's small black eyes seemed glazed in retrospect.

The newspaperman put in suddenly, from his corner, "And then we came?"

"And then you came," the Cepheid agreed simply. "It changed everything. Energy was ours for the asking. A new world, congenial and, indeed, ideal, was ours even without asking. If our problems of society had long been solved by ourselves, our more difficult problems of environment were suddenly solved for us, no less completely."

"Well?" urged Antyok.

"Well—it was somehow not well. For centuries our ancestors had fought towards the stars, and now the stars suddenly proved to be the property of others. We had fought for life, and it had become a present handed to us by others. There is no longer any reason to fight. There is no longer anything to attain. All the universe is the property of your race."

"This world is yours," said Antyok, gently.

"By sufferance. It is a gift. It is not ours by right."

"You have earned it, in my opinion."

And now the Cepheid's eyes were sharply fixed on the other's countenance. "You mean well, but I doubt that you understand. We have nowhere to go, save this gift of a world. We are in a blind alley. The function of life is striving, and that is taken from us. Life can no longer interest us. We have no offspring—voluntarily. It is our way of removing ourselves from your way."

Absent-mindedly, Antyok had removed the fluoroglobe from the window seat, and spun it on its base. Its gaudy surface reflected light as it spun and its three-foot-high bulk floated with incongruous grace and lightness in the air.

Antyok said, "Is that your only solution? Sterility?"

"We might escape still," whispered the Cepheid, "but where in the Galaxy is there place for us? It is all yours."

"Yes, there is no place for you nearer than the Magellanic Clouds if you wished independence. The Magellanic Clouds—"

"And you would not let us go of yourselves. You mean kindly, I know."

"Yes, we mean kindly—but we could not let you go."

"It is a mistaken kindness."

"Perhaps, but could you not reconcile yourselves? You have a world."

"It is something past complete explanations. Your mind is different. We could not reconcile ourselves. I believe, administrator, that you have thought of all this before. The concept of the blind alley we find ourselves trapped in is not new to you."

Antyok looked up, startled, and one hand steadied the fluoro-globe. "Can you read my mind?"

"It is just a guess. A good one, I think."

"Yes—but *can* you read my mind? The minds of humans in general, I mean. It is an interesting point. The scientists say you cannot, but sometimes I wonder if it is that you simply will not. Could you answer that? I am detaining you, unduly, perhaps."

"No . . . no—" But the little Cepheid drew his enveloping robe closer, and buried his face in the electrically-heated pad at the collar for a moment. "You other-worldlings speak of reading minds. It is not so at all, but it is assuredly hopeless to explain."

Antyok mumbled the old proverb, "One cannot explain sight to a man blind from birth."

"Yes, just so. This sense which you call 'mind reading,' quite erroneously, cannot be applied to other-worldlings. It is not that we cannot receive the proper sensations, it is that your people do not transmit them, and we have no way of explaining to you how to go about it."

"Hm-m-m."

"There are times, of course, of great concentration or emotional tension on the part of an other-worldling when some of us who are more expert in this sense— more sharp-eyed, so to speak—detect vaguely *something*. It is uncertain; yet I myself have at times wondered—"

Carefully, Antyok began spinning the fluoro-globe once more. His pink face was set in thought, and his eyes were fixed upon the Cepheid. Gustiv Bannerd stretched his fingers and reread his notes, his lips moving silently.

The fluoro-globe spun, and slowly the Cepheid seemed to grow tense as well, as his eyes shifted to the colorful sheen of the globe's fragile surface.

The Cepheid said, "What is that?"

Antyok started, and his face smoothed into an almost chuckling placidity. "This? A Galactic fad of three years ago; which means that it is a hopelessly old-fashioned relic this year. It is a useless device but it looks pretty. Bannerd, could you adjust the windows to nontransmission?"

There was the soft click of a contact, and the windows became curved regions of darkness, while in the center of the room, the fluoro-globe was suddenly the focus of a rosy effulgence that seemed to leap outward in streamers. Antyok, a scarlet figure in a scarlet room, placed it upon the table and spun it with a hand that dripped red. As it spun, the colors changed with a slowly increasing rapidity, blended and fell apart into more extreme contrasts.

Antyok was speaking in an eerie atmosphere of molten, shifting rainbow. "The surface is of a material that exhibits variable fluorescence. It is almost weightless, extremely fragile, but gyroscopically balanced so that it rarely falls with ordinary care. It is rather pretty, don't you think?"

From somewhere the Cepheid's voice came. "Extremely pretty."

"But it has outworn its welcome; outlived its fashionable existence."

The Cepheid's voice was abstracted. "It is very pretty."

Bannerd restored the light at a gesture, and the colors faded.

The Cepheid said, "That is something my people would enjoy." He stared at the globe with fascination.

And now Antyok rose. "You had better go. If you stay longer, the atmosphere may have bad effects. I thank you humbly for your kindness."

"I thank you humbly for yours." The Cepheid had also risen.

Antyok said, "Most of your people, by the way, have accepted our offers to them to study the make-up of our modern spaceships. You understand, I suppose, that the purpose was to study the reactions of your people to our technology. I trust that conforms with your sense of propriety."

"You need not apologize. I, myself, have now the makings of a human pilot. It was most interesting. It recalls our own efforts—and reminds us of how nearly on the right track we were."

The Cepheid left, and Antyok sat, frowning.

"Well," he said to Bannerd, a little sharply. "You remember our agreement, I hope. This interview can't be published."

Bannerd shrugged. "Very well."

Antyok was at his seat, and his fingers fumbled with the small metal figurine upon his desk. "What do you think of all this, Bannerd?"

"I am sorry for them. I think I understand how they feel. We must educate them out of it. The Philosophy can do it."

"You think so?"

"Yes."

"We can't let them go, of course."

"Oh, no. Out of the question. We have too much to learn from them. This feeling of theirs is only a passing stage. They'll think differently, especially when we allow them the completest independence."

"Maybe. What do you think of the fluoro-globes, Bannerd? He liked them. It might be a gesture of the right sort to order several thousand of them. The Galaxy knows they're a drug on the market right now, and cheap enough."

"Sounds like a good idea," said Bannerd.

"The Bureau would never agree, though. I know them."

The newsman's eyes narrowed. "But it might be just the thing. They need new interests."

"Yes? Well, we *could* do something. I could include your transcript of the interview as part of a report and just emphasize the matter of the globes a bit. After all, you're a member of The Philosophy and might have influence with important people, whose word with the Bureau might carry much more weight than mine. You understand—?"

"Yes," mused Bannerd. "Yes."

From: AdHQ-Ceph18

To: BuOuProv

Subject: OuProv Project 2910, Part II; Birth rate of non-Humans on Cepheus 18, Investigation of.

Reference:

(a) BuOuProv letr. Ceph-N-CM/car, 115097, dated 223/977 G.E.

Enclosure:

1. Transcript of conversation between L. Antyok of AdHQ-Ceph18, and Ni-San, High Judge of the non-Humans on Cepheus 18.

1. Enclosure 1 is forwarded herewith for the information of the BuOuProv.

2. The investigation of the subject project undertaken in response to the authorization of reference (a) is being pursued along the new lines indicated in Enclosure 1. The BuOuProv is assured that every means will be used to combat the harmful psychological at-

titude at present prevalent among the non-Humans.

3. It is to be noted that the High Judge of the non-Humans on Cepheus 18 expressed interest in fluoro-globes. A preliminary investigation into this fact of non-Human psychology has been initiated.

L. ANTYOK, Superv. AdHQ-Ceph18, 272/977 G.E.

From: BuOuProv
To: AdHQ-Ceph18
Subject: OuProv Project 2910; Birth rate of non-Humans on Cepheus 18, Investigation of.
Reference:
        (a) AdHQ-Ceph18 letr. AA-LA/mn, dated 272/977 G.E.

1. With reference to Enclosure 1 of reference (a), five thousand fluoro-globes have been allocated for shipment to Cepheus 18, by the Department of Trade.

2. It is instructed that AdHQ-Ceph18 make use of all methods of appeasing non-Humans' dissatisfaction consistent with the necessities of obedience to Imperial proclamation.

C. MORILY, Chief, BuOuProv, 283/977 G.E.

v

The dinner was over, the wine had been brought in, and the cigars were out. The groups of talkers had formed and the captain of the merchant fleet was the center of the largest. His brilliant white uniform quite outsparkled his listeners.

He was almost complacent in his speech: "The trip was nothing. I've had more than three hundred ships under me before this. Still, I've never had a cargo quite like this. What do you want with five thousand fluoro-globes on this desert, by the Galaxy?"

Loodun Antyok laughed gently. He shrugged. "For the non-Humans. It wasn't a difficult cargo, I hope."

"No, not difficult. But bulky. They're fragile, and I couldn't carry more than twenty to a ship with all the government regulations concerning packing and precautions against breakage. But it's the government's money, I suppose."

Zammo smiled grimly. "Is this your first experience with government methods, captain?"

"Galaxy, no," exploded the spaceman. "I try to avoid it, of course, but you can't help getting entangled on occasion. And it's an abhorrent thing when you are, and that's the truth. The red tape! The paper work! It's enough to stunt your growth and curdle your circulation. It's a tumor, a cancerous growth on the Galaxy. I'd wipe out the whole mess."

Antyok said, "You're unfair, captain. You don't understand."

"Yes? Well, now, as one of these bureaucrats," and he smiled amiably at the word, "suppose you explain your side of the situation, administrator."

"Well, now," Antyok seemed confused, "government is a serious and complicated business. We've got thousands of planets to worry about in this Empire of ours and billions of people. It's almost past human ability to supervise the business of governing without the tightest sort of organization. I think there are something like four hundred million men today in the Imperial Administrative Service alone and in order to co-ordinate their efforts and to pool their knowledge, you *must* have what you call red tape and paper work. Every bit of it, senseless though it may seem, annoying though it may be, has its uses. Every piece of paper is a thread binding the labors of four hundred million humans. Abolish the Administrative Service and you abolish the Empire; and with it, interstellar peace, order, and civilization."

"Come—" said the captain.

"No. I mean it." Antyok was earnestly breathless. "The rules and system of the Administrative set-up must be sufficiently all-embracing and rigid, so that in case of incompetent officials, and sometimes one *is* appointed . . . you may laugh, but there are incompetent scientists, and news men, and captains too . . . in case of incompetent officials, I say, little harm will be done. For at the worst, the system can move by itself."

"Yes," grunted the captain, sourly, "and if a capable administrator should be appointed? He is then caught by the same rigid web and is forced into mediocrity."

"Not at all," replied Antyok, warmly. "A capable man can work within the limits of the rules and accomplish what he wishes."

"How?" asked Bannerd.

"Well . . . well—" Antyok was suddenly ill at ease. "One method is to get yourself an A-priority project, or double-A, if possible."

The captain leaned his head back for laughter, but never quite made it, for the door was flung open and frightened men were pouring in. The shouts made no sense at first. Then:

"Sir, the ships are gone. These non-Humans have taken them by force."

"What? All?"

"Every one. Ships and creatures—"

It was two hours later that the four were together again, alone in Antyok's office now.

Antyok said coldly, "They've made no mistakes. There's not a ship left behind, not even your training ship, Zammo. And there isn't a government ship available in this entire half of the Sector. By the time we organize a pursuit, they'll be out of the Galaxy and halfway to the Magellanic Clouds. Captain, it was your responsibility to maintain an adequate guard."

The captain cried, "It was our first day out of space. Who could have known—"

Zammo interrupted fiercely, "Wait a while, captain. I'm beginning to understand. Antyok," his voice was hard, "you engineered this."

"I?" Antyok's expression was strangely cool, almost indifferent.

"You told us this evening that a clever administrator

got an A-priority project assigned to accomplish what he wished. You got such a project in order to help the non-Humans escape."

"I did? I beg your pardon, but how could that be? It was you yourself in one of your reports that brought up the problem of the failing birth rate. It was Bannerd, here, whose sensational articles frightened the Bureau into making a double-A priority project out of it. I had nothing to do with it."

"*You* suggested that I mention the birth rate," said Zammo violently.

"Did I?" said Antyok, composedly.

"And for that matter," roared Bannerd, suddenly, "you suggested that I mention the birth rate in my articles."

The three ringed him now and hemmed him in. Antyok leaned back in his chair and said easily, "I don't know what you mean by suggestions. If you are accusing me, please stick to evidence—legal evidence. The laws of the Empire go by written, filmed, or transcribed material, or by witnessed statements. All my letters as administrator are on file here, at the Bureau, and at other places. I never asked for an A-priority project. The Bureau assigned it to me, and Zammo and Bannerd are responsible for that. In print, at any rate."

Zammo's voice was an almost inarticulate growl. "You hoodwinked me into teaching the creatures how to handle a spaceship."

"It was *your* suggestion. I have your report proposing they be studied in their reaction to human tools on file. So has the Bureau. The evidence—the *legal* evidence, is plain. I had nothing to do with it."

"Nor with the globes?" demanded Bannerd.

The captain howled suddenly, "You had my ships brought here purposely. Five thousand globes! You knew it would require hundreds of craft."

"I never asked for globes," said Antyok, coldly. "That was the Bureau's idea, although I think Bannerd's friends of The Philosophy helped that along."

Bannerd fairly choked. He spat out, "You were asking that Cepheid leader if he could read minds. You were telling him to express interest in the globes."

"Come now. You prepared the transcript of the conversation yourself, and that, too, is on file. You can't prove it." He stood up. "You'll have to excuse me. I must prepare a report for the Bureau."

At the door, Antyok turned. "In a way, the problem of the non-Humans is solved, even if only to their own satisfaction. They'll breed now, and have a world they've earned themselves. It's what they wanted.

"Another thing. Don't accuse me of silly things. I've been in the Service for twenty-seven years, and I assure you that my paper work is proof enough that I have been thoroughly correct in everything I have done. And, captain, I'll be glad to continue our discussion of earlier this evening at your convenience and explain how a capable administrator can work through red tape and still get what he wants."

It was remarkable that such a round, smooth babyface could wear a smile quite so sardonic.

From: BuOuProv

To: Loodun Antyok, Chief Public Administrator, A-8

Subject: Administrative Service, Standing in.

Reference:

(a) AdServ Court Decision 22874-Q, dated 1/978 G.E.

1. In view of the favorable opinion handed down in reference (a) you are hereby absolved of all responsibility for the flight of non-Humans on Cepheus 18. It is requested that you hold yourself in readiness for your next appointment.

R. HORPRITT, Chief, AdServ, 15/978 G.E.

POUL ANDERSON

THE HELPING HAND

> *With this story, we enter a future in which mankind has spread itself far out into the galaxy of which Earth's sun— and Earth itself, of course—are such microscopically small bits of dust. In Anderson's concept, most life forms encountered seem to be essentially humanoid. In this story, indeed, they are not only humanoid, but measurably "human" in their psychological reactions. If one wanted to draw some comparisons, one could, I suppose, compare Cundaloa in this tale with the islands of the Pacific, and Skontar with the Scandinavian countries. Sweden, for example, is Swedish through and through. Hawaii? Whatever Hawaii is, and it sounds wonderful for a vacation, it surely no longer belongs to the original Hawaiians . . . You will get the point of this analogy as you read on, of course.*

A MELLOW bell tone was followed by the flat voice of the roboreceptionist: "His Excellency Valka Vahino, Special Envoy from the League of Cundaloa to the Commonwealth of Sol."

The Earthlings rose politely as he entered. Despite the heavy gravity and dry chill air of terrestrial conditions, he moved with the flowing grace of his species, and many of the humans were struck anew by what a handsome people his race was.

People—yes, the folk of Cundaloa were humanoid enough, mentally and physically, to justify the term. Their differences were not important; they added a certain charm, the romance of alienness, to the comforting reassurance that there was no really basic strangeness.

Ralph Dalton let his eyes sweep over the ambassador. Valka Vahino was typical of his race—humanoid mammal, biped, with a face that was very manlike, differing only in its beauty of finely chiseled features, high cheekbones, great dark eyes. A little smaller, more slender than the Earthlings, with a noiseless, feline ease of movement. Long shining blue hair swept back from his high forehead to his slim shoulders, a sharp and pleasing contrast to the rich golden skin color. He was dressed in the ancient ceremonial garb of Luai on Cundaloa—shining silvery tunic, deep-purple cloak from which little sparks of glittering metal swirled like fugitive stars, gold-worked boots of soft leather. One slender six-fingered hand held the elaborately carved staff of office which was all the credentials his planet had given him.

He bowed, a single rippling movement which had nothing of servility in it, and said in excellent Terrestrial, which still retained some of the lilting, singing accent of his native tongue: "Peace on your houses! The Great House of Cundaloa sends greetings and many well-wishings to his brothers of Sol. His unworthy member Valka Vahino speaks for him in friendship."

Some of the Earthlings shifted stance, a little embarrassed. It did sound awkward in translation, thought Dalton. But the language of Cundaloa was one of the most beautiful sounds in the Galaxy.

He replied with an attempt at the same grave formality. "Greetings and welcome. The Commonwealth of Sol receives the representative of the League of

Cundaloa in all friendship. Ralph Dalton, Premier of the Commonwealth, speaking for the people of the Solar System."

He introduced the others then—cabinet ministers, technical advisers, military staff members. It was an important assembly. Most of the power and influence in the Solar System was gathered here.

He finished: "This is an informal preliminary conference on the economic proposals recently made to your gov . . . to the Great House of Cundaloa. It has no legal standing. But it is being televised, and I daresay the Solar Assembly will act on a basis of what is learned at these and similar hearings."

"I understand. It is a good idea." Vahino waited until the rest were seated before taking a chair.

There was a pause. Eyes kept going to the clock on the wall. Vahino had arrived punctually at the time set, but Skorrogan of Skontar was late, thought Dalton. Tactless, but then the manners of the Skontarans were notoriously bad. Not at all like the gentle deference of Cundaloa, which in no way indicated weakness.

There was aimless conversation, of the "How do you like it here?" variety. Vahino, it developed, had visited the Solar System quite a few times in the past decade. Not surprising, in view of the increasingly close economic ties between his planet and the Commonwealth. There were a great many Cundaloan students in Earthian universities, and before the war there had been a growing tourist traffic from Sol to Avaiki. It would probably revive soon—especially if the devastation were repaired and—

"Oh, yes," smiled Vahino. "It is the ambition of all young *anamai*, men on Cundaloa, to come to Earth, if only for a visit. It is not mere flattery to say that our admiration for you and your achievements is boundless."

"It's mutual," said Dalton. "Your culture, your art and music, your literature—all have a large following in the Solar System. Why, many men, and not just scholars, learn Luaian simply to read the *Dvanagoa-Epai* in the original. Cundaloan singers, from concert artists to night-club entertainers, get more applause than any others." He grinned. "Your young men here have some difficulty keeping our terrestrial coeds off their necks. And your few young women here are besieged by invitations. I suppose only the fact that there cannot be issue has kept the number of marriages as small as it has been."

"But seriously," persisted Vahino, "we realize at home that your civilization sets the tone for the known Galaxy. It is not just that Solarian civilization is the most advanced technically, though that has, of course, much to do with it. *You* came to *us*, with your spaceships and atomic energy and medical science and all else—but, after all, we can learn that and go on with you from there. It is, however, such acts as . . . well, as your present offer of help: to rebuild ruined worlds light-years away, pouring your own skill and treasure into our homes, when we can offer you so little in return—it is that which makes you the leading race in the Galaxy."

"We have selfish motives, as you well know," said Dalton a little uncomfortably. "Many of them. There is, of course, simple humanitarianism. We could not let races very like our own know want when the Solar System and its colonies have more wealth than they know what to do with. But our own bloody history has taught us that such programs as this economic-aid plan redound to the benefit of the initiator. W' ɛn we have built up Cundaloa and Skontar, got them producing again, modernized their backward industry, taught them our science—they will be able to trade with us. And our economy is still, after all these centuries, primarily mercantile. Then, too, we will have knitted them too closely together for a repetition of the disastrous war just ended. And they will be allies for us against some of the really alien and menacing cultures in the Galaxy, planets and systems and empires against which we may one day have to stand."

"Pray the High One that that day never comes," said Vahino soberly. "We have seen enough of war."

The bell sounded again, and the robot announced in its clear inhuman tones: "His Excellency Skorrogan Valthak's son, Duke of Kraakahaym, Special Envoy from the Empire of Skontar to the Commonwealth of Sol."

They got up again, a little more slowly this time, and Dalton saw the expressions of dislike on several faces, expressions which smoothed into noncommittal blankness as the newcomer entered. There was no denying that the Skontarans were not very popular in the Solar System just now, and partly it was their own fault. But most of it they couldn't help.

The prevailing impression was that Skontar had been at fault in the war with Cundaloa. That was plainly an error. The misfortune was that the suns Skang and Avaiki, forming a system about half a light-year apart, had a third companion which humans usually called Allan, after the captain of the first expedition to the system. And the planets of Allan were uninhabited.

When terrestrial technology came to Skontar and Cundaloa, its first result had been to unify both planets —ultimately—both systems into rival states which turned desirous eyes on the green new planets of Allan. Both had had colonies there, clashes had followed, ultimately the hideous five years' war which had wasted both systems and ended in a peace negotiated with terrestrial help. It had been simply another conflict of rival imperialisms, such as had been common enough in human history before the Great Peace and the formation of the Commonwealth. The terms of the treaty were as fair as possible, and both systems were exhausted. They would keep the peace now, especially when both were eagerly looking for Solarian help to rebuild.

Still—the average human liked the Cundaloans. It was almost a corollary that he should dislike the Skontarans and blame them for the trouble. But even before the war they had not been greatly admired. Their isolationism, their clinging to outmoded traditions, their harsh accent, their domineering manner, even their appearance told against them.

Dalton had had trouble persuading the Assembly to let him include Skontar in the invitation to economic-aid conferences. He had finally persuaded them that it was essential—not only would the resources of Skang be a material help in restoration, particularly their minerals, but the friendship of a potentially powerful and hitherto aloof empire could be gained.

The aid program was still no more than a proposal. The Assembly would have to make a law detailing who should be helped, and how much, and then the law would have to be embodied in treaties with the planets concerned. The initial informal meeting here was only the first step. But—crucial.

Dalton bowed formally as the Skontaran entered. The envoy responded by stamping the butt of his huge spear against the floor, leaning the archaic weapon against the wall, and extending his holstered blaster handle first. Dalton took it gingerly and laid it on the desk. "Greeting and welcome," he began, since Skorrogan wasn't saying anything. "The Commonwealth—"

"Thank you." The voice was a hoarse bass, somehow metallic, and strongly accented. "The Valtam of the Empire of Skontar sends greetings to the Premier of Sol by Skorrogan Valthak's son, Duke of Kraakahaym."

He stood out in the room, seeming to fill it with his strong, forbidding presence. In spite of coming from a world of higher gravity and lower temperature, the Skontarans were a huge race, over two meters tall and so broad that they seemed stocky. They could be classed as humanoid, in that they were bipedal mammals, but there was not much resemblance beyond that. Under a wide, low forehead and looming eyebrow ridges, the eyes of Skorrogan were fierce and golden, hawk's eyes. His face was blunt-snouted, with a mouthful of fangs in the terrific jaws; his ears were blunt and set high on the massive skull. Short brown fur covered his muscular body to the end of the long restless tail, and a ruddy mane flared from his head and throat. In spite of the, to him, tropical temperature, he wore the furs and skins of state occasions at home, and the acrid reek of his sweat hung about him.

"You are late," said one of the ministers with thin politeness. "I trust you were not detained by any difficulties."

"No, I underestimated the time needed to get here," answered Skorrogan. "Please to excuse me." He did not sound at all sorry, but lowered his great bulk into the nearest chair and opened his portfolio. "We have business now, my sirs?"

"Well . . . I suppose so." Dalton sat down at the head of the long conference table. "Though we are not too concerned with facts and figures at this preliminary discussion. We want simply to agree on general aims, matters of basic policy."

"Naturally, you will wish a full account of the available resources of Avaiki and Skang, as well as the Allanian colonies," said Vahino in his soft voice. "The agriculture of Cundaloa, the mines of Skontar, will contribute much even at this early date, and, of course, in the end there must be economic self-sufficiency."

"It is a question of education, too," said Dalton. "We will send many experts, technical advisers, teachers—"

"And, of course, some question of military resources will arise—" began the Chief of Staff.

"Skontar have own army," snapped Skorrogan. "No need of talk there yet."

"Perhaps not," agreed the Minister of Finance mildly. He took out a cigarette and lit it.

"Please, sir!" For a moment Skorrogan's voice rose to a bull roar. "No smoke. You know Skontarans allergic to tobacco—"

"Sorry!" The Minister of Finance stubbed out the cylinder. His hand shook a little and he glared at the envoy. There had been little need for concern, the air-conditioning system swept the smoke away at once. And in any case—you don't shout at a cabinet minister. Especially when you come to ask him for help—

"There will be other systems involved," said Dalton hastily, trying with a sudden feeling of desperation to smooth over the unease and tension. "Not only the colonies of Sol. I imagine your two races will be expanding beyond your own triple system, and the resources made available by such colonization—"

"We will have to," said Skorrogan sourly. "After treaty rob us of all fourth planet— No matter. Please to excuse. Is bad enough to sit at same table with enemy without being reminded of how short time ago he *was* enemy."

This time the silence lasted a long while. And Dalton realized, with a sudden feeling almost of physical illness, that Skorrogan had damaged his own position beyond repair. Even if he suddenly woke up to what he was doing and tried to make amends—and who ever heard of a Skontaran noble apologizing for anything —it was too late. Too many millions of people, watching their telescreens, had seen his unpardonable arrogance. Too many important men, the leaders of Sol, were sitting in the same room with him, looking into his contemptuous eyes and smelling the sharp stink of unhuman sweat.

There would be no aid to Skontar.

With sunset, clouds piled up behind the dark line of cliffs which lay to the east of Geyrhaym, and a thin, chill wind blew down over the valley with whispers of winter. The first few snowflakes were borne on it, whirling across the deepening purplish sky, tinted pink by the last bloody light. There would be a blizzard before midnight.

The spaceship came down out of darkness and settled into her cradle. Beyond the little spaceport, the old town of Geyrhaym lay wrapped in twilight, huddling together against the wind. Firelight glowed ruddily from the old peak-roofed houses, but the winding cobbled streets were like empty canyons, twisting up the hill on whose crest frowned the great castle of the old barons. The Valtam had taken it for his own use, and little Geyrhaym was now the capital of the Empire. For proud Skirnor and stately Thruvang were radioactive pits, and wild beasts howled in the burned ruins of the old palace.

Skorrogan Valthak's son shivered as he came out of the airlock and down the gangway. Skontar was a cold planet. Even for its own people it was cold. He wrapped his heavy fur cloak more tightly about him.

They were waiting near the bottom of the gangway, the high chiefs of Skontar. Under an impassive exterior, Skorrogan's belly muscles tightened. There might be death waiting in that silent, sullen group of men. Surely disgrace—and he couldn't answer—

The Valtam himself stood there, his white mane blowing in the bitter wind. His golden eyes seemed luminous in the twilight, hard and fierce, a deep sullen hate smoldering behind them. His oldest son, the heir apparent, Thordin, stood beside him. The last sunlight gleamed crimson on the head of his spear; it seemed to drip blood against the sky. And there were the other mighty men of Skang, counts of the provinces on Skontar and the other planets, and they all stood waiting for him. Behind them was a line of imperial household guards, helmets and corselets shining in the dusk, faces in shadow, but hate and contempt like a living force radiating from them.

Skorrogan strode up to the Valtam, grounded his spear butt in salute, and inclined his head at just the proper degree. There was silence then, save for the whimpering wind. Drifting snow streamed across the field.

The Valtam spoke at last, without ceremonial greeting. It was like a deliberate slap in the face: "So you are back again."

"Yes, sire." Skorrogan tried to keep his voice stiff. It was difficult to do. He had no fear of death, but it was cruelly hard to bear this weight of failure. "As you know, I must regretfully report my mission unsuccessful."

"Indeed. We receive telecasts here," said the Valtam acidly.

"Sire, the Solarians are giving virtually unlimited aid to Cundaloa. But they refused any help at all to Skontar. No credits, no technical advisers—nothing. And we can expect little trade and almost no visitors."

"I know," said Thordin. "And *you* were sent to get their help."

"I tried, sire." Skorrogan kept his voice expressionless. He had to say something—*but be forever damned if I'll plead!* "But the Solarians have an unreasonable prejudice against us, partly related to their wholly emotional bias toward Cundaloa and partly, I suppose, due to our being unlike them in so many ways."

"So they do," said the Valtam coldly. "But it was not great before. Surely the Mingonians, who are far less human than we, have received much good at Solarian hands. They got the same sort of help that Cundaloa will be getting and that we might have had.

"We desire nothing but good relations with the mightiest power in the Galaxy. We might have had more than that. I know, from first-hand reports, what the temper of the Commonwealth was. They were ready to help us, had we shown any cooperativeness at all. We could have rebuilt, and gone farther than that—" His voice trailed off into the keening wind.

After a moment he went on, and the fury that quivered in his voice was like a living force: "I sent you as my special delegate to get that generously offered help. You, whom I trusted, who I thought was aware of our cruel plight—Arrrgh!" He spat. "And you spent your whole time there being insulting, arrogant, boorish. You, on whom all the eyes of Sol were turned, made yourself the perfect embodiment of all the humans think worst in us. No wonder our request was refused! You're lucky Sol didn't declare war!"

"It may not be too late," said Thordin. "We could send another—"

"No." The Valtam lifted his head with the inbred iron pride of his race, the haughtiness of a culture where for all history face had been more important than life. "Skorrogan went as our accredited representative. If we repudiated him, apologized for—not for any overt act but for bad manners!—if we crawled before the Galaxy—no! It isn't worth that. We'll just have to do without Sol."

The snow was blowing thicker now, and the clouds were covering the sky. A few bright stars winked forth in the clear portions. But it was cold, cold.

"And what a price to pay for honor!" said Thordin wearily. "Our folk are starving—food from Sol could keep them alive. They have only rags to wear—Sol would send clothes. Our factories are devastated, are obsolete, our young men grow up in ignorance of Galactic civilization and technology—Sol would send us machines and engineers, help us rebuild. Sol would send teachers, and we could become great— Well, too late, too late." His eyes searched through the gloom, puzzled, hurt. Skorrogan had been his friend. "But why did you do it? Why did you do it?"

"I did my best," said Skorrogan stiffly. "If I was not fitted for the task, you should not have sent me."

"But you were," said Valtam. "You were out best diplomat. Your wiliness, your understanding of extra-Skontaran psychology, your personality—all were invaluable to our foreign relations. And then, on this simple and most tremendous mission— No more!" His voice rose to a shout against the rising wind. "No more will I trust you. Skontar will know you failed."

"Sire—" Skorrogan's voice shook suddenly. "Sire, I

have taken words from you which from anyone else would have meant a death duel. If you have more to say, say it. Otherwise let me go."

"I cannot strip you of your hereditary titles and holdings," said the Valtam. "But your position in the imperial government is ended, and you are no longer to come to court or to any official function. Nor do I think you will have many friends left."

"Perhaps not," said Skorrogan. "I did what I did, and even if I could explain further, I would not after these insults. But if you ask my advice for the future of Skontar—"

"I don't," said the Valtam. "You have done enough harm already."

". . . then consider three things." Skorrogan lifted his spear and pointed toward the remote glittering stars. "First, those suns out there. Second, certain new scientific and technological developments here at home—such as Dyrin's work on semantics. And last—look about you. Look at the houses your fathers built, look at the clothes you wear, listen, perhaps, to the language you speak. And then come back in fifty years or so and beg my pardon!"

He swirled his cloak about him, saluted the Valtam again, and went with long steps across the field and into the town. They looked after him with incomprehension and bitterness in their eyes.

There was hunger in the town. He could almost feel it behind the dark walls, the hunger of ragged and desperate folk crouched over their fires, and wondered whether they could survive the winter. Briefly he wondered how many would die—but he didn't dare follow the thought out.

He heard someone singing and paused. A wandering bard, begging his way from town to town, came down the street, his tattered cloak blowing fantastically about him. He plucked his harp with thin fingers, and his voice rose in an old ballad that held all the harsh ringing music, the great iron clamor of the old tongue, the language of Naarhaym on Skontar. Mentally, for a moment of wry amusement, Skorrogan rendered a few lines into Terrestrial:

> *Wildly the winging*
> *War birds, flying*
> *wake the winter-dead*
> *wish for the sea-road.*
> *Sweetheart, they summon me,*
> *singing of flowers*
> *fair for the faring.*
> *Farewell, I love you.*

It didn't work. It wasn't only that the metallic rhythm and hard barking syllables were lost, the intricate rhyme and alliteration, though that was part of it —but it just didn't make sense in Terrestrial. The concepts were lacking. How could you render, well, such a word as *vorkansraavin* as "faring" and hope to get more than a mutilated fragment of meaning? Psychologies were simply too different.

And there, perhaps, lay his answer to the high chiefs. But they wouldn't know. They couldn't. And he was alone, and winter was coming again.

Valka Vahino sat in his garden and let sunlight wash over his bare skin. It was not often, these days, that he got a chance to *aliacaui*— What was that old Terrestrial word? "Siesta"? But that was wrong. A resting Cundaloan didn't sleep in the afternoon. He sat or lay outdoors, with the sun soaking into his bones or a warm rain like a benediction over him, and he let his thoughts run free. Solarians called that daydreaming, but it wasn't, it was, well—they had no real word for it. Psychic recreation was a clumsy term, and the Solarians never understood.

Sometimes it seemed to Vahino that he had never rested, not in an eternity of years. The grinding urgencies of wartime duty, and then his hectic journeys to

Sol—and since then, in the past three years, the Great House had appointed him official liaison man at the highest level, assuming that he understood the Solarians better than anyone else in the League.

Maybe he did. He'd spent a lot of time with them and liked them as a race and as individuals. But—by all the spirits, how they worked! How they drove themselves! As if demons were after them.

Well, there was no other way to rebuild, to reform the old obsolete methods and grasp the dazzling new wealth which only lay waiting to be created. But right now it was wonderfully soothing to lie in his garden, with the great golden flowers nodding about him and filling the summer air with their drowsy scent, with a few honey insects buzzing past and a new poem growing in his head.

The Solarians seemed to have some difficulty in understanding a whole race of poets. When even the meanest and stupidest Cundaloan could stretch out in the sun and make lyrics—well, every race has its own peculiar talents. Who could equal the gadgeteering genius which the humans possessed?

The great soaring, singing lines thundered in his head. He turned them over, fashioning them, shaping every syllable, and fitting the pattern together with a dawning delight. This one would be—good! It would be remembered, it would be sung a century hence, and they wouldn't forget Valka Vahino. He might even be remembered as a masterversemaker—*Alia Amaui cauianriho, valana, valana, vro!*

"Pardon, sir." The flat metal voice shook in his brain, he felt the delicate fabric of the poem tear and go swirling off into darkness and forgetfulness. For a moment there was only the pang of his loss; he realized dully that the interruption had broken a sequence which he would never quite recapture.

"Pardon, sir, but Mr. Lombard wishes to see you."

It was a sonic beam from the roboreceptionist which Lombard himself had given Vahino. The Cundaloan had felt the incongruity of installing its shining metal among the carved wood and old tapestries of his house, but he had not wanted to offend the donor—and the thing was useful.

Lombard, head of the Solarian reconstruction commission, the most important human in the Avaikian System. Just now Vahino appreciated the courtesy of the man's coming to him rather than simply sending for him. Only—why did he have to come exactly at this moment?

"Tell Mr. Lombard I'll be there in a minute."

Vahino went in the back way and put on some clothes. Humans didn't have the completely casual attitude toward nakedness of Cundaloa. Then he went into the forehall. He had installed some chairs there for the benefit of Earthlings, who didn't like to squat on a woven mat—another incongruity. Lombard got up as Vahino entered.

The human was short and stocky, with a thick bush of gray hair above a seamed face. He had worked his way up from laborer through engineer to High Commissioner, and the marks of his struggle were still on him. He attacked work with what seemed almost a personal fury, and he could be harder than tool steel. But most of the time he was pleasant, he had an astonishing range of interests and knowledge, and, of course, he had done miracles for the Avaikian System.

"Peace on your house, brother," said Vahino.

"How do you do," clipped the Solarian. As his host began to signal for servants, he went on hastily: "Please, none of your ritual hospitality. I appreciate it, but there just isn't time to sit and have a meal and talk cultural topics for three hours before getting down to business. I wish . . . well, you're a native here and I'm not, so I wish you'd personally pass the word around—tactfully, of course—to discontinue this sort of thing."

"But . . . they are among our oldest customs—"

"That's just it! Old—backward—delaying progress. I don't mean to be disparaging, Mr. Vahino. I wish we

Solarians had some customs as charming as yours. But —not during working hours. Please."

"Well . . . I dare say you're right. It doesn't fit into the pattern of a modern industrial civilization. And that is what we are trying to build, of course." Vahino took a chair and offered his guest a cigarette. Smoking was one of Sol's characteristic vices, perhaps the most easily transmitted and certainly the most easily defensible. Vahino lit up with the enjoyment of the neophyte.

"Quite. Exactly. And that is really what I came here about, Mr. Vahino. I have no specific complaints, but there has accumulated a whole host of minor difficulties which only you Cundaloans can handle for yourselves. We Solarians can't and won't meddle in your internal affairs. But you must change some things, or we won't be able to help you at all."

Vahino had a general idea of what was coming. He'd been expecting it for some time, he thought grayly, and there was really nothing to be done about it. But he took another puff of smoke, let it trickle slowly out, and raised his eyebrows in polite inquiry. Then he remembered that Solarians weren't used to interpreting nuances of expression as part of a language, and said aloud, "Please say what you like. I realize no offense is meant, and none will be taken."

"Good." Lombard leaned forward, nervously clasping and unclasping his big work-scarred hands. "The plain fact is that your whole culture, your whole psychology, is unfitted to modern civilization. It can be changed, but the change will have to be drastic. You can do it—pass laws, put on propaganda campaigns, change the educational system, and so on. But it *must* be done.

"For instance, just this matter of the siesta. Right now, all through this time zone on the planet, hardly a wheel is turning, hardly a machine is tended, hardly a man is at his work. They're all lying in the sun making poems or humming songs or just drowsing. There's a whole civilization to be built, Vahino! There are plantations, mines, factories, cities abuilding—you just can't do it on a four-hour working day."

"No. But perhaps we haven't the energy of your race. You are a hyperthyroid species, you know."

"You'll just have to learn. Work doesn't have to be backbreaking. The whole aim of mechanizing your culture is to release you from physical labor and the uncertainty of dependence on the land. And a mechanical civilization can't be cluttered with as many old beliefs and rituals and customs and traditions as yours is. There just isn't time. Life is too short. And it's too incongruous. You're still like the Skontarans, lugging their silly spears around after they've lost all practical value."

"Tradition *makes* life—the meaning of life—"

"The machine culture has its own tradition. You'll learn. It has its own meaning, and I think that is the meaning of the future. If you insist on clinging to outworn habits, you'll never catch up with history. Why, your currency system—"

"It's practical."

"In its own field. But how can you trade with Sol if you base your credits on silver and Sol's are an abstract actuarial quantity? You'll have to convert to our system for purpose of trade—so you might as well change over at home, too. Similarly, you'll have to learn the metric system if you expect to use our machines or make sense to our scientists. You'll have to adopt . . . oh, everything!

"Why, your very society— No wonder you haven't exploited even the planets of your own system when every man insists on being buried at his birthplace. It's a pretty sentiment, but it's no more than that, and you'll have to get rid of it if you're to reach the stars.

"Even your religion . . . excuse me . . . but you must realize that it has many elements which modern science has flatly disproved."

"I'm an agnostic," said Vahino quietly. "But the religion of Mauiroa means a lot to many people."

THE HELPING HAND 225

"If the Great House will let us bring in some missionaries, we can convert them to, say, Neopantheism. Which, I, for one, think has a lot more personal comfort and certainly more scientific truth than your mythology. If your people are to have faith at all, it must not conflict with facts which experience in a modern technology will soon make self-evident."

"Perhaps. And I suppose the system of familial bonds is too complex and rigid for modern industrial society. . . . Yes, yes—there is more than a simple conversion of equipment involved."

"To be sure. There's a complete conversion of minds," said Lombard. And then, gently, "After all, you'll do it eventually. You were building spaceships and atomic-power plants right after Allan left. I'm simply suggesting that you speed up the process a little."

"And language—"

"Well, without indulging in chauvinism, I think all Cundaloans should be taught Solarian. They'll use it at some time or other in their lives. Certainly all your scientists and technicians will have to use it professionally. The languages of Laui and Muara and the rest are beautiful, but they just aren't suitable for scientific concepts. Why, the agglutination alone— Frankly, your philosophical books read to me like so much gibberish. Beautiful, but almost devoid of meaning. Your language lacks—*precision*."

"Aracles and Vranamaui were always regarded as models of crystal thought," said Vahino wearily. "And I confess to not quite grasping your Kant and Russell and even Korzybski—but then, I lack training in such lines of thought. No doubt you are right. The younger generation will certainly agree with you.

"I'll speak to the Great House and may be able to get something done now. But in any case you won't have to wait many years. All our young men are striving to make themselves what you wish. It is the way to success."

"It is," said Lombard; and then, softly, "Sometimes I

wish success didn't have so high a price. But you need only look at Skontar to see how necessary it is."

"Why—they've done wonders in the last three years. After the great famine they got back on their feet, they're rebuilding by themselves, they've even sent explorers looking for colonies out among the stars." Vahino smiled wryly. "I don't love our late enemies, but I must admire them."

"They have courage," admitted Lombard. "But what good is courage alone? They're struggling in a tangle of obsolescence. Already the over-all production of Cundaloa is three times theirs. Their interstellar colonizing is no more than a feeble gesture of a few hundred individuals. Skontar can live, but it will always be a tenth-rate power. Before long it'll be a Cundaloan satellite state.

"And it's not that they lack resources, natural or otherwise. It's that, having virtually flung our offer of help back in our faces, they've taken themselves out of the main stream of Galactic civilization. Why, they're even trying to develop scientific concepts and devices we knew a hundred years ago, and are getting so far off the track that I'd laugh if it weren't so pathetic. Their language, like yours, just isn't adapted to scientific thought, and they're carrying chains of rusty tradition around. I've seen some of the spaceships they've designed themselves, for instance, instead of copying Solarian models, and they're ridiculous. Half a hundred different lines of approach, trying desperately to find the main line we took long ago. Spheres, ovoids, cubes—I hear someone even thinks he can build a tetrahedral spaceship!"

"It might just barely be possible," mused Vahino. "The Riemannian geometry on which the interstellar drive itself is based would permit—"

"No, no! Earth tried that sort of thing and found it didn't work. Only a crank—and, isolated, the scientists of Skontar are becoming a race of cranks—would think so.

"We humans were just fortunate, that's all. Even we had a long history before a culture arose with the mentality appropriate to a scientific civilization. Before that, technological progress was almost at a standstill. Afterward, we reached the stars. Other races can do it, but first they'll have to adopt the proper civilization, the proper mentality—and without our guidance, Skontar or any other planet isn't likely to evolve that mentality for many centuries to come.

"Which reminds me—" Lombard fumbled in a pocket. "I have a journal here, from one of the Skontaran philosophical societies. A certain amount of communication still does take place, you know; there's no official embargo on either side. It's just that Sol has given Skang up as a bad job. Anyway"—he fished out a magazine—"there's one of their philosophers, Dyrin, who's doing some new work on general semantics which seems to be arousing quite a furor. You read Skontaran, don't you?"

"Yes," said Vahino. "I was in military intelligence during the war. Let me see—" He leafed through the journal to the article and began translating aloud:

"The writer's previous papers show that the principle of nonelementalism is not itself altogether a universal, but must be subject to certain psychomathematical reservations arising from consideration of the *broganar*—that's a word I don't understand—field, which couples to electronic wave-nuclei and—"

"What is that jabberwocky?" exploded Lombard.

"I don't know," said Vahino helplessly. "The Skontaran mind is as alien to me as to you."

"Gibberish," said Lombard. "With the good old Skontaran to-hell-with-you dogmatism thrown in." He threw the magazine on the little bronze brazier, and fire licked at its thin pages. "Utter nonsense, as anyone with any knowledge of general semantics, or even an atom of common sense, can see." He smiled crookedly, a little sorrowfully, and shook his head. "A race of cranks!"

"I wish you could spare me a few hours tomorrow," said Skorrogan.

"Well—I suppose so." Thordin XI, Valtam of the Empire of Skontar, nodded his thinly maned head. "Though next week would be a little more convenient."

"Tomorrow—please."

The note of urgency could not be denied. "All right," said Thordin. "But what will be going on?"

"I'd like to take you on a little jaunt over to Cundaloa."

"Why there, of all places? And why must it be tomorrow, of all times?"

"I'll tell you—then." Skorrogan inclined his head, still thickly maned though it was quite white now, and switched off his end of the telescreen.

Thordin smiled in some puzzlement. Skorrogan was an odd fellow in many ways. But . . . well . . . we old men have to stick together. There is a new generation, and one after that, pressing on our heels.

No doubt thirty-odd years of living in virtual ostracism had changed the old joyously confident Skorrogan. But it had, at least, not embittered him. When the slow success of Skontar had become so plain that his own failure could be forgotten, the circle of his friends had very gradually included him again. He still lived much alone, but he was no longer unwelcome wherever he went. Thordin, in particular, had discovered that their old friendship could be as alive as ever before, and he was often over to the Citadel of Kraakahaym, or Skorrogan to the palace. He had even offered the old noble a position back in the High Council, but it had been refused, and another ten years—or was it twenty?—had gone by with Skorrogan fulfilling no more than his hereditary duties as duke. Until now, for the first time, something like a favor was being asked. . . . Yes, he thought, I'll go tomorrow. To blazes with work. Monarchs deserve holidays, too.

Thordin got up from his chair and limped over to

the broad window. The new endocrine treatments were doing wonders for his rheumatism, but their effect wasn't quite complete yet. He shivered a little as he looked at the wind-driven snow sweeping down over the valley. Winter was coming again.

The geologists said that Skontar was entering another glacial epoch. But it would never get there. In another decade or so the climate engineers would have perfected their techniques and the glaciers would be driven back into the north. But meanwhile it was cold and white outside, and a bitter wind hooted around the palace towers.

It would be summer in the southern hemisphere now, fields would be green, and smoke would rise from freeholders' cottages into a warm blue sky. Who had headed that scientific team?—Yes, Aesgayr Haasting's son. His work on agronomics and genetics had made it possible for a population of independent smallholders to produce enough food for the new scientific civilization. The old freeman, the backbone of Skontar in all her history, had not died out.

Other things had changed, of course. Thordin smiled wryly as he reflected just how much the Valtamate had changed in the last fifty years. It had been Dyrin's work in general semantics, so fundamental to all the sciences, which had led to the new psychosymbological techniques of government. Skontar was an empire in name only now. It had resolved the paradox of a libertarian state with a nonelective and efficient government. All to the good, of course, and really it was what past Skontaran history had been slowly and painfully evolving toward. But the new science had speeded up the process, compressed centuries of evolution into two brief generations. As physical and biological science had accelerated beyond belief— But it was odd that the arts, music, literature had hardly changed, that handicraft survived, that the old High Naarhaym was still spoken.

Well, so it went. Thordin turned back toward his

desk. There was work to be done. Like that matter of
the colony on Aesric's Planet— You couldn't expect to
run several hundred thriving interstellar colonies without some trouble. But it was minor. The empire was
safe. And it was growing.

They'd come a long way from the day of despair
fifty years ago, and from the famine and pestilence and
desolation which followed. A long way— Thordin
wondered if even he realized just how far.

He picked up the microreader and glanced over the
pages. His mind training came back to him and he
arrished the material. He couldn't handle the new techniques as easily as those of the younger generation,
trained in them from birth, but it was a wonderful help
to arrish, complete the integration in his subconscious,
and incolate the probabilities. He wondered how he
had ever survived the old days of reasoning on a purely
conscious level.

Thordin came out of the warp just outside Kraakahaym Citadel. Skorrogan had set the point of emer-
gence there, rather than indoors, because he liked the
view. It was majestic, thought the Valtam, but dizzying—a wild swoop of gaunt gray crags and wind-riven
clouds down to the far green valley below. Above him
loomed the old battlements, with the black-winged
kraakar which had given the place its name hovering
and cawing in the sky. The wind roared and boomed
about him, driving dry white snow before it.

The guards raised their spears in salute. They were
unarmed otherwise, and the vortex guns on the castle
walls were corroding away. No need for weapons in
the heart of an empire second only to Sol's dominions.
Skorrogan stood waiting in the courtyard. Fifty years
had not bent his back much or taken the fierce golden
luster from his eyes. It seemed to Thordin today,
though, that the old being wore an air of taut and in-
wardly blazing eagerness: he seemed somehow to be
looking toward the end of a journey.

Skorrogan gave conventional greeting and invited him in. "Not now, thanks," said Thordin. "I really am very busy. I'd like to start the trip at once."

The duke murmured the usual formula of polite regret, but it was plain that he could hardly wait, that he could ill have stood an hour's dawdling indoors. "Then please come," he said. "My cruiser is all set to go."

It was cradled behind the looming building, a sleek little roboship with the bewildering outline of all tetrahedral craft. They entered and took their seats at the center, which, of course, looked directly out beyond the hull.

"Now," said Thordin, "perhaps you'll tell me why you want to go to Cundaloa today?"

Skorrogan gave him a sudden look in which an old pain stirred.

"Today,' he said slowly, "it is exactly fifty years since I came back from Sol."

"Yes—?" Thordin was puzzled and vaguely uncomfortable. It wasn't like the taciturn old fellow to rake up that forgotten score.

"You probably don't remember," said Skorrogan, "but if you want to vargan it from your subconscious, you'll perceive that I said to them, then, that they could come back in fifty years and beg my pardon."

"So now you want to vindicate yourself." Thordin felt no surprise—it was typically Skontaran psychology—but he still wondered what there was to apologize for.

"I do. At that time I couldn't explain. Nobody would have listened, and in any case I was not perfectly sure myself that I had done right." Skorrogan smiled, and his thin hands set the controls. "Now I am. Time has justified me. And I will redeem what honor I lost then by showing you, today, that I didn't really fail.

"Instead, I succeeded. You see, I alienated the Solarians on purpose."

He pressed the main-drive stud, and the ship flashed through half a light-year of space. The great blue shield of Cundaloa rolled majestically before them, shining softly against a background of a million blazing stars.

Thordin sat quietly, letting the simple and tremendous statement filter through all the levels of his mind. His first emotional reaction was a vaguely surprised realization that, subconsciously, he had been expecting something like this. He hadn't ever really believed, deep down inside himself, that Skorrogan could be an incompetent.

Instead—no, not a traitor. But—what, then? What had he meant? Had he been mad, all these years, or—

"You haven't been to Cundaloa much since the war, have you?" asked Skorrogan.

"No—only three times, on hurried business. It's a prosperous system. Solar help put them on their feet again."

"Prosperous . . . yes, yes, they are." For a moment a smile tugged at the corners of Skorrogan's mouth, but it was a sad little smile, it was as if he were trying to cry but couldn't quite manage it. "A bustling, successful little system, with all of three colonies among the stars."

With a sudden angry gesture he slapped the short-range controls and the ship warped down to the surface. It landed in a corner of the great spaceport at Cundaloa City, and the robots about the cradle went to work, checking it in and throwing a protective force-dome about it.

"What—now?" whispered Thordin. He felt, suddenly, dimly afraid; he knew vaguely that he wouldn't like what he was going to see.

"Just a little stroll through the capital," said Skorrogan. "With perhaps a few side trips around the planet. I wanted us to come here unofficially, incognito, because that's the only way we'll ever see the real world, the day-to-day life of living beings which is so much more important and fundamental than any number of statistics and economic charts. I want to show you what I saved Skontar from." He smiled again, wryly. "I gave my life for my planet, Thordin. Fifty years of it, anyway—fifty years of loneliness and disgrace."

They emerged into the clamor of the great steel and concrete plain and crossed over the gates. There was a steady flow of beings in and out, a never-ending flux, the huge restless energy of Solarian civilization. A large proportion of the crowd was human, come to Avaiki on business or pleasure, and there were some representatives of other races. But the bulk of the throng was, naturally, native Cundaloans. Sometimes one had a little trouble telling them from the humans. After all, the two species looked much alike, and with the Cundaloans all wearing Solarian dress—

Thordin shook his head in some bewilderment at the roar of voices. "I can't understand," he shouted to Skorrogan. "I know Cundaloan, both Laui and Muara tongues, but—"

"Of course not," answered Skorrogan. "Most of them here are speaking Solarian. The native languages are dying out fast."

A plump Solarian in shrieking sports clothes was yelling at an impassive native storekeeper who stood outside his shop. "Hey, you boy, gimme him fella souvenir chop-chop—"

"Pidgin Solarian," grimaced Skorrogan. "It's on its way out, too, what with all young Cundaloans being taught the proper speech from the ground up. But tourists never learn." He scowled, and for a moment his hand shifted to his blaster.

But no—times changed. You did not wipe out someone who simply happened to be personally objectionable, not even on Skontar. Not any more.

The tourist turned and bumped him. "Oh, so sorry," he exclaimed, urbanely enough. "I should have looked where I was going."

"Is no matter," shrugged Skorrogan.

The Solarian dropped into a struggling and heavily accented High Naarhaym: "I really must apologize, though. May I buy you a drink?"

"No matter," said Skorrogan, with a touch of grimness.

"What a Planet! Backward as . . . as Pluto! I'm going on to Skontar from here. I hope to get a business contract—you know how to do business, you Skontarans!"

Skorrogan snarled and swung away, fairly dragging Thordin with him. They had gone half a block down the motilator before the Valtam asked, "What happened to your manners? He was trying hard to be civil to us. Or do you just naturally hate humans?"

"I like most of them," said Skorrogan. "But not their tourists. Praise the Fate, we don't get many of that breed on Skontar. Their engineers and businessmen and students are all right. I'm glad that relations between Sol and Skang are close, so we can get many of that sort. But keep out the tourists!"

"Why?"

Skorrogan gestured violently at a flashing neon poster. "That's why." He translated the Solarian:

SEE THE ANCIENT MAUIROA
CEREMONIES!

COLORFUL! AUTHENTIC! THE
MAGIC OF OLD CUNDALOA!

AT THE TEMPLE OF THE HIGH ONE
ADMISSION REASONABLE

"The religion of Mauiroa meant something, once," said Skorrogan quietly. "It was a noble creed, even if it did have certain unscientific elements. Those could have been changed— But it's too late now. Most of the natives are either Neopantheists or unbelievers, and they perform the old ceremonies for money. For a show."

He grimaced. "Cundaloa hasn't lost all its picturesque old buildings and folkways and music and the rest of its culture. But it's become conscious that they are picturesque, which is worse."

"I don't quite see what you're so angry about," said Thordin. "Times have changed. But they have on Skontar, too."

"Not in this way. Look around you, man! You've never been in the Solar System, but you must have seen pictures from it. Surely you realize that this is a typical Solarian city—a little backward, maybe, but typical. You won't find a city in the Avaikian System which isn't essentially—*human*.

"You won't find significant art, literature, music here any more—just cheap imitations of Solarian products, or else an archaistic clinging to outmoded native traditions, romantic counterfeiting of the past. You won't find science that isn't essentially Solarian, you won't find machines basically different from Solarian, you'll find fewer homes every year which can be told from human houses. The old society is dead; only a few fragments remain now. The familial bond, the very basis of native culture, is gone, and marriage relations are as casual as on Earth itself. The old feeling for the land is gone. There are hardly any tribal farms left; the young men are all coming to the cities to earn a million credits. They eat the products of Solarian-type food factories, and you can only get native cuisine in a few expensive restaurants.

"There are no more handmade pots, no more handwoven cloths. They wear what the factories put out. There are no more bards chanting the old lays and making new ones. They look at the telescreen now. There are no more philosophers of the Araclean or Vranamauian schools, there are just second-rate commentaries on Aristotle versus Korzybski or the Russell theory of knowledge—"

Skorrogan's voice trailed off. Thordin said softly, after a moment, "I see what you're getting at. Cundaloa has made itself over to fit the Solarian pattern."

"Just so. It was inevitable from the moment they accepted help from Sol. They'd *have* to adopt Solar science, Solar economics, ultimately the whole Solar culture. Because that would be the only pattern which would make sense to the humans who were taking the lead in reconstruction. And, since that culture was obviously successful, Cundaloa adopted it. Now it's too late. They can never go back. They don't even want to go back.

"It's happened before, you know. I've studied the history of Sol. Back before the human race even reached the other planets of its system, there were many cultures, often radically different. But ultimately one of them, the so-called Western society, became so overwhelmingly superior technologically that . . . well, no others could coexist with it. To compete, they had to adopt the very approach of the West. And when the West helped them from their backwardness, it necessarily helped them into a Western pattern. With the best intentions in the world, the West annihilated all other ways of life."

"And you wanted to save us from that?" asked Thordin. "I see your point, in a way. Yet I wonder if the sentimental value of old institutions was equal to some millions of lives lost, to a decade of sacrifice and suffering."

"It was more than sentiment!" said Skorrogan tensely. "Can't you see? Science is the future. To amount to anything, we *had* to become scientific. But was Solarian science the only way? Did we have to become second-rate humans to survive—or could we strike out on a new path, unhampered by the overwhelming helpfulness of a highly developed but essentially alien way of life? I thought we could. I thought we would have to.

"You see, no nonhuman race will ever make a really successful human. The basic psychologies—metabolic rates, instincts, logical patterns, *everything*—are too different. One race *can* think in terms of another's mentality, but never too well. You know how much trouble there's been in translating from one language to another. And all thought is in language, and language reflects the basic patterns of thought. The most precise, rigorous, highly thought out philosophy and science of one species will never quite make sense to another race. Because they are making somewhat different abstractions from the same great basic reality.

"I wanted to save us from becoming Sol's spiritual dependents. Skang was backward. It *had* to change its ways. But—why change them into a wholly alien pattern? Why not, instead, force them rapidly along the natural path of evolution—our own path?"

Skorrogan shrugged. "I did," he finished quietly. "It was a tremendous gamble, but it worked. We saved our own culture. It's *ours*. Forced by necessity to become scientific on our own, we developed our own approach.

"You know the result. Dyrin's semantics was developed—Solarian scientists would have laughed it to abortion. We developed the tetrahedral ship, which human engineers said was impossible, and now we can cross the Galaxy while an old-style craft goes from Sol to Alpha Centauri. We perfected the spacewarp, the psychosymbology of our own race—not valid for any other—the new agronomic system which preserved the freeholder who is basic to our culture—everything! In fifty years Cundaloa has been revolutionized, Skontar has revolutionized itself. There's a universe of difference.

"And we've therefore saved the intangibles which are our own, the art and handicrafts and essential folkways, music, language, literature, religion. The *élan* of our success is not only taking us to the stars, making us one of the great powers in the Galaxy, but it is producing a renaissance in those intangibles equaling any Golden Age in history.

"And all because we remained ourselves."

He fell into silence, and Thordin said nothing for a while. They had come into a quieter side street, an old quarter where most of the buildings antedated the coming of the Solarians, and many ancient-style native clothes were still to be seen. A party of human tourists was being guided through the district and had clustered about an open pottery booth.

"Well?" said Skorrogan after a while. "Well?"

"I don't know." Thordin rubbed his eyes, a gesture of confusion. "This is all so new to me. Maybe you're right. Maybe not. I'll have to think a while about it."

"I've had fifty years to think about it," said Skorrogan bleakly. "I suppose you're entitled to a few minutes."

They drifted up to the booth. An old Cundaloan sat in it among a clutter of goods, brightly painted vases and bowls and cups. Native work. A woman was haggling over one of the items.

"Look at it," said Skorrogan to Thordin. "Have you ever seen the old work? This is cheap stuff made by the thousands for the tourist trade. The designs are corrupt, the workmanship's shoddy. But every loop and line in those designs had meaning once."

Their eyes fell on one vase standing beside the old boothkeeper, and even the unimpressionable Valtam drew a shaky breath. It glowed, that vase. It seemed almost alive; in a simple shining perfection of clean lines and long smooth curves, someone had poured all his love and longing into it. Perhaps he had thought: This will live when I am gone.

Skorrogan whistled. "That's an authentic old vase," he said. "At least a century old—a museum piece! How'd it get in this junk shop?"

The clustered humans edged a little away from the two giant Skontarans, and Skorrogan read their expressions with a wry inner amusement: They stand in some awe of us. Sol no longer hates Skontar; it admires us. It sends its young men to learn our science and language. But who cares about Cundaloa any more?

But the woman followed his eyes and saw the vase glowing beside the old vendor. She turned back to him: "How much?"

"No sell," said the Cundaloan. His voice was a dusty whisper, and he hugged his shabby mantle closer about him.

"You sell." She gave him a bright artificial smile. "I give you much money. I give you ten credits."

"No sell."

"I give you hundred credits. Sell!"

"This mine. Fambly have it since old days. No sell."

"Five hundred credits!" She waved the money before him.

He clutched the vase to his thin chest and looked up with dark liquid eyes in which the easy tears of the old were starting forth. "No sell. Go 'way. No sell *oamaui*."

"Come on," mumbled Thordin. He grabbed Skorrogan's arm and pulled him away. "Let's go. Let's get back to Skontar."

"So soon?"

"Yes. Yes. You were right, Skorrogan. You were right, and I am going to make public apology, and you are the greatest savior of history. But let's get home!"

They hurried down the street. Thordin was trying hard to forget the old Cundaloan's eyes. But he wondered if he ever would.

ERIC FRANK RUSSELL

ALLAMAGOOSA

*For the information of those not in the
know, an "offog" is an allamagoosa, also
known as a thingumajig, a whatchama-
callit, and a dingus. . . . I suppose it is a
bit cynical to end this batch of stories
about man's glorious expansion into the
immediate neighborhood of our galaxy,
from our own personal Moon to the vicinity of Sirius and other nearby stars,
with a tale about the interstellar calami-
ties resulting from a silly misprint in an
inventory list, but—there it is. That's the
way the editor arranged it, and the pub-
lisher let him get away with it, too!*

IT WAS A LONG TIME since the *Bustler* had been so silent.
She lay in the Sirian spaceport, her tubes cold, her shell
particle-scarred, her air that of a long-distance runner
exhausted at the end of a marathon. There was good
reason for this: she had returned from a lengthy trip
by no means devoid of troubles.

Now, in port, well-deserved rest had been gained if
only temporarily. Peace, sweet peace. No more both-
ers, no more crises, no more major upsets, no more dire
predicaments such as crop up in free flight at least
twice a day. Just peace.

Hah!

Captain McNaught reposed in his cabin, feet up on
desk, and enjoyed the relaxation to the utmost. The

engines were dead, their hellish pounding absent for
the first time in months. Out there in the big city four
hundred of his crew were making whoopee under a
brilliant sun. This evening, when First Officer Gregory
returned to take charge, he was going to go into the
fragrant twilight and make the rounds of neon-lit
civilization.

That was the beauty of making landfall at long last.
Men could give way to themselves, blow off surplus
steam, each according to his fashion. No duties, no
worries, no dangers, no responsibilities in spaceport. A
haven of safety and comfort for tired rovers.

Again, hah!

Burman, the chief radio officer, entered the cabin.
He was one of the half-dozen remaining on duty and
bore the expression of a man who can think of twenty
better things to do.

"Relayed signal just come in, sir." Handing the paper
across he waited for the other to look at it and perhaps dictate a reply.

Taking the sheet, McNaught removed the feet from
his desk, sat erect and read the message aloud.

Terran Headquarters to Bustler. *Remain Siriport
pending further orders. Rear Admiral Vane W. Cassidy
due there seventeenth. Feldman. Navy Op. Command,
Sirisec.*

He looked up, all happiness gone from his leathery
features, and groaned.

"Something wrong?" asked Burman, vaguely alarmed.

McNaught pointed at three thin books on his desk.
"The middle one. Page twenty."

Leafing through it, Burman found an item that said:
*Vane W. Cassidy, R-Ad. Head Inspector Ships and
Stores.*

Burman swallowed hard. "Does that mean—?"

"Yes, it does," said McNaught without pleasure.
"Back to training-college and all its rigmarole. Paint
and soap, spit and polish." He put on an officious expression, adopted a voice to match it. "Captain, you

have only seven ninety-nine emergency rations. Your allocation is eight hundred. Nothing in your log-book accounts for the missing one. Where is it? What happened to it? How is it that one of the men's kits lacks an officially issued pair of suspenders? Did you report his loss?"

"Why does he pick on us?" asked Burman, appalled. "He's never chivvied us before."

"That's why," informed McNaught, scowling at the wall. "It's our turn to be stretched across the barrel." His gaze found the calendar. "We have three days—and we'll need 'em! Tell Second Officer Pike to come here at once."

Burman departed gloomily. In short time Pike entered. His face reaffirmed the old adage that bad news travels fast.

"Make out an indent," ordered McNaught, "for one hundred gallons of plastic paint, Navy-gray, approved quality. Make out another for thirty gallons of interior white enamel. Take them to spaceport stores right away. Tell them to deliver by six this evening along with our correct issue of brushes and sprayers. Grab up any cleaning material that's going for free."

"The men won't like this," remarked Pike, feebly.

"They're going to love it," McNaught asserted. "A bright and shiny ship, all spic and span, is good for morale. It says so in that book. Get moving and put those indents in. When you come back, find the stores and equipment sheets and bring them here. We've got to check stocks before Cassidy arrives. Once he's here we'll have no chance to make up shortages or smuggle out any extra items we happened to find in our hands."

"Very well, sir." Pike went out wearing the same expression as Burman's.

Lying back in his chair McNaught muttered to himself. There was a feeling in his bones that something was sure to cause a last-minute ruckus. A shortage of any item would be serious enough unless covered by a previous report. A surplus would be bad, very bad. The former implied carelessness or misfortune. The latter suggested barefaced theft of government property in circumstances condoned by the commander.

For instance, there was that recent case of Williams of the heavy cruiser *Swift*. He'd heard of it over the spacevine when out around Bootes. Williams had been found in unwitting command of eleven reels of electric-fence wire when his official issue was ten. It had taken a court-martial to decide that the extra reel— which had formidable barter-value on a certain planet —had not been stolen from space-stores, or, in sailor jargon, "teleportated aboard." But Williams had been reprimanded. And that did not help promotion.

He was still rumbling discontentedly when Pike returned bearing a folder of foolscap sheets.

"Going to start right away, sir?"

"We'll have to." He heaved himself erect, mentally bidded good-by to time off and a taste of the bright lights. "It'll take long enough to work right through from bow to tail. I'll leave the men's kit inspection to the last."

Marching out of the cabin, he set forth toward the bow, Pike following with broody reluctance.

As they passed the open main lock Peaslake observed them, bounded eagerly up the gangway and joined behind. A pukka member of the crew, he was a large dog whose ancestors had been more enthusiastic than selective. He wore with pride a big collar inscribed: *Peaslake—Property of S. S. Bustler.* His chief duties, ably performed, were to keep alien rodents off the ship and, on rare occasions, smell out dangers not visible to human eyes.

The three paraded forward, McNaught and Pike in the manner of men grimly sacrificing pleasure for the sake of duty, Peaslake with the panting willingness of one ready for any new game no matter what.

Reaching the bow-cabin, McNaught dumped himself in the pilot's seat, took the folder from the other.

"You know this stuff better than me—the chart room is where I shine. So I'll read them out while you look them over." He opened the folder, started on the first page. "K1. Beam compass, type D, one of."

"Check," said Pike.

"K2. Distance and direction indicator, electronic, type JJ, one of."

"Check."

"K3. Port and starboard gravitic meters, Casini models, one pair."

"Check."

Peaslake planted his head in McNaught's lap, blinked soulfully and whined. He was beginning to get the others' viewpoint. This tedious itemizing and checking was a hell of a game. McNaught consolingly lowered a hand and played with Peaslake's ears while he ploughed his way down the list.

"K187. Foam rubber cushions, pilot and co-pilot, one pair."

"Check."

By the time First Officer Gregory appeared they had reached the tiny intercom cubby and poked around it in semidarkness. Peaslake had long departed in disgust.

"M24. Spare minispeakers, three inch, type T2, one set of six."

"Check."

Looking in, Gregory popped his eyes and said, "What's going on?"

"Major inspection due soon." McNaught glanced at his watch. "Go see if stores has delivered a load and if not why not. Then you'd better give me a hand and let Pike take a few hours off."

"Does this mean land-leave is canceled?"

"You bet it does—until after Hizonner has been and gone." He glanced at Pike. "When you get into the city search around and send back any of the crew you can find. No arguments or excuses. Also no alibis and/or delays. It's an order."

Pike registered unhappiness. Gregory glowered at him, went away, came back and said, "Stores will have the stuff here in twenty minutes' time." With bad grace he watched Pike depart.

"M47. Intercom cable, woven-wire protected, three drums."

"Check," said Gregory, mentally kicking himself for returning at the wrong time.

The task continued until late in the evening, was resumed early next morning. By that time three-quarters of the men were hard at work inside and outside the vessel, doing their jobs as though sentenced to them for crimes contemplated but not yet committed.

Moving around the ship's corridors and catwalks had to be done crab-fashion, with a nervous sidewise edging. Once again it was being demonstrated that the Terran life form suffers from ye fear of wette paynt. The first smearer would have ten years willed off his unfortunate life.

It was in these conditions, in midafternoon of the second day, that McNaught's bones proved their feelings had been prophetic. He recited the ninth page while Jean Blanchard confirmed the presence and actual existence of all items enumerated. Two-thirds of the way down they hit the rocks, metaphorically speaking, and commenced to sink fast.

McNaught said boredly, "V1097. Drinking bowl, enamel, one of."

"Is zis," said Blanchard, tapping it.

"V1098. Offog, one."

"*Quoi?*" asked Blanchard, staring.

"V1098. Offog, one," repeated McNaught. "Well, why are you looking thunderstruck? This is the ship's galley. You're the head cook. You know what's supposed to be in the galley, don't you? Where's this offog?"

"Never hear of heem," stated Blanchard, flatly.

"You must have. It's on this equipment-sheet in

plain, clear type. Offog, one, it says. It was here when we were fitted-out four years ago. We checked it ourselves and signed for it."

"I signed for nossings called offog," Blanchard denied. "In the cuisine zere is no such sing."

"Look!" McNaught scowled and showed him the sheet.

Blanchard looked and sniffed disdainfully. "I have here zee electronic oven, one of. I have jacketed boilers, graduated capacities, one set. I have bain marie pans, seex of. But no offog. Never heard of heem. I do not know of heem." He spread his hands and shrugged. "No offog."

"There's got to be," McNaught insisted. "What's more, when Cassidy arrives there'll be hell to pay if there isn't."

"You find heem," Blanchard suggested.

"You got a certificate from the International Hotels School of Cookery. You got a certificate from the Cordon Bleu College of Cuisine. You got a certificate with three credits from the Space-Navy Feeding Center," McNaught pointed out. "All that—and you don't know what an offog is."

"*Nom d'un chien!*" ejaculated Blanchard, waving his arms around. "I tell you ten t'ousand time zere is no offog. Zere never was an offog. Escoffier heemself could not find zee offog of vich zere is none. Am I a magician perhaps?"

"It's part of the culinary equipment," McNaught maintained. "It must be because it's on page nine. And page nine means its proper home is in the galley, care of the head cook."

"Like hail it does," Blanchard retorted. He pointed at a metal box on the wall. "Intercom booster. Is zat mine?"

McNaught thought it over, conceded, "No, it's Burman's. His stuff rambles all over the ship."

"Zen ask heem for zis bloody offog," said Blanchard, triumphantly.

"I will. If it's not yours it must be his. Let's finish this checking first. If I'm not systematic and thorough Cassidy will jerk off my insignia." His eyes sought the list. "V1099. Inscribed collar, leather, brass studded, dog, for the use of. No need to look for that. I saw it myself five minutes ago." He ticked the item, continued, "V1100. Sleeping basket, woven reed, one of."

"Is zis," said Blanchard, kicking it into a corner.

"V1101. Cushion, foam rubber, to fit sleeping basket, one of."

"Half of," Blanchard contradicted. "In four years he has chewed away other half."

"Maybe Cassidy will let us indent for a new one. It doesn't matter. We're O. K. so long as we can produce the half we've got." McNaught stood up, closed the folder. "That's the lot for here. I'll go see Burman about this missing item."

The inventory party moved on.

Burman switched off a UHF receiver, removed his earplugs and raised a questioning eyebrow.

"In the galley we're short an offog," explained Mc-Naught. "Where is it?"

"Why ask me? The galley is Blanchard's bailiwick."

"Not entirely. A lot of your cables run through it. You've two terminal boxes in there, also an automatic switch and an intercom booster. Where's the offog?"

"Never heard of it," said Burman, baffled.

McNaught shouted, "Don't tell me that! I'm already fed up hearing Blanchard saying it. Four years back we had an offog. It says so here. This is our copy of what we checked and signed for. It says we signed for an offog. Therefore we must have one. It's got to be found before Cassidy gets here."

"Sorry, sir," sympathized Burman. "I can't help you."

"You can think again," advised McNaught. "Up in the bow there's a direction and distance indicator. What do *you* call it?"

"A didin," said Burman, mystified.

"And," McNaught went on, pointing at the pulse transmitter, "what do you call *that?*"

"The opper-popper."

"Baby names, see? Didin and opper-popper. Now rack your brains and remember what you called an offog four years ago."

"Nothing," asserted Burman, "has ever been called an offog to my knowledge."

"Then," demanded McNaught, "why did we sign for one?"

"I didn't sign for anything. You did all the signing."

"While you and others did the checking. Four years ago, presumably in the galley, I said, 'Offog, one,' and either you or Blanchard pointed to it and said, 'Check.' I took somebody's word for it. I have to take other specialists' words for it. I am an expert navigator, familiar with all the latest navigational gadgets but not with other stuff. So I'm compelled to rely on people who know what an offog is—or ought to."

Burman had a bright thought. "All kinds of oddments were dumped in the main lock, the corridors and the galley when we were fitted-out. We had to sort through a deal of stuff and stash it where it properly belonged, remember? This offog-thing might be any place today. It isn't necessarily my responsibility or Blanchard's."

"I'll see what the other officers say," agreed McNaught, conceding the point. "Gregory, Worth, Sanderson or one of the others may be coddling the item. Wherever it is, it's got to be found. Or accounted for in full if it's been expended."

He went out. Burman pulled a face, inserted his ear-plugs, resumed fiddling with his apparatus. An hour later McNaught came back wearing a scowl.

"Positively," he announced with ire, "there is no such thing on the ship. Nobody knows of it. Nobody can so much as guess at it."

"Cross it off and report it lost," Burman suggested.

"What, when we're hard aground? You know as well as I do that loss and damage must be signaled at time of occurrence. If I tell Cassidy the offog went west in space, he'll want to know when, where, how and why it wasn't signaled. There'll be a real ruckus if the contraption happens to be valued at half a million credits. I can't dismiss it with an airy wave of the hand."

"What's the answer then?" inquired Burman, innocently ambling straight into the trap.

"There's one and only one," McNaught announced. "*You* will manufacture an offog."

"Who? Me?" said Burman, twitching his scalp.

"You and no other. I'm fairly sure the thing is your pigeon, anyway."

"Why?"

"Because it's typical of the baby names used for your kind of stuff. I'll bet a month's pay that an offog is some sort of scientific allamagoosa. Something to do with fog, perhaps. Maybe a blind-approach gadget."

"The blind-approach transceiver is called 'the fumbly,'" Burman informed.

"There you are!" said McNaught as if that clinched it. "So you will make an offog. It will be completed by six tomorrow evening and ready for my inspection then. It had better be convincing, in fact pleasing. In fact its function will be convincing."

Burman stood up, let his hands dangle, and said in hoarse tones, "How can I make an offog when I don't even know what it is?"

"Neither does Cassidy know," McNaught pointed out, leering at him. "He's more of a quantity surveyor than anything else. As such he counts things, looks at things, certifies that they exist, accepts advice on whether they are functionally satisfactory or worn out. All we need do is concoct an imposing allamagoosa and tell him it's the offog."

"Holy Moses!" said Burman, fervently.

"Let us not rely on the dubious assistance of Biblical

characters," McNaught reproved. "Let us use the brains that God has given us. Get a grip on your soldering-iron and make a topnotch offog by six tomorrow evening. That's an order!"

He departed, satisfied with this solution. Behind him, Burman gloomed at the wall and licked his lips once, twice.

Rear Admiral Vane W. Cassidy arrived right on time. He was a short, paunchy character with a florid complexion and eyes like those of a long-dead fish. His gait was an important strut.

"Ah, captain, I trust that you have everything ship-shape."

"Everything usually is," assured McNaught, glibly. "I see to that." He spoke with conviction.

"Good!" approved Cassidy. "I like a commander who takes his responsibilities seriously. Much as I regret saying so, there are a few who do not." He marched through the main lock, his cod-eyes taking note of the fresh white enamel. "Where do you prefer to start, bow or tail?"

"My equipment-sheets run from bow backward. We may as well deal with them the way they're set."

"Very well." He trotted officiously toward the nose, paused on the way to pat Peaslake and examine his collar. "Well cared-for, I see. Has the animal proved useful?"

"He saved five lives on Mardia by barking a warning."

"The details have been entered in your log, I suppose?"

"Yes, sir. The log is in the chart room awaiting your inspection."

"We'll get to it in due time." Reaching the bow-cabin, Cassidy took a seat, accepted the folder from McNaught, started off at businesslike pace. "K1. Beam compass, type D, one of."

"This is it, sir," said McNaught, showing him.

"Still working properly?"

"Yes, sir."

They carried on, reached the intercom-cubby, the computer room, a succession of other places back to the galley. Here, Blanchard posed in freshly laundered white clothes and eyed the newcomer warily.

"V147. Electronic oven, one of."

"Is zis," said Blanchard, pointing with disdain.

"Satisfactory?" inquired Cassidy, giving him the fishy-eye.

"Not beeg enough," declared Blanchard. He encompassed the entire galley with an expressive gesture. "Nossings beeg enough. Place too small. Eversings too small. I am chef de cuisine an' she is a cuisine like an attic."

"This is a warship, not a luxury liner," Cassidy snapped. He frowned at the equipment-sheet. "V148. Timing device, electronic oven, attachment thereto, one of."

"Is zis," spat Blanchard, ready to sling it through the nearest port if Cassidy would first donate the two pins.

Working his way down the sheet, Cassidy got nearer and nearer while nervous tension built up. Then he reached the critical point and said, "V1098. Offog, one."

"*Morbleu!*" said Blanchard, shooting sparks from his eyes, "I have say before an' I say again, zere never was—"

"The offog is in the radio room, sir," McNaught chipped in hurriedly.

"Indeed?" Cassidy took another look at the sheet. "Then why is it recorded with galley equipment?"

"It was placed in the galley at time of fitting-out, sir. It's one of those portable instruments left to us to fix up where most suitable."

"Hm-m-m! Then it should have been transferred to the radio room list. Why didn't you transfer it?"

"I thought it better to wait for your authority to do so, sir."

The fish-eyes registered gratification. "Yes, that is quite proper of you, captain. I will transfer it now." He crossed the item from sheet nine, initialed it, entered it on sheet sixteen, initialed that. "V1099. Inscribed collar, leather . . . oh, yes, I've seen that. The dog was wearing it."

He ticked it. An hour later he strutted into the radio room. Burman stood up, squared his shoulders but could not keep his feet or hands from fidgeting. His eyes protruded slightly and kept straying toward McNaught in silent appeal. He was like a man wearing a porcupine in his britches.

"V1098. Offog, one," said Cassidy in his usual tone of brooking no nonsense.

Moving with the jerkiness of a slightly uncoördinated robot, Burman pawed a small box fronted with dials, switches and colored lights. It looked like a radio ham's idea of a fruit machine. He knocked down a couple of switches. The lights came on, played around in intriguing combinations.

"This is it, sir," he informed with difficulty.

"Ah!" Cassidy left his chair and moved across for a closer look. "I don't recall having seen this item before. But there are so many different models of the same things. Is it still operating efficiently?"

"Yes, sir."

"It's one of the most useful things in the ship," contributed McNaught, for good measure.

"What does it *do?*" inquired Cassidy, inviting Burman to cast a pearl of wisdom before him.

Burman paled.

Hastily, McNaught said, "A full explanation would be rather involved and technical but, to put it as simply as possible, it enables us to strike a balance between opposing gravitational fields. Variations in lights indicate the extent and degree of unbalance at any given time."

"It's a clever idea," added Burman, made suddenly reckless by this news, "based upon Finagle's Constant."

"I see," said Cassidy, not seeing at all. He resumed his seat, ticked the offog and carried on. "Z44. Switchboard, automatic, forty-line intercom, one of."

"Here it is, sir."

Cassidy glanced at it, returned his gaze to the sheet. The others used his momentary distraction to mop perspiration from their foreheads.

Victory had been gained.

All was well.

For the third time, hah!

Rear Admiral Vane W. Cassidy departed pleased and complimentary. Within one hour the crew bolted to town. McNaught took turns with Gregory at enjoying the gay lights. For the next five days all was peace and pleasure.

On the sixth day Burman brought in a signal, dumped it upon McNaught's desk and waited for the reaction. He had an air of gratification, the pleasure of one whose virtue is about to be rewarded.

Terran Headquarters to Bustler. *Return here immediately for overhaul and refitting. Improved power plant to be installed. Feldman. Navy Op. Command. Sirisec.*

"Back to Terra," commented McNaught, happily. "And an overhaul will mean at least one month's leave." He eyed Burman. "Tell all officers on duty to go to town at once and order the crew aboard. The men will come running when they know why."

"Yes, sir," said Burman, grinning.

Everyone was still grinning two weeks later when the Siriport had receded far behind and Sol had grown to a vague speck in the sparkling mist of the bow starfield. Eleven weeks still to go, but it was worth it. Back to Terra. Hurrah!

In the captain's cabin the grins abruptly vanished one

evening when Burman suddenly developed the willies. He marched in, chewed his bottom lip while waiting for McNaught to finish writing in the log.

Finally, McNaught pushed the book away, glanced up, frowned. "What's the matter with you? Got a bellyache or something?"

"No, sir. I've been thinking."

"Does it hurt that much?"

"I've been thinking," persisted Burman in funereal tones. "We're going back for overhaul. You know what that means? We'll walk off the ship and a horde of experts will walk onto it." He stared tragically at the other. "Experts, I said."

"Naturally they'll be experts," McNaught agreed. "Equipment cannot be tested and brought up to scratch by a bunch of dopes."

"It will require more than a mere expert to bring the offog up to scratch," Burman pointed out. "It'll need a genius."

McNaught rocked back, swapped expressions like changing masks. "Jumping Judas! I'd forgotten all about that thing. When we get to Terra we won't blind *those* boys with science."

"No, sir, we won't," endorsed Burman. He did not add "any more" but his face shouted aloud, "You got me into this. You get me out of it." He waited a time while McNaught did some intense thinking, then prompted, "What do you suggest, sir?"

Slowly the satisfied smile returned to McNaught's features as he answered, "Break up the contraption and feed it into the disintegrator."

"That doesn't solve the problem," said Burman. "We'll still be short an offog."

"No we won't. Because I'm going to signal its loss owing to the hazards of space-service." He closed one eye in an emphatic wink. "We're in free flight right now." He reached for a message-pad and scribbled on it while Burman stood by vastly relieved.

Bustler *to Terran Headquarters. Item V1098, Offog*

one, came apart under gravitational stress while pass-
ing through twin-sun field Hector Major-Minor. Ma-
terial used as fuel. McNaught, Commander. Bustler.

Burman took it to the radio room and beamed it
Earthward. All was peace and progress for another
two days. The next time he went to the captain's
cabin he went running and worried.

"General call, sir," he announced breathlessly and
thrust the message into the other's hands.

Terran Headquarters for relay all sectors. Urgent
and Important. All ships grounded forthwith. Vessels
in flight under official orders will make for nearest
spaceport pending further instructions. Welling. Alarm
and Rescue Command. Terra.

"Something's gone bust," commented McNaught,
undisturbed. He traipsed to the chart room, Burman
following. Consulting the charts, he dialed the intercom phone, got Pike in the bow and ordered, "There's
a panic. All ships grounded. We've got to make for
Zaxtedport, about three days' run away. Change course
at once. Starboard seventeen degrees, declination ten."
Then he cut off, griped, "Bang goes that sweet month
on Terra. I never did like Zaxted, either. It stinks. The
crew will feel murderous about this and I don't blame
them."

"What d'you think has happened, sir?" asked Burman. He looked both uneasy and annoyed.

"Heaven alone knows. The last general call was
seven years ago when the *Starider* exploded halfway
along the Mars run. They grounded every ship in
existence while they investigated the cause." He rubbed
his chin, pondered, went on, "And the call before that
one was when the entire crew of the *Blowgun* went
nuts. Whatever it is this time, you can bet it's serious."

"It wouldn't be the start of a space war?"

"Against whom?" McNaught made a gesture of contempt. "Nobody has the ships with which to oppose
us. No, it's something technical. We'll learn of it

eventually. They'll tell us before we reach Zaxted or soon afterward."

They did tell him. Within six hours. Burman rushed in with face full of horror.

"What's eating you now?" demanded McNaught, staring at him.

"The offog," stuttered Burman. He made motions as though brushing off invisible spiders.

"What of it?"

"It's a typographical error. In your copy it should read off. dog."

The commander stared owlishly.

"Off. dog?" echoed McNaught, making it sound like foul language.

"See for yourself." Dumping the signal on the desk, Burman bolted out, left the door swinging. McNaught scowled after him, picked up the message.

Terran Headquarters to Bustler. *Your report V1098, ship's official dog Peaslake. Detail fully circumstances and manner in which animal came apart under gravitational stress. Cross-examine crew and signal all coincidental symptoms experienced by them. Urgent and Important. Welling. Alarm and Rescue Command. Terra.*

In the privacy of his cabin McNaught commenced to eat his nails. Every now and again he went a little cross-eyed as he examined them for nearness to the flesh.

LIBRARY OF CONGRESS CATALOG CARD NUMBER: 63-15124

TEMPO BOOKS EDITION, 1963

FIRST PRINTING, JULY 1963

SECOND PRINTING, DECEMBER 1965

COPYRIGHT ACKNOWLEDGMENTS

Poul Anderson, THE HELPING HAND. Copyright 1950 by Street and Smith Publications, Inc. Reprinted by permission of the author and the author's agent, Scott Meredith Literary Agency, Inc., from *Astounding Science Fiction,* May, 1950.

Isaac Asimov, BLIND ALLEY. Copyright 1945 by Street and Smith Publications, Inc. Reprinted by permission of the author from *Astounding Science Fiction,* March, 1945.

Jerome Bixby, THE HOLES AROUND MARS. Copyright 1954 by Galaxy Publishing Corp. Reprinted by permission of the author from *Galaxy Science Fiction,* January, 1954.

Ray Bradbury, KALEIDOSCOPE. Copyright 1949 by Standard Magazines, Inc. Reprinted by permission of the author and Harold Matson Co. from *Thrilling Wonder Stories,* October, 1949.

Arthur C. Clarke, A WALK IN THE DARK. Copyright 1950 by Standard Magazines, Inc. Reprinted by permission of the author and the author's agents, Scott Meredith Literary Agency, Inc., from *Thrilling Wonder Stories,* August, 1950.

Lester del Rey, WINGS OF NIGHT. Copyright 1942 by Street and Smith Publications, Inc. Reprinted by permission of the author and the author's agents, Scott Meredith Literary Agency, Inc., from *Astounding Science Fiction,* March, 1942.

Damon Knight, CABIN BOY. Copyright 1951 by Galaxy Publishing Corp. Reprinted by permission of the author and the author's agent, Robert P. Mills, General Artists Corp., from *Galaxy Science Fiction.*

Murray Leinster, PROPAGANDIST. Copyright 1947 by Street and Smith Publications, Inc. Reprinted by permission of Will Jenkins from *Astounding Science Fiction,* August, 1947.

Eric Frank Russell, ALLAMAGOOSA. Copyright 1955 by Street and Smith Publications, Inc. Reprinted by permission of the author and the author's agents, Scott Meredith Literary Agency, Inc., from *Astounding Science Fiction,* May, 1955.

A. E. Van Vogt, FAR CENTAURUS. Copyright 1944 by Street and Smith Publications, Inc.; 1952 by A. E. Van Vogt. Reprinted by permission of the author and the author's agent, Forrest J. Ackerman, from *Astounding Science Fiction,* January, 1944.

Jack Vance, I'LL BUILD YOUR DREAM CASTLE. Copyright 1947 by Street and Smith Publications, Inc. Reprinted by permission of the author and the author's agents, Scott Meredith Literary Agency, Inc., from *Astounding Science Fiction,* September, 1947.

EDITED BY GROFF CONKLIN

GREAT STORIES
OF SPACE TRAVEL

TEMPO
BOOKS

A TEMPO BOOKS *Original*

GROSSET & DUNLAP

NEW YORK

You will find the same absorbing reading and high quality in other TEMPO BOOKS. Look for them wherever books are sold. If your dealer does not have the TEMPO BOOKS you want, you may order them by mail, enclosing the list price plus 10¢ a copy to cover mailing. A complete list of titles is available free from TEMPO BOOKS, Grosset & Dunlap, Inc., 51 Madison Avenue, New York, New York 10010.

ANOTHER TEMPO BOOKS
SCIENCE FICTION ANTHOLOGY
Edited by GROFF CONKLIN

INVADERS OF EARTH. Seventeen hair-rais-   **T6** **60¢**
ing stories by science-fiction's most thought-provoking writers.

IT HASN'T HAPPENED.........................Not yet.

But who knows in the years to come what strange things will confront those brave Earthlings who dare to invade the far reaches of outer space . . . and beyond?

Mind now, there is no certainty that the seemingly fantastic things you will read in this book will come true . . . but no one can prove that they will not. No one, that is, except one who has journeyed into time and space and has returned, alive, to tell about it.

Have you been there? Do you know? For sure?

If not, take this journey into the distant worlds of the unknown future. It will be the experience of a lifetime. (Lifetime? Quaint expression.) Let us go then, and don't be afraid. There is no danger . . . nothing can happen . . . **don't be afra. . . .**